Pug Hill

"I adored *Pug Hill* . . . I can't remember when I've seen such sensitive and funny writing about dogs."   —Jennifer Weiner

"All at once touching, witty, and so very smart . . . There's a terrific comedic eye at work here, and a tender heart."
—Elinor Lipman

If Andy Warhol Had a Girlfriend

"Poignant and very funny . . ."   —*The Washington Post*

"This book is GENIUS! I stayed up all night laughing hyena-style."   —Jill Kargman

Through Thick and Thin

"[C]raftily portrays the balancing act between work and play, family (be it four-legged or two) and friends, and food and fasting."   —*Publishers Weekly*

City Dog

"Pace exhibits a keen eye for characters, both human and canine."   —*The Newark Star-Ledger*

A Pug's Tale

"[A] winningly affectionate tribute to art, love, New York City, and pugs."   —*Booklist*

pug hill

alison pace

BERKLEY BOOKS, NEW YORK

THE BERKLEY PUBLISHING GROUP
Published by the Penguin Group
Penguin Group (USA) Inc.
375 Hudson Street, New York, New York 10014, USA
Penguin Group (Canada), 90 Eglinton Avenue East, Suite 700, Toronto, Ontario M4P 2Y3, Canada
(a division of Pearson Penguin Canada Inc.)
Penguin Books Ltd., 80 Strand, London WC2R 0RL, England
Penguin Group Ireland, 25 St. Stephen's Green, Dublin 2, Ireland (a division of Penguin Books Ltd.)
Penguin Group (Australia), 250 Camberwell Road, Camberwell, Victoria 3124, Australia
(a division of Pearson Australia Group Pty. Ltd.)
Penguin Books India Pvt. Ltd., 11 Community Centre, Panchsheel Park, New Delhi—110 017, India
Penguin Group (NZ), 67 Apollo Drive, Rosedale, Auckland 0632, New Zealand
(a division of Pearson New Zealand Ltd.)
Penguin Books (South Africa) (Pty.) Ltd., 24 Sturdee Avenue, Rosebank, Johannesburg 2196,
South Africa

Penguin Books Ltd., Registered Offices: 80 Strand, London WC2R 0RL, England

PUG HILL

A Berkley Book / published by arrangement with the author

PRINTING HISTORY
Berkley trade paperback edition / May 2006
Berkley mass-market edition / November 2011

ISBN: 978-0-425-24505-7

BERKLEY®
Berkley Books are published by The Berkley Publishing Group,
a division of Penguin Group (USA) Inc.,
375 Hudson Street, New York, New York 10014.
BERKLEY® is a registered trademark of Penguin Group (USA) Inc.
The "B" design is a trademark of Penguin Group (USA) Inc.

PRINTED IN THE UNITED STATES OF AMERICA

10 9 8 7 6 5 4 3 2 1

For Mom and Dad
(Happy Anniversary)

acknowledgments

This book might never have been started without the enthusiasm of Allison McCabe, and it certainly never would have been finished without the endless encouragement and thoughtful advice offered to me by my agent and friend, Joe Veltre. Tremendous thanks to you both.

Endless appreciation goes to my wonderful, talented, and ever-patient editor, Susan Allison, who made revisions seem like a fun new adventure, and who was so available to me throughout the entire process with her invaluable ideas and insights.

I am very grateful to Jessica Wade, Julia Fleischaker, and everyone at Berkley Books for all their hard work on my behalf; and to Karen Schifano, Grace Shin, Mark Greenberg, Boris Sternberg and Simon Parkes at Simon Parkes Art Conservation for the glimpse into their careers.

For listening to all of my stories and for always making me laugh, special thanks to Cynthia Zabel, Joanna Schwartz, Christine Ciampa, Jennifer Geller, Sarah Melinger, Francis Tucci, Zander Byers, Kerry Dolan, Kimberly Bohner, Peter Bohner, Wendy Tufano, Jessica Goodman, and, of course, Crankyface.

And most of all, always, love and thanks to my sister, Joey, who has never once said she'd like to join a commune; to Mom, for being much nicer than Hope's mom, for instilling in me a great love of dogs, and for reading every last page of my early drafts; and to Dad, for always reminding me to stop and smell the roses, while wearing sunscreen.

Someday we'll find it.
—Kermit the Frog

prologue

For Holly Golightly, there was always Tiffany's. No matter what was going wrong in her life, she always had Tiffany's. For me, there's always Pug Hill. For as long as I've lived in New York, whenever I've wanted to think, or relax, or be happy, or even sad, my destination of choice has been, without fail, Pug Hill.

Pug Hill, if you haven't heard, is a hill in Central Park, over on the east side around Seventy-fourth Street, where pugs from all over New York City convene. Just as I imagine Holly Golightly was in it much more for the diamonds than for the big building on the corner of Fifty-seventh Street and Fifth Avenue, I'm in it much more for the pugs than for Central Park. It's not that I don't like the serenity and tranquility of Central Park as much as the next New Yorker, it's just that I've always had a pretty big thing for dogs.

Dogs have always been a great presence in my life, have always affected it in ways you might call deeply. I simply can't imagine my life without them. I wonder if it must speak volumes about me that I've never had one of my own.

What I do have right now are all the same reasons as all the other people in New York who love dogs but don't have one: I work too much, I'm not home enough, my apartment is too small, it's *never* the right time. But one day, and I don't doubt this at all—or at least, I try not to doubt it—it will be. And of all the dogs there are to love, pugs are, by far, my favorite.

So until that day, when the right time begins, I try to content myself with all the many versions of my favorite, all the endlessly comforting pugs of Pug Hill. I know all the regulars. I know their names and the colors of their harnesses and I know which pugs to expect if I visit on a Saturday or if I visit on a Sunday. Most of the time I'm the only person at Pug Hill without a pug. And that might seem kind of sad, but actually, it's not. I like to think that, in its own way, it's kind of hopeful really, if you think about it.

chapter one

The End

"Conservation," Elliot says quietly as he picks up the phone, and then, a moment later, "Okay, hold on a sec, please." I watch Elliot, focusing intently on the flick of his wrist as he hits the hold button and puts down the receiver. I watch Elliot a lot; it's a problem, it might be a bit stalkerish, this I know.

"Hope," he says, looking over at me, "it's your dad."

I look away, embarrassed, regretful. I tell myself it isn't my fault. I had, after all, no way of knowing the call was going to be for me. Really, I had no way of knowing that Elliot wasn't going to look across the room right then, not at me, but at our coworker, Sergei, or at our boss, May— people who the call could have much more likely been for. Nobody calls me at work. People e-mail me, or they instant message me when I turn on the IM during lunch, but they refrain for the most part from calling. It's generally understood that I don't like the phone. It causes me anxiety.

"Thanks," I say without looking up and reach for the phone. As I do so, it occurs to me that Dad, even more than anyone else, doesn't ever call me at work. Dad thinks talking on the phone while at the workplace is slacking. Though I don't think he uses that actual word, Dad doesn't approve of slacking and does not wish to be an accessory to it.

"Hi, Dad," I say, worried now, wondering if maybe Dad is breaking his rule of never calling because something is wrong.

"Hi, Hope, how are you?" he says, very much *not* like anything at all is wrong. Dad's voice is calm and clear and assured, as it almost always is. For as long as I can remember, I have always felt so assured from just the sound of Dad's voice.

"I'm good. Is everything okay?" I ask just to be sure there isn't actually something wrong and I have just been lulled into a false complacency by the very soothing and comforting nature of my dad's voice.

"Oh, everything's fine," he says, "I'm not disturbing you at work, am I?" I tell him, no, not at all.

"Well, good then, I'm calling because I have some exciting news and wanted to talk to you about it right away." I wonder if this exciting news has something to do with my older sister, Darcy. In my family, a lot of things have to do with Darcy. I try my best to push the thought from my mind.

"Sure, what's up?"

"Well, Mom and I have decided to have a party for our fortieth wedding anniversary. May seventh is a Saturday this year; we'll have it right on the actual date," he tells me happily.

"That's great," I say, and I think to myself, not for the first time, *Wow, forty years.*

"Oh, yes, we're already really looking forward to it. Mom's already all caught up in the planning. You know how she loves a project."

Oh, I know, I think, *believe me, I know.*

"Yes," I say in lieu of anything that could be construed as hostile.

"Well, Hope," he says and pauses for a moment, "Mom and I were thinking how nice it would be if, at the party, you made a speech."

A speech.

I say nothing. I stare blankly ahead of me as the word *speech* scrapes through my brain like nails on a chalkboard.

Well, Hope, I think to myself, because suddenly all I want in the world is to go back to the part of the conversation where Dad hadn't said anything about a speech, where he'd only said, *Well, Hope.* I want to go back to *Well, Hope* and have something, anything, even something about Darcy come after it.

"I'm sorry?" I say in a last-ditch effort to allow myself to think that I didn't hear what I thought I just heard, a last-ditch effort to delude myself into believing that this couldn't really be happening. But, sadly, tragically even, Dad simply says the same thing again.

"Mom and I were thinking how nice it would be for you to make a speech at the party."

He says it happily, in anticipation, it seems, of all the niceness that will surely be my speech. He says it all just like it's any other sentence, any other perfectly harmless sentence. He says it all as if what he's just said won't, in its own quiet way, kill me.

"A speech?" I ask and the words don't sound like nails on a chalkboard anymore, now they sound very much like the first two bars of the theme song from *Jaws*.

Duh-duh!

My heart has stopped beating. I put my hand to my chest.

"A speech, yes," he says it yet again. I listen to the *duh-duh!* getting louder and louder in the background.

I sit frozen, phone in hand, and along with the music, I listen to this voice in my head: it's listening to the *Jaws* music, too, and it's shouting at me, quite loudly, "Get your drunk, naked ass out of the ocean, you are about to be eaten alive by a motherfucking GREAT WHITE SHARK!"

And then, there is another voice in my head, one that apparently isn't listening to the music. This one speaks calmly, softly. It says to me, "Look, so you've had this one thing, public speaking, that has scared you more than anything else for your entire life. So it's your Great White Shark, so it's your BIG SCARY THING, it's also your parents' fortieth wedding anniversary." The voice pauses for a moment, maybe just to be sure that what it has said has sunk in, and then continues, "You love your parents and your dad has asked this important favor of you, and really," the voice asks me, "*who* says no to such a request?"

"Really," it says again, *"who?"*

I think for a minute that maybe *I* do, that maybe *I* am the person who says no to such a request.

The shark is approaching, faster and faster, bigger and bigger, but somehow, I manage to think how saying no would be so ungrateful, so flippant, and so disrespectful of forty years of marriage. Saying no seems kind of hostile and churlish and as right as I want it to be, I know it would be wrong.

"I'd love to, Dad," I say, and wonder how much time has actually passed.

Dad says, "Wonderful."

Somehow I refrain from explaining to him that this is all pretty damn far away from wonderful. Instead, I say, "Great," and then I say, "okay."

The *okay,* I know, is more to calm myself than for any other reason.

"Great."

There is no more *Jaws* music. The voices in my head, the frantic one, along with the calm, cool, and collected one, have both fallen silent. I listen, helpless, hopeless, alone, as Dad says, "Okay, then, back to work. Love you, Hope. Talk to you soon."

"Love you, too, Dad. Bye," I say, and put down the phone. My heart has started beating, though I wonder if it will ever beat in quite the same way again.

I stare blankly at my computer screen. I try to think how long I've been trying to prevent this from happening. Ever since Mr. Brogrann's tenth grade English class, and the disaster that was my oral report on *The Grapes of Wrath,* I've been petrified, horrified really, of even just the *thought* of public speaking. Since then, I've taken great pains to avoid any sort of public speaking; in fact many decisions in my life, it could be said, have been predicated on keeping this fear at bay. It may seem like a lot, like too much really has stemmed from that day in tenth grade English that began with my freezing in front of the class and ended some horrible twenty minutes later with my throwing up, locked safely in a bathroom stall. But that's how it happened.

The waves of repercussion from that ill-fated speech, they started right away. In eleventh grade, I dropped Advanced Placement Topics in European History as soon as I saw the soul-shattering words, *forty-minute final presentation,* on the last page of the syllabus. And pretty much, it all just snowballed from there. To tell you the truth, at this point, it's a pretty big snowball. That I work in Paintings Conservation is not exactly a coincidence. Yes, it is the result not only of a lot of training and study and genuine, real interest on my part, but it is also quite closely related to the fact that early on in college I realized how much time an Art History student spent sitting quietly in a darkened room, watching slide shows.

A professor told me once, in a way I believe was meant to deter me, that an MFA in Paintings Conservation was not all hands-on practical application, but actually entailed quite a lot of research, quite a lot of sitting in libraries, chasing down footnotes. It sounded to me at the time very much like an earthly heaven.

One decision slyly led to the next, not unlike the way sand will bury your feet and then your ankles if you stand at the beach, a little ways back from where the waves break. But that might not be the best analogy, because with the sand it's different. With the sand there's something reassuring in knowing that you can walk away, in knowing that you won't actually be buried alive.

The further away I got from that oral report in Mr. Brogrann's class, the more determined I was to make sure I never went back. And as the years went on, I felt more and more sure I never would. I made it through high school, college, and graduate school. I had a job as a paintings restorer at the Metropolitan Museum of Art, a very good job that I actually loved, and that would never require me to make a speech. I'd been a bridesmaid a few times, but all those brides had sisters so I'd never been a maid of honor, a speech-making danger zone if ever there was one. And then, at last, I'd believed that I was safe. I'd somehow managed to lull myself into complacency; I became so certain it would never come up again, that I'd almost forgotten all about it. Until today. Today, regardless of everything I have done over the years to keep this fear at bay, here it is, leering at me like a scary birthday party clown.

The IM symbol, the little yellow man with the blue triangle, starts jumping, up and down, at the bottom of my computer screen. I reach for my mouse and click on the bouncing yellow man. An IM window pops up on my screen.

> EVAN2020: *You remember that I'm playing squash tonight with Brandon and then we're having dinner with him and his fiancée after at the club? Like eight?*

I quit out of IM without answering. Then I do the only thing I can think of, the only thing I can think of that makes any sense. I leave.

chapter two

There Are No Pugs
at Pug Hill

I leave my desk, I leave the museum, I leave Elliot. As soon as I'm outside, I feel guilty for leaving work so abruptly. I worry that maybe I should have said something, that maybe I should consider going back. But I can't. I walk quickly, south for a while, down Fifth. It's not as crowded now, in the late afternoon. I'm sweating, but not because it's hot outside; though it is warm out for February, "warm for February," in my mind, is just not that warm. I think how maybe the sweat is really just fear, just trying to get out of my body any way it can. I welcome it, I walk faster; it makes me feel a little less like I'm about to die.

At Seventy-sixth Street, I turn right and walk into the park. I see the *Alice in Wonderland* sculpture, the one with the mushroom and Alice and the Mad Hatter and the rabbit. I remember how for so long I thought the story was about someone named Allison Wonderland, and how even after I knew that it wasn't, I always thought it should be. I always thought it made so much more sense that way.

I turn left and step over a low wrought-iron fence. I stand for a full minute, just over the fence, and listen to my breathing as it slows down. Slowly, I walk up Pug Hill through the wet leaves; Central Park is so quiet and I think it smells so much like mulch. I don't know why I think mulch because I don't know if I've ever smelled mulch before. In fact, I'm pretty sure I haven't. As I walk, I look down at my feet, at my UGG boots, and I feel a twinge of disappointment, not because they're already out of style, but because I've gotten water spots on them from walking through the wet leaves. I'm struck by that not completely unfamiliar feeling, that feeling like maybe I'm about to cry. And I know it's not the dark marks all over the shearling boots that make me feel like I want to cry, but The Speech, the Great White Shark, the BIG SCARY THING.

I get to the top of the hill and I sit down on one of the benches that I sit on when it's too cold or too wet to sit on the grass by the pine tree. The grass by the pine tree is better. There, you get so many more of the renegade pugs, the ones who will break away from the group and run toward you, panting hard, running as fast as they can in their little harnesses—purple, and green, and pink, and even once I saw a zebra-striped harness on a beautiful black pug. There, by the tree, you get the pugs who'll stop to sit with you for a moment, tongues out, heads bobbing, looking up at you and then in the same direction as you, back at all their pug compatriots.

It isn't until I've been sitting for a moment that the silence I was thinking about before, right before the mulch, hits me. There is no snorting. No panting. No "Jasper!" No "Fresa!" No "Derby, Roxy, Buster, Vince, come here!"

No pugs. Not even one. I lean back against the bench, hoping it might help me not sink under the heavy weight that is the gravity of the situation. I close my eyes.

There are no pugs at Pug Hill.

Not today, I think. *Today is not the day I want to learn that there aren't always pugs at Pug Hill.* I don't want this knowledge. What I want is to go back in time; back to before there was a *speech,* back to when I lived in a world where the pugs would be here any instant I needed them. I guess I've just never thought about it before. I guess they just come here on the weekends. I count back in my head: nine years. Nine years I've lived in New York and I don't think I've ever been in Central Park during the week.

I close my eyes. I try not to think about the speech. Because the speech, you see, it's too big of a problem. I try to think about other things. Sometimes I've found that when you are faced with what seems like an unsolvable problem, it helps to take stock of the other problems in your life. I've found that if you look at the other problems, ones that are maybe, possibly, if you *really* put your mind to it, solvable, you'll feel a little bit better about the problem you can't ever imagine solving. While not necessarily the most cheering of pursuits, it does take your mind off the unsolvable problem for a little while.

Okay. I mean, it's not like I woke up this morning and felt very much like a light, carefree person, like a person who wanted to lie on her back and kick her feet in the air with delight. It's not like I woke up this morning feeling like a person without some problems that needed solving. Lately, to be truthful, there have been a few.

There's my boyfriend, Evan, for starters. I don't think it's working out with Evan. I have been trying to ignore this fact. I have been trying to believe that we are just going through a bad phase, but the more I tell myself that, the more

I suspect it isn't really true. I try to remember the way I felt when I first met him, when he called me after our first date and said to my voice mail, "I'm having a drink with some friends, but the only thing I want to do in the world right now is have another drink with you." I try to remember how, when he said that, I just melted. I try to remember how I felt like maybe all the less-than-stellar boyfriends who had happened before him had happened so I'd meet Evan right at the right time, right when I was ready, so that everything might be a little bit perfect. But lately, the more I try to remember all that, the less I can. And mostly, the more I try to think that maybe he really is the one, the more it's just so completely clear that he isn't. There's that.

And then, there is, of course, Elliot. There is always, always Elliot. I seem to be very infatuated with Elliot.

Just this very morning, as I walked up Columbus Avenue, to stop back at my apartment to get ready for work, as I do not have any of my stuff at Evan's, I think I thought *then* that I had too many problems. And I think I even thought that I had *no idea* how to solve them. Some sort of problem god must have heard me think this and he must've said, "Oh, no, sister, you think you've got problems? You think these are problems you can't solve? I'll show you problems."

I look down at my watch, and a wave of guilt washes over me for busting out of work in the middle of the day in the dramatic way that I just have. The guilt at least takes my mind off all the problems, solvable and not so. As I stand up, take one last look around to make sure there isn't maybe just one pug, I think that at least I can count on something. I can count on the guilt. I'm half Jewish and half Catholic; I've got the market on guilt pretty well covered. And anyway, I can't think any more about any of it. It just isn't the same sorting out your problems at Pug Hill when the pugs aren't here. I make a mental note to come back over the weekend. I hope Evan hasn't already made plans to go ice fishing or something equally as fun.

I get up and turn away from the hill, the hill so very free of any sweet, snorting pugs. I don't walk back down the hill, back across more empty lawn covered with leaves. Instead, I walk on the other side, along the cement path. I do this, I know, because I don't want to inflict any additional water damage on my UGG boots. Before every fashion victim in New York and L.A. wore them, UGG boots were originally worn by Australian surfers. The surfers like them because the sheepskin is warm in the winter and cool in the summer. I picture surfer dudes in Australia carrying surfboards into the ocean, waves lapping at UGG boots left on the shore. I look down at my boots again and wonder if I have, as I fear I have with so many things, perhaps quite completely missed the point.

chapter three

You May Feel Sad

I walk quickly away from Pug Hill and back up to the Met. I hurry past the Paul Manship sculpture of the three bears, trying not to think that the absence of the pugs is a bad omen. Usually I'm not in this much of a hurry; usually I stop for a minute and look at the sculpture. Though I'm beginning to realize that, today, nothing is usual. I reenter the museum through the south side employee entrance; I take a left, a right, go through a long snaking underground hallway, and I'm back at the door to the Conservation Studio.

I walk back into the Conservation Studio, this room that houses so many beautiful, priceless (if slightly worse-for-wear) masterpieces of art, and the first thing I see is Elliot. Lately, I could walk into a room that held a million more beautiful, priceless, timeless objects than this one does and if Elliot were in it, he would, time and again, be the first thing I see. I pad silently over to my work space, trying to draw as little attention as possible to myself, to the fact that I have, most recently, been gone. It's not very difficult. One of the things about paintings restorers (technically you can say paintings restorer or paintings conservator, but I prefer restorer; I find conservator to be a bit of a mouthful) is that they have to concentrate so much on their paintings in order to properly restore them that generally, they are much more wrapped up in their paintings than they are in their coworkers. Unless, of course, the paintings restorer in question happens to be me. Then, of course, it's a whole different story. Lately, I've been having a bit of trouble with concentrating. It's harder and harder, what with Elliot always being right there.

I settle into my chair and look over again at Elliot, hunched studiously over an Old Master landscape, as oblivious to me and to everyone else as he usually is. He reaches up to brush his curly light brown hair—a light brown color that I like to think is almost red—away from his forehead. I sigh quietly and turn away from him. I turn toward my easel to contemplate Mark Rothko's *No. 13 (White, Red on Yellow)*, the painting I've just begun to work on. It's a large canvas, a field of luminous yellow with a white rectangle at the top and a red rectangle at the bottom. What's happened to this Rothko is that sometime before the painting made its way to the Met, it was stored in a place where the humidity level wasn't quite right and the canvas expanded and contracted, and the paint on it didn't. Dry paint isn't flexible, isn't malleable at all; it can't expand and contract the way a canvas can. So now, there are a few flecks of missing paint in each section, and my job is to match the color exactly, to fill in the missing spots. With something like a Rothko, where color is so important, where color might just be everything, there isn't any room for error. Everything you do has to be perfect, just as everything you add has to be reversible, and I have to admit, I think the restoration of this painting, the precision that it will demand, might take me forever. I haven't been sure of where to begin and I'm certainly not sure now.

As I stare at it, losing focus, for a moment all I can see is red, and I decide, a bit brazenly really, to start with the red. I flip through my paintbrushes, looking for the smallest, thinnest one. I don't know if I should attempt much more, after the finding of the paintbrush, because right now I'm finding it harder and harder to be sure of anything. The only thing I'm sure of is that after the knowledge that I will have to make a speech—a real, actual speech in front of people!—in the near enough future, and after the disappointment that is Pug Hill when the pugs aren't there, the last thing I really want to do is spend the last few hours of the day swimming in the sea of unprofessed love that work has become.

It wasn't always like this. The sea of unprofessed love used to be known only as the Conservation Studio at the Metropolitan Museum of Art. Debilitating crush on coworker notwithstanding, the Metropolitan Museum of Art, of all the wonderful places in New York, has always been my favorite place. When I find myself alone here, after hours, walking through the Egyptian wing, wandering in the sculpture rooms, the halls after halls of European and American paintings, I'm still, after so many years, struck by the sheer awesomeness, the real beauty of it all. I've always loved the museum. I've always loved the type of concentrated, focused work that I do here, restoring masterpieces of art, erasing any imperfections. The museum has always been such a sanctuary to me. That is until Elliot showed up and my sanctuary became a place where, sometimes, if you listened really carefully, you could hear Patsy Cline singing "Crazy" in the background.

I turn away from Elliot. I put on my magnifying visor, pull the magnifying part down over my eyes and look at the red part of my Rothko. I wonder briefly if maybe I shouldn't start with the white part or the yellow part, rather than the red. The red, and I know this, has a way of being so hard.

At 5:30 exactly, the phone rings. I try my best to ignore it.

"Conservation." I hear Sergei's heavy voice from across the room, and then louder, projecting, "Elliot, it is Claire!"

"Thanks, man," Elliot says. He turns away from his easel, reaches for his phone and brings it to his mouth. "Hey," he says, his voice softer, sweeter than it generally is. Claire.

Right, there's that. There's Claire. Maybe I should have mentioned it. There's another thing about the impossibility of there ever being a Hope and Elliot, the happy couple so destined to be together, so clearly, clearly right for each other. Other than the fact that I have a boyfriend, and the fact that Elliot generally doesn't notice me, there is the fact that Elliot has a girlfriend, Claire.

Claire. *Claire.* Anyone who grew up in the eighties, anyone who was raised on John Hughes movies knows that Claire is a fat girl's name.

I turn away from the Rothko and begin to gather my things. Usually, on days when the sky is not so clearly about to fall, I don't leave work so early. No one leaves work this early. Elliot, I think, never leaves work, ever. On top of being intense and sexy and deep and meaningful and really very handsome, Elliot is also quite diligent. Try as I might to get to work ahead of him, I never have. As late as I have toiled at times into the night, Elliot has always stayed later. It's actually almost annoying enough to make me not head over heels in lust with him. But not quite.

Today though, I want to leave at 5:30, because I have dinner at The Union Club with squash-playing fiancé at 8:00, and I just really feel that I need to go home and chill out for an hour or two, need to, you know, give myself a minute. I think it's important sometimes to give yourself a minute. Because it's so early and everyone's so busy, I don't say good night to anyone, not even to Elliot. Well, especially not to Elliot. I shut down my computer and slip silently out the door.

* * *

At Eighty-sixth and Central Park West, I get off the cross-town bus and head down to Eighty-fifth Street, then toward Columbus. In the distance, I can see the steps that lead up to my brownstone. I look at those steps and I smile in spite of myself, in spite of my belief that, among other things, I may never live to see the other side of this speech. I've always loved that my building has outdoor steps; loved this more I imagine than you'd think a person would.

I speed up and soon enough I'm walking up the beloved outdoor steps and then up the three flights of interior stairs. The interior stairs are far less beloved: they are actually a bit skanky. I unlock the door to my apartment and walk in. I let out a breath I didn't even realize I'd been holding, and look around at the familiar room. *This is good right now,* I think, as I shut the door behind me. I inhale the lingering scent of the Soku Lime relaxation candle I was burning at some point over the weekend, before today happened, before I had any idea how much I really needed to relax. I put my bag down on the floor by the door and cross the room to put my keys in the dish on my mantelpiece. It's an unspoken agreement I have with my apartment: if I leave the keys on top of the mantelpiece I will find them again when I have to leave. If I put them anywhere else it will take me hours.

I rest my hand on the mantelpiece and look down at the white-painted bricks that were put in place, sometime long before I got here, to board up the fireplace. Like many brownstone-dwelling Upper West Siders, I have the ubiquitous "decorative" fireplace. "Decorative," on the Upper West Side means "doesn't work." I wonder if there is any symbolic significance to the fact that Evan and I both live on the Upper West Side.

I look away from the boarded-up fireplace, stare instead for a moment at the wall. I do not have the ubiquitous Upper West Side exposed brick wall. Having never actually been a fan of the exposed brick wall, I'm really okay with that. What I do have are beautiful moldings and closet doors with proper handles. I have built-in bookcases and an archway that leads from the living room area of the apartment to the sleeping area of the apartment. In the front I have a bay window, and off the back of my kitchen, I have that ever-so-elusive element of New York real estate, *outdoor space*: a tiny balcony that has room enough for exactly two small folding chairs. I look out at the chairs, all-weather chairs so it's perfectly safe for them to stay out there all winter. I really like those chairs, the way they sit so close together, looking out at the backs of all the other brownstones. Sometimes I imagine them as a happy couple, sitting so close on the balcony, happy together through the coldest of winters. Today they just seem smug.

I walk away from them, through the archway, into the sleeping area. It's cold; it always is at first, when the heat's been off all day while I'm gone, but I don't turn the heat on. I strip down to my underwear (I have a pretty big thing about clothes that have been outside in the city being inside the bed). I push the pillows that are just for show, but not ever used (two white European squares and actually two others), into the space between the bed and the wall. I pull back the quilt and the sheet, and I scoot inside and underneath as quickly as I can. I hate the cold. I hate being cold, have less of a threshold for it than I think I should, but I've always quite liked being under the covers in bed in a slightly-colder-than-you'd-ideally-want-it apartment. This is the only thing I like about winter.

Eventually I get warm, almost but not quite hot; this inevitably happens if you wait long enough. I pull the covers down from over my head, to chest level, freeing my arms. As I smooth the sheet around me like a strapless dress, it occurs to me what this might look like if anyone were watching. Sometimes when I'm bored, I like to imagine someone's watching me. I do this also when I like someone new. I'll say to myself, Okay, starting right now, he's watching, and then I try to imagine what he must see. If someone were watching me right now, let's say, Elliot, for example, I might look very much like an actress on TV or in a PG-rated movie who has just had a much more entertaining afternoon than I, in reality, have had.

I jump out of bed, reach behind the dresser and turn the heat on. A girl has to think about the future, and my future, as unappealing as it seems, does entail getting out of bed. Just not right now. Back in bed, I resituate my sheet, prop myself up on two of the three remaining pillows and reach over to the night table for the remote.

I want to see my commercial. If I can't see the pugs today, at the very least, I would like to see my commercial. It's been on a lot lately. I wonder if it's been on so much lately because of some cosmic coincidence; because some force somewhere knew the speech was coming and knew that it might help things if I started seeing the commercial more and more often. Or maybe they'd just increased their marketing budget.

I saw it the other night, I think, right in the middle of *Law & Order*. My DVR is set to record *Law & Order*! I click over to list and there it is, right at the top: *Law & Order*. I hit select and play, and think, as I often do, that DVR, the cable company's much easier-to-install version of TiVo (mostly, I guess, because someone comes and does it for you) is just fantastic. I listen to the first *duh-duh* of *Law & Order*. It is so similar in tone to the music from *Jaws;* I'm surprised I've never noticed this before. I hit fast forward until I see the first frame of my commercial. I hit play and turn the volume up a bit. I sit up a little straighter on my pillow.

There is the little sad egg on the TV screen. There is a rain cloud over his head, just like there always is. I watch the sad egg sigh as he propels himself forward across the screen. A voice-over comes on and soothingly explains, "You may feel sad." The sad egg: he hears this, he nods.

"You may feel panicky," the voice-over tells him. "You may feel isolated, overwhelmed, embarrassed in groups." And the sad egg, he sighs again.

Then the voice-over tells the sad egg all about Zoloft; he tells it that Zoloft can help. The rain cloud disappears. I lean back, a bit more relaxed into my pillow. I watch as sunshine spreads out over the egg, I notice that the one previously out-of-place hair on its head has been smoothed (confidence and the lessening of anxiety apparently works well as a styling balm, too). And the sad egg smiles.

I hit rewind. I watch it again. I watch it two more times. Whenever the sad egg sighs, I do, too.

chapter four

Single Jewish Male, 32, Likes: Squash; Hedge Funds; WASPs; Long Purposeful Walks in the Cold

As uplifting an activity as staying under the covers for the remainder of the evening, watching the Zoloft commercial again and again, would be, at a little after seven, I reluctantly accept the fact that my night holds other forms of fun in store for me.

Slowly, I emerge from under the covers. I sit on the edge of my bed, holding on to it, not quite ready to commit to getting out of it. Though commit, I know I must. I walk the one and a half steps to my dresser and pull a T-shirt from the middle drawer, the in-the-apartment/gym-T-shirt drawer as opposed to the nice T-shirt drawer. Pulling it over my head, I look down and contemplate my pile of clothing on the floor.

I wonder if I should pick out a different outfit to wear to dinner at The Union Club. I pick up my pants off the floor, smooth them, and lay them on the bed. I retrieve the sweater and fold it. Even though said sweater and pants are perfectly fine, more than acceptable, I figure I should pick out a different outfit. The thing about The Union Club is that it's the type of place that always makes you wish you'd picked out a different outfit, no matter what it is you happen to be wearing. Well, there are lots of things about The Union Club, that's just one of them. I look at the green numbers on my alarm clock: 7:14 glows back at me in a way that I would not describe as helpful. I turn toward my closet, focusing first on my shoes. "Clearly," I say to myself in my best snooty voice, "one does not wear UGG boots to *The Union Club*," and that makes me hate everything a little bit more.

* * *

Just before eight, I turn off Sixty-ninth Street and into the dark wood and marble entrance of The Union Club. The same man who's always there, a man with gray hair and sad-looking eyes, gets up from this stool he has to sit in, in this little marble nook right off the foyer, and walks a few steps toward me, slowly.

"May I take your coat, ma'am?" he asks and, as I do whenever I'm here, I hate that he calls me *ma'am*. I hate it not in the way that women in their thirties usually hate to be called *ma'am*, because it makes them feel old, but because I know it's in this man's job description to call people *sir* and *ma'am*.

Some Biffy guy coming up from the downstairs locker room passes by and says, "Hey, Clarence," to the guy waiting to take my coat. He says back, "Hi, Mr. Ward." And really, I think I so often miss the mark. I will waste all this time and energy feeling sorry that this man's job is taking the coats of squash-playing Republicans (I don't play squash nor am I a Republican, but I think you'd be safe in assuming that pretty much everyone else here does, and is). What I should really feel bad about, if I'm inclined to feel bad about something, is the fact that I've been here fifteen, twenty times and this man has always taken my coat, and I've never asked his name. That's another thing about The Union Club: it always makes me feel bad.

I take off my coat and hand it to him, to Clarence. I say, "Thanks, Clarence," as he takes it. Clarence is now looking at me strangely. I smile back at him and it takes me a minute to realize he's waiting.

"Oh, right," I say quickly, "I'm here to meet Evan Russell." I say this not only because I want him to know that I myself do not belong here, that I myself am not a squash-playing Republican, but because Clarence won't let me in unless I'm meeting a member.

"Mr. Russell is in the library," he tells me and then, making it all so much worse, he kind of shuffles away with my coat. I thank him again and wonder if Evan is the type of club member who gives good tips. He told me once after he'd gotten a massage that he hadn't tipped the masseuse because she'd stopped after fifty minutes. He hadn't seemed remorseful at all, not in the least, when I told him that I thought most hour-long massages only last for fifty minutes.

I start up the grand sweeping staircase, a *Gone with the Wind*–type staircase if ever there was one. I wonder, as I climb up one of two graceful, sweeping sides of the staircase, what it is that actually bothers me: The Union Club itself, or the fact that I have been willingly dating for the past six months (which, especially when you're thirty-one, isn't a nothing amount of time) someone who belongs to The Union Club. I know that in the end we all must take a certain, if not a complete, measure of responsibility for our actions, and for our circumstances. And I endeavor to do that, I do. For right now, though, I blame Pamela.

I should explain. I need a minute anyway before I head into the library to meet Evan and Brandon and his fiancée.

My friend Pamela told me about a year ago, right after my then-boyfriend Rick had broken up with me (Rick, by the way, was not a great boyfriend, but the man could wear a Barbour jacket like nobody else), that she felt I should get out more.

"You need to embrace being single," Pamela told me one day. "You need to get out more. You need to date!" she pronounced, captain of the cheerleading squad for single Manhattanites everywhere. Pamela, professionally, is a party planner, and pretty much I've always thought of her as a professional dater, too.

"Maybe you should go on JDate," she suggested.

"I do *not* want to go on JDate," I told her, and by JDate, just so you know, in the context of the conversation, I swear, I meant JDate, Match.com, Nerve.com, eHarmony, the whole lot of them. I feel it is important to clarify that I was expressing my lack of interest in Internet dating altogether, not a lack of interest in Internet-dating Jewish people.

"You shun your Judaism," she told me. "This has always bothered me about you." Shunning my Judaism? I thought that was taking it a bit far.

"I think," I told her, "that's taking it a bit far."

"I don't," she said, getting her back rather up, taking it, I thought, a little ridiculously personally. "I think most people don't even know you're Jewish."

Pamela had a point with that, but I thought that was more of a factor of my name than of any overt shunning on my part. As my nana has told every single person she has ever introduced me to, I'm the only Jewish girl she's ever heard of with the name Hope, and the only Jewish girl in the history of the world, she's sure of it, with the name *Hope McNeill*. Nana's also quite fond of explaining that along with my shiksa name, I got the red hair, the fair skin, and the lack of bust from my father's side of the family.

"I think that's a really judgmental thing to say," I said to Pamela, who can at times be very judgmental.

"Well, that's what I think." And rather inflexible, too.

"Well, Pam-e-la," I said, exhaling, stretching out her name as a way to point out my displeasure at her condemnation, "As you know, I wasn't raised Jewish so I don't really think it's something you can just come right out and say I *shun*," I pointed out.

So right, in addition to being Jewish and Catholic, I'm also kind of neither. After all the grandparents freaked out over the interfaith marriage, or maybe even before, my parents decided they'd raise me and my sister, Darcy, without religion. And I'm sure they thought this was a good idea. I'm sure they thought that this was for the best. It's just that sometimes, I'm not so sure. I'm not sure if they thought that through, if they realized that being no religion doesn't erase the fact that you are two. And I'm not sure, since it wasn't something either of them ever experienced, that they realized what an identity crisis being two religions, *and* being no religion, could be. Or at least could be for me.

"Well, I don't think that has anything to do with it," she said.

"Pamela, it does."

"Well, I think you shun your Judaism," Pamela said again and I think she sneered at me, a little bit like I'd failed her, like I'd failed *all* my people.

I did, I imagine, what anyone would have done. I stopped returning Pamela's phone calls for a while, and about four months later I signed up on JDate. It wasn't just Pamela, it was a tribute to Nana, too. She used to love to tell me that she was pretty sure I'd never be happy if I didn't stop dating the *goyim*. She just didn't understand how I could date non-Jew after non-Jew in good conscience. The fact my father wasn't Jewish never seemed to play into her logic. But even so, it had gotten to the point where I'd had to wonder, where I'd begun to believe that if the last ten years of dating were any indication, maybe she was on to something.

Evan was the first and only JDate I ever went on. I used to think that it was all so easy for us: how we e-mailed, and met, and then he made that really nice phone call to me, and I melted, and then pretty soon we were dating exclusively. I used to think that maybe, except for the whole being half-Catholic thing, I could be the poster child for JDate, because it all worked out so well for me. I don't think that anymore.

At the top of the stairs, I turn left and walk into the library. It's impossible, even if you hate having dinner at The Union Club, not to be taken in, even if it is ever so briefly, by the breathtaking woodwork, the four-hundred-foot-high ceiling, and the grand leaded glass windows that look out onto Park Avenue. I see Evan at the far end of the room, sitting on a couch with a blond couple, one of those couples who look, from across a very large room at least, like they are brother and sister. As I approach, I notice that the sister/fiancée is wearing a headband. I can hear Evan *caw-caw*-ing all the way from here. Evan has a *caw-caw*-sounding laugh, and apparently someone has just said something funny. Everyone stands as I reach them. The brother and sister (and I should stop calling them that; I should start right now calling them the affianced) are both ten feet tall.

"Hope, hi, I'm Courteney. Evan has told us so much about you," says the sister, I mean the fiancée, I mean Courteney, as she reaches out her hand to me. Evan has not reached out to kiss me, to say hello, yet. He hangs back; it is because he wants to observe the interaction between Courteney and me. Evan is judgmental, too.

"Hi, Courteney," I say with a (slightly fake) smile, "it's so nice to meet you, too." We shake hands. She is so tall, and thin, and long-limbed, and blond, and I don't want to feel threatened by that, but I am. I try to push any comparative thoughts from my mind as Evan reaches over, places his hand on the small of my back, leans in and pecks me on the cheek.

"You remember Brandon, right?" he asks.

"Yes, hi, Brandon."

"Hope, great to see you."

"Shall we?" Evan asks. *Shall we?* And we head together to the elevators, up to the fourth floor to the dining room.

Courteney turns to face me, once we are seated. The table is square and I am next to her, and Brandon is across from me, next to Evan.

"Evan tells us you're from Long Island."

"Yes."

"Whereabouts?" she asks, perky, bright-eyed.

"Huntington?" I ask it, I don't say it, and I wish I didn't do this. "It's about an hour outside of the city," I say, more assertively, wishing to appear as someone who is more informed about where she is from than I just have.

"Is that near Locust Valley?"

"Kind of."

"Do you belong to Piping Rock Club?" she asks, her eyes all lit up. The Piping Rock Club, a country club in Locust Valley, is for WASPy people what Pug Hill is for pugs. It is the Mecca, if you'll excuse the really poor analogy.

"No," I tell her.

"Oh, Creek Club then?" she asks, slightly tempered but still enthusiastic.

"No," I say, and she smiles at me, maybe a little sadly, and reaches a hand over to Brandon, places it on top of one of his.

"Brandon shot skeet at Piping just last weekend."

Brandon looks up at Courteney, and into her eyes, and the way he looks at her, it just says, "I love you, Muffin," and I have this feeling that when Brandon and Courteney get married, they'll be very happy. She takes a sip of water and smiles back at him yet again. She is one of those women, the kind who have the magical ability to keep all of her lipstick on her lips, leaving none of it on her glass.

A waiter comes to take our drink orders. I order a white wine spritzer. I look over at Evan and smile. His eyes aren't all lit up for me like Brandon's are for Courteney. His eyes don't say, "I love you, Muffin." His eyes say something more along the lines of, "Why can't you order a normal cocktail?" Evan thinks a white wine spritzer is not a normal cocktail. Evan thinks it's the kind of drink a person orders when they want everyone to be ashamed of them.

"So, how'd you two meet again?" Courteney asks me, and I can see Evan's jaw tense up. He leans forward, jumping in to answer, in case I've forgotten.

"We met at the Met. Hope works there."

Evan thinks it's just *easier* all around to say we met at the Met. He thinks this is a nice story, and perfectly plausible, as if, on occasion, I did leave the Conservation Studio in the middle of the day, to stroll leisurely around the museum, striking up conversations with random passersby. As if Evan were the type of person to be at a museum, which he isn't, ever, let alone in the middle of the workweek, which is when, ostensibly, I would have been there, you know, making new friends left and right.

"That's so nice," Courteney says.

Evan looks over at me, and smiles, and then stealthily winks. He crunches down on an ice cube from his Scotch. I've always hated the smell of Scotch, but when I first met Evan I thought it would be a good idea to not let the Scotch bother me. I don't think that anymore. I don't smile back at him, or wink or lend any of the previously lent agreement, any of the previously lent feelings of, oh, look at us, aren't we bonded because we have this secret, which really isn't a secret so much as it is a lie.

I notice that the light from the tremendous chandelier in the center of the room is bouncing off the gold buttons on Evan's navy blue blazer. It's a rip-off really, if you think about it, to go on JDate in the hopes that you might find yourself a nice Jewish boyfriend, and wind up six months later at The Union Club with Evan. I mean, someone like Evan, in my mind, he's lucky. He's one religion and not two. Why not just be Jewish? *Why the WASPy squash club,* I wonder, obviously not for the first time. *Why add all that in?*

I listen to the *caw-caw* around the table, rising up above us and heading to the chandelier. Evan and Brandon are laughing now about something that has to do with a hedge fund. Evan, by the way, works at a hedge fund, and I think Brandon does, too. To be completely honest, I have no idea what actually goes on at a hedge fund, no idea how all these people who work at hedge funds actually spend their days. It's been explained to me; it's just one of those things that refuses to sink in. *A little bit like love,* I think, even though thinking things like that can't possibly help anything. I smile, and occasionally I ask Courteney a polite question or two about the upcoming nuptials, less because I'm interested and more so that later Evan doesn't say, "Hope, you really weren't being very friendly at all."

Evan's talking about pheasant hunting now, and I try as hard as I can not to hear. I stare at the melting ice cubes in my drink and wonder if the identity crisis so deeply ingrained within me is what drew to me Evan in the first place, as Evan is so clearly in the middle of one.

*   *   *

On our way home in the taxi, Evan reaches over and strokes the back part of my upper arm. Don't be fooled. The way he does it is not in a way that is affectionate or kind. It is, I'm sure of this, much more in a way that wants to say, do you ever use those arm weights I got for you? I've wondered quite seriously at times if he and my mom are somehow in this together. Had one of them called the other and had they aligned themselves into some nefarious Evan/Mom axis of evil? Had Mom said, "I'll stick with her thighs and the fact that she seems completely incapable of matching her foundation to her skin tone," and had Evan then wholeheartedly agreed and said, "That sounds good, Mom [because so bonded are they in their Evan/Mom axis of evil that at some point Mom said to Evan, "Oh, Evan, please, just call me *Mom*"], I'll stick with the fat on the backs of her upper arms"?

And it's not that I embrace the criticism from Mom, I certainly don't, but from her at least I can understand it. Mom is an interior decorator. It's in her nature to want everything to be pretty. And also, no matter what the religion of the man she married, she is also *very much* a Jewish mother; some might say it's in her nature to be critical in, of course, a loving, albeit slightly annoying way. I don't have an excuse for Evan.

The taxi pulls up outside of Evan's building, and, as has been happening lately, I am overwhelmed by the desire to be in my own apartment. And maybe that doesn't necessarily have to be a comment on how I feel about Evan, maybe it's just because all my stuff is there, and Evan has really bad pillows. Once we are on the sidewalk, I turn to him.

"I think I'm just going to head home. I think I'm just going to stay at my apartment tonight."

"Why?" he asks back quickly, right away.

"I don't know. I mean, it's not a big deal, it's just my stuff is there, and it's easier for me." I look behind him, across Columbus Avenue and into the store that's right across the street. I focus on the mannequins in the window: they're not whole mannequins, they're just the legs, wearing pants.

"Maybe it's not always about being easy for you," Evan says, drawing my attention back to him, away from the pants. "Maybe you'd just want to sleep at my apartment because sometimes it's nice for me to stay at my apartment? Maybe you'd just want to sleep at my apartment to do something nice for me?" He stares at me, eyes bulging accusingly. I can see that this is not the exact best time to say that generally we do stay at his apartment, and that if you counted all the times he's slept at my apartment, and then counted all the times I've slept at his apartment, his apartment—with all the messiness everywhere, covering every single surface, with the complete lack of any pillows that are either decorative or soft—would come out on top.

Evan's eyes debulge ever so slightly and he asks, "I mean when was the last time you did something just to be nice to me?"

I stare back at him. I think how just yesterday I received a *CNN Breaking News* e-mail about how a cow in the United States had tested positive for mad cow disease. Evan is very disciplined with his low-carb diet; I have never seen him eat so much as a grain of rice, yet I have seen him eat countless hamburgers. I forwarded that e-mail to him right away. I am about to point this out, but I feel we are just moments away from jumping onto the hamster wheel that is late-night arguing and not getting any sleep at either of our apartments, and there's something to be said, I think, for not doing that. There's something to be said for not always having to be alone in your apartment, or I guess, come to think of it, the world.

"You're right," I say and watch his expression soften. I take a step in the direction of Evan's apartment, and he falls right in step beside me.

chapter five

Set Me Free,
Why Don't You, Babe

On Sunday morning, I wake up not at Evan's apartment, but at mine; but still, I don't feel right. It's been four days now that I've known about the speech, and every morning when I wake up, without a solution appearing out of thin air, I feel a little bit more like the walls are closing in.

I look over at the sleeping Evan: so still, so quiet, so nonjudgmental, so much easier to get along with this way. So as not to wake him, I slide silently out of bed and into the bathroom. And after the ease that is getting oneself together when one has all their stuff so easily accessible, I actually feel quite appreciative of Evan, appreciative that at the end of the night last night, he just gave the taxi driver my address, in a gesture I have to admit was pretty much a very nice one.

In the spirit of reciprocity, I head into the kitchen and start a pot of coffee. Yes, I am making the coffee for myself, too, but also for Evan. Surely the making of coffee for someone while they are still sleeping counts as something nice? I stand and stare at the coffee as it drips into the pot, and as soon as I've prepared a mug for myself, I bring it over to my desk.

I shuffle through the mail that has piled up over the week, not really expecting to find anything monumental, mail always being such a letdown. Then my eyes fall on a glossy postcard. Suddenly, I have this really fleeting feeling—one that's already almost gone, which I guess is what makes it fleeting—that everything is about to change. I stare at the postcard: it has a bright blue background with green lettering that says, across the top, THE NEW SCHOOL. The New School is downtown, and I think they have an undergraduate program, but mostly it's this great center, this Pug Hill if you will, of continuing education. I took a cooking class there once; Pamela has taken writing classes there; and I know that my boss, May, who likes to dabble in decorative painting, once taught a decorative painting class there. Really, you can take any sort of class you could ever think of at The New School: journalism, acting, French, basket-weaving, anything.

I pick up the card and turn it over in my hand. I focus on the smaller, white words: *It's not too late to register for spring classes!* A thought fills my head, a thought I'm not entirely sure I want there. *I could take a public speaking class.* I turn the card over again, to the other side, to see if maybe the thought will go away. It doesn't. I go so far as to wonder if there might be a public speaking class that hasn't started yet. I mean, clearly there must be lots of classes that haven't started yet, otherwise, why even send the postcard? And then, for a moment, I feel just the slightest bit peaceful.

I hear Evan getting out of bed, making stretching noises; I listen to his feet shuffle across the floor and into the living room.

"Hey, Hope," he says sleepily, yawning, I notice, without covering his mouth.

"Hey, I made coffee," I announce, gesturing proudly in the direction of the kitchen. Evan heads in the direction of the coffee, makes himself a cup, and brings it out to the couch with him. I swivel around in my chair to face him.

"What do you want to do today?" he asks. I lean forward quickly and grab the remote from the coffee table. I turn on New York One to check the weather: thirty-seven degrees. *Damn.*

"Well, maybe let's go to brunch and then see a movie?" I suggest. "It's really cold out."

"Nothing good is playing," he counters back instantly, "and I have squash at four. Want to get brunch and walk over to the Boat Basin and then down by the water? Or maybe," he says brightly, a lightbulb popping up over his head, "there's still some snow on the ground, maybe we could walk around the park and see if we can watch the kids sledding?"

"Watch sledding?" I repeat, with very little enthusiasm.

"Yeah, it'll be fun."

It occurs to me that if it turns out I'm actually more Catholic than I am Jewish, if the Catholic part actually wins out in the end and my eternal soul winds up in hell (for, let's say, being a completely sulky and unenthusiastic girlfriend), then that hell for me will be to spend all eternity with someone whose idea of fun is to freeze his ass off in Central Park WATCHING OTHER PEOPLE SLEDDING!

"Ummm," I say, "what about we get some brunch, and then maybe do you want to go to that place on Amsterdam where you can paint pottery?" I do not actually think this is something that Evan would like to do; I am more just trying to make a point.

Evan doesn't say anything. Evan just looks at me in much

the same way as he looks at me when I've just ordered a white wine spritzer. I look down at the card in my hand.

"What's that?" he asks.

"It's nothing," I say, tossing the postcard back onto the stack of mail. "Do you want to go to Columbus Bakery and then we'll play the rest of the day by ear? Let's do that, that sounds like a good plan," I suggest with what I hope is a tone of finality.

"And then do you want to go for a walk in the park before my squash game?" Evan, as you may have noticed, is not so great at dropping things.

I exhale heavily before answering back, "Why don't we play that part *by ear*?"

Right, dropping things; I might not be so good at that either.

*   *   *

After brunch at Columbus Bakery, Evan and I spent an hour walking around in the park before his squash game. Due to the fact that it had warmed up considerably, combined with the fact that I wore five thousand layers, it was not as cold as I was worrying it would be. During what had to be our millionth long, purposeful walk in the cold, I even briefly considered the possibility that I may envision things (public speaking excepted, of course) to be worse than they actually are. Later, when Evan headed over to the east side for his squash game, I waited until he was out of sight, and headed that way, too. Though I headed east for a very different reason: not to go to The Union Club, but to go to Pug Hill.

As I arrive at Pug Hill, there are actually five or six people here, their pugs all running around in a jumble. All the pugs are in blankets, coats, and sweaters, which sometimes makes it harder to tell who is who. Before I can really look at anything else, before I can pay any sort of attention to all the other wonderful pugs, I look over toward the pine tree. There, sitting on one hip, with his legs splayed jauntily out to the side, proudly showing off his rounded belly, is my favorite pug. Even though he's in a bright green sweater, I recognize him. He's a black pug. Black pugs, just so you know, are my favorite kind of pugs. Black pugs, if you ask me (and really, at this point, who else are you going to ask?), are the very best kind of pugs. When *I* get a pug, I often think, it'll be a black one. This pug, my favorite, he's also so much smaller than the other pugs; his name is Kermit. Kermit, as much as he reminds me of happiness, reminds me of my parents' dog, Annabelle, whom, by the way, I also adore. Annabelle is a French bulldog, but secretly I think she might be a magical black-and-white spotted pug. Just like Annabelle, little Kermit, this little black pug that I adore, is very rough-and-tumble and always looking for an adventure, though he always manages to hold his own.

But right now, Kermit isn't cruising with the other pugs, all of whom are running in circles around each other at the other end of the clearing. Right now, Kermit is just sitting peacefully, right by the pine tree, in this way that makes me think he's waiting for me. I walk toward him.

"Hi, Kermit," I say, leaning down to pet him. He tilts his head to one side, a bit of his pink tongue slipping out the other side. He looks up at me and fixes me in his mesmerizing gaze. I like to believe he's smiling at me, just as I like to believe that sometimes he waits for me, right here by the pine tree. I tilt my head in the same direction as Kermit's and smile back at him. Kermit snorts at me jubilantly, wiggles his curled piglet tail, and dashes off. And just like that, just as I always do when I see a pug, I feel calmer, better than I did before. I feel free.

I watch happily as Kermit's tail bounds in the direction of his owner. I watch, still happily, but also a bit enviously as Kermit's owner reaches down to clip a leash to Kermit's harness. Kermit flattens his ears and coyly shrinks away from the leash, compacting himself into a much smaller pug than he already is. Kermit, you can tell, doesn't want to leave. But even though Kermit's owner, at present, is taking him away, it should be noted that Kermit's owner is one of the cool owners, one of the owners who rarely yells after his pug, who respects that Pug Hill time is important in so many ways, and that pugs need lots of things and that those things do not always include its person braying after it all afternoon.

As a rule though, I try not to pay too much attention to the owners; I try not to go out of my way to figure out which person belongs to which pug. I feel like it cheapens the whole thing, at the least, and at the very most it completely diminishes the serenity. Pug Hill is about so much for me, but I try not to have it be about the people.

I do not, especially not here, want to draw attention to myself. There's part of me that worries a bit that if I did, all the Pug Hill people would start to know me, and think of me as weird, or as a dog stalker, or a little bit sad. I worry sometimes that they'd start to think of me as some crazy pug-watching lady who lives under Bow Bridge. And then, as the years wore on, I'd become a crazy pug-watching lady who lives under Bow Bridge and has no teeth. You can see, I imagine, why it is best that Pug Hill be about the pugs, much more than about the people. I have enough trouble in all the other places of my life with people. I think it's important that I don't have it here.

I head to the bench, take a seat, do my best to forget about having no teeth, and just watch the pugs for a while. I watch them as they spin themselves around in circles, approach one another, jerk back cautiously, and reapproach. I watch them as they stop—almost midstride—to lie on their stomachs, legs out in front, legs out behind as if they are covering a hole in the ground. I listen to them snort, and make other strange but endearing noises for which I'm not sure there are words. And for what's left of the afternoon, I stay on the bench and soak up just a little of their unconditional sweetness.

My whole life I've always felt better in the presence of dogs. And luckily for me, there have always been dogs, even before I was born. Before I was born there was Morgan. Morgan was not a pug, but a Saint Bernard. As I stare out at all the pugs here today, I remember Morgan.

Morgan spent a tremendous amount of her life running through our neighborhood and jumping in other people's swimming pools. My father spent a tremendous amount of Morgan's life tracking her down. But when Morgan was actually at home, I always felt like she looked out for me. When I was a baby and Darcy came into my room and picked me up out of my crib and dropped me on the floor, it was Morgan who barked to wake my parents, even before I had started crying. I always think she must have known what I was up against, being up against Darcy. And later, Morgan used to sit with me for hours on the yellow shag carpet in my room, letting me stick pieces of yarn up her nose.

When the sky starts to get dark, I take one last look out at the pugs, before I reluctantly start to head back to the west side. As I pass the playground that's right there, right when you walk out of the park, I pause for a moment to look at the pewter metal plaque by its gate: THE DIANA ROSS PLAYGROUND. Suddenly, song lyrics pop into my head like so many sequin-clad Supremes: *Set me free why don't you, babe? Get out my life why don't you, babe?* I think I know why. As I cross Central Park West though, I wonder if I've even got it right, wonder, *Did Diana Ross even sing that?*

When I get to Columbus Avenue, instead of heading to

my apartment, I keep walking west, over to Broadway. I have decided to fight with the hysterical, asylum-bound people who like to shop at Fairway on Sunday evening. Fairway, in case you don't know, is this Upper West Side market where they have just about everything edible you could ever think of, and also, you can get a good deal there. Because of that combination, it is the most crowded, frantic market in all of New York. Sometimes, even, I imagine Fairway to be the most frantic market, with the most unpleasant clientele, in all the world. Though I'm probably wrong about that. Being generally more interested in peace and quiet than I am interested in a good price on my produce, I don't go to Fairway very often. Pretty much, I can't handle Fairway, but after a while with the pugs, I think it will be easier.

And you might be wondering why I have decided to fight the hysterical, asylum-bound people at Fairway. It's not actually because I think I'm about to become one of them. But rather because Evan is the type of guy who gets all excited if you have a plate of cheese and crackers out for him. Evan will be coming over later, and I'm still thinking how he said I never do anything nice for him. I'm thinking that maybe I have more to do with this bad place we're in than I generally acknowledge, and I'm thinking that maybe all with Evan might not need to be lost.

And what better way to say, "I'd really like everything to work out," than with a nice plate of crackers and cheese? Though, come to think of it, Evan won't eat the carb-laden crackers. But still, there'll be the cheese.

chapter six

Elliot, My Elliot

I can see the IM man bouncing out of the corner of my eye.
I should never have turned it on. I should, most likely, not
have IM at all. Or at the very least, I should angle my easel
in a way so that it is behind my desk, and not off to the side
of it, so that when the bouncing yellow man starts bouncing
so insistently, so impatiently, I am unaware.

I swivel on my stool, grab my mouse, and click.

EVAN2020: *Are you mad?*

I stare for a moment at the IM window, at all that empty
white space in which to answer Evan. But I don't want to
talk to Evan right now. I don't for that matter want to talk
about Evan. Suffice it to say, though the cheese was much
appreciated, last night did not go well. I stare for a few

moments more, and as I do so, it occurs to me that Evan is the only person who ever IM's me. I quit out of IM without answering and turn back to my easel.

I work diligently through lunch, seldom taking my eyes off the Rothko, a vision, if you will, of concentration. I've been trying to match the exact shade of red that Rothko used. I've been mixing together different reds—vermillion and alizarin—on my palette, painting it over different shades of yellow and white in an effort to find a perfect match. Though I haven't been able to match the exact color just yet, I'm slightly optimistic. I think, with a little more concentration, that I might be getting close.

At three, May announces with an air of mystery that she's leaving for an important meeting and will not be back. As soon as she is out the door, I notice Sergei over there on the other side of the room, making a beeline for his desk. Sergei doesn't work at his desk, since he's the structural guy and has to lay his canvases out flat, and be near the heating table and such. I think how it might be nicer to have Sergei's job, how it might be nicer to be always away from my desk, away from the computer and the lure of the IM. There's something to be said, I think, for being "the structural guy," something to be said for not spending as much time as I do staring at only surfaces.

It's clear now that I'm out of my groove. So I do what I always try not to do, just as much as it is what I always want to do. I look across the room at Elliot.

He's holding his paintbrush lightly against his chest. He takes a step back, oblivious to anything else around him, and stares, so intently, with all the focus in the world at the canvas in front of him. *Oh, God*, I think, *to be that canvas. Or at the very least, to be that paintbrush.*

It's not altogether my fault. The whole Elliot thing, it all really took me by surprise. In my defense, I was taken a little offguard. It's not like my place of employment is one that is typically crawling with cute, hot, smart, hip, eligible men. Before Elliot Death (it's pronounced Deeth, just so you know), with all his qualifications and accolades, arrived here three months ago, I'd never once been confronted by a cute and eligible coworker. It was just something I never thought would happen, ever. Until, of course, it did.

Most people apply to the Met, like I did, like Sergei did. Elliot was wooed here from the Brooklyn Museum, because he's so good at what he does. Wooed by the Met, can you imagine? I couldn't before I met Elliot. But then, as soon as I did, I realized instantly that such is the way of Elliot. Elliot Death is just that type of guy. He is the type of guy whose very focused and studious presence will make you forget everything else around you. He is the type of guy who makes you hear Natalie Merchant singing in your background, and makes you see *New York Times* wedding announcements in your future. Granted, they are wedding announcements that include the words, "The bride will be keeping her name," but they are wedding announcements all the same.

But I digress. It's kind of hard these days not to. So, anyway, Elliot arrived here, wooed, and I tried not to get all infatuated with him, knowing it was unprofessional at best to be infatuated with a coworker, but I did anyway. And then, perhaps not so coincidentally, once things recently started going to the bad place with Evan, I just fell that much harder. And it hasn't worked out well for me.

Sergei walks by me, carrying a tacking iron. He looks at me quizzically and I wonder if he knows I am secretly (or not so) in lust with Elliot. I smile at Sergei, feeling slightly embarrassed, and as I turn back to the now endless-seeming sea of red on my Rothko, I feel a little bit like a slacker for thinking so much about Elliot when there is so much work that needs to be done. I'm so tired right now of looking at the Rothko, but undoubtedly it is a better bet than looking over anymore at Elliot. I grab my magnifying visor and pull it down over my eyes. I think maybe that might help. I think, pretty much, *something's* got to.

Lately, I've been beginning to realize that in addition to being the endless object of my fascination, Elliot Death also happens to be the personification of why people tell you not to fall head over heels in lust with your coworkers. Granted, people generally might more often say, "Don't date your coworkers," but if they knew falling head over heels in lust with your coworkers without even dating them was a risk, they'd warn you against that, too.

Trust me on this one. Look around you, any cute coworkers? If so, there is only one thing to do: shun them. Because if it doesn't work out, because let's say he doesn't seem to take any notice of you at all *and* he has a girlfriend, *and* you have a boyfriend, having to see him every day, day in and day out, by virtue of the fact that you are in the same place as him day in and day out (seeing as you are coworkers and all) will make the whole "it's not gonna happen" thing an entirely harder ballgame. It will all be so much harder than it would be if the person whom you lusted after went every day to, say, Bhutan, as opposed to a desk not ten feet away from you. I know this now.

Perhaps I knew this before, perhaps it was clear to me the second I met Elliot—the second I looked up and said to myself, "No way, a cute, hot, straight paintings restorer?" But I, when it comes to matters of the heart, am nothing if not a slow learner.

I force myself to focus in a bit closer on the Rothko, and think to myself, as I think about so many things these days,

Why is it so hard? I've spent basically my whole career as a paintings restorer dealing mostly with the nineteenth century and earlier. I've spruced up more Hudson River School landscapes than you could shake a stick at. But actually, don't really shake a stick, because shaking sticks, they can break loose and fly right onto the surface of a painting that I worked really hard and long and meticulously to get right. I've gotten to the point at last where I feel pretty confident in my ability to diagnose and fix all the problems of the seventeenth-century Dutch paintings, the eighteenth century, the nineteenth century; but the modern stuff, the contemporary stuff—which at this late date is still so frighteningly new to me—is a whole different story. With paintings restoration, the problems of today are a lot trickier to fix than the ones of the distant past; you'd think that the reverse might be true, but trust me it's not.

When I need to look away from my easel again, I don't look across the room at Elliot, but instead I look down at the floor. There on the floor is my bag, and as I look at it, I'm so aware of what's inside it: the postcard from The New School. I reach in, fish around, and pull it out. I flip the card over in my hand. I read the crisp, white lettering: *It's not too late to sign up for spring classes!* And then, suddenly, everything flips. I'd been so sure that the problem of the speech was the one problem I surely couldn't do anything to solve. That, I realize, just might not be entirely true. It occurs to me right now that maybe my biggest problem, bigger than Evan or Elliot, or even the speech, is that I refuse to face my fears, and that I never want to confront my issues. With the way the world has been lately caving in on me, it's become really clear that something's got to give. It occurs to me that now, *right now,* is as good a time as any to start facing my fears.

I all but lunge for my mouse. I click open the IM again.

hopemcneill: *Evan?*
EVAN2020: *y?*
hopemcneill: *I'm not mad, but I'm really sorry but I don't
    think I can make it to dinner tonight.*
EVAN2020: *why?*
hopemcneill: *I have to go downtown*

I sign off before there can be more, before there can be
anything else.

chapter seven

Overcoming Presentation Anxiety

For the rest of the afternoon, I manage to only think, "Elliot Death, light of my light, heart of my heart," once. And yes, I know that such a phrase isn't quite as poetic as it could be, but if you think about it, these days, so few things are.

And then, as an added bonus, when I leave the museum, it isn't even so cold out at all. I walk down Fifth, all the way to Central Park South. I stop and look at The Plaza, wishing briefly, as I always do, that instead of me, I were Eloise. I persevere in my mission, get on the R train and take it down to Union Square. After a dread-filled but brief subway ride, I'm walking down Twelfth Street, and then I'm standing right outside The New School.

I take a deep breath, and walk in. And there it is, a wall display, just teeming with Spring Bulletins. Slowly, I approach; even more slowly, I reach out and take one. Back out on the

street again, Spring Bulletin in hand, I open it up and start
flipping through the pages of course offerings, hoping and
not hoping all at the same time, that there might be the right
class.

There is a class called Overcoming Presentation Anxiety.
I like that name: so Zoloft-like in spirit, it makes so much
more sense to me than something generic and simple, like
Public Speaking I. There is still part of me that hopes there
won't be a class that fits into my schedule. Because wouldn't
it be nice to attempt to face your fears but be momentarily
off the hook because scheduling-wise, it just wasn't going
to work out? But alas, Overcoming Presentation Anxiety
meets every Thursday night for six weeks, and it starts next
week.

It all seems so perfect, so terrifyingly perfect; the last
class is in the last week of April, just a week before my parents' party. If I sign up for this class, I will be training in the
complexities of public speaking, dealing with my fear of it,
right up to the point where I will actually have to face it. I fold
down the page the class is on, along with the page that explains
how to register for the class via phone, fax, or Internet. It
occurs to me that so much of this—the timing of the class,
the duration of the class, the very Zoloft-esque name of the
class—it all really seems like it might be meant to be. There
is part of me, though, that wishes it wasn't.

I head to the bus stop to catch the uptown bus. Though
the bus is perhaps not the most efficient means of getting
oneself from the Village to the Upper West Side, I prefer it.
And even though in the interest of time, I take trains up and
downtown much more often than I take the bus, I'm actually
a little bit afraid of trains. An express bus pulls up, oxymo-
ron that it is, and I get on; luckily, as I've got a ways to go,
I find a seat. I wonder, as the bus heads sluggishly uptown,
about all the things that are meant to be, and how it seems

with me that there is always somewhere between a slight to enormous disconnect between what is meant to be and what I think I would like so much better.

*   *   *

On the top step of the outdoor steps of my brownstone, I stop for a minute and look down again at The New School catalog in my hand. I angle the cover toward me just to see it better, just to remind myself that this is real, that this is what I am going to do. *It is,* I tell myself, tightening my grip on the catalog, tightening my resolve. *Sometimes*, I tell myself firmly, *people just really need to confront their issues.*

My cell phone beeps twice as if in agreement with the fact that sometimes people really do need to confront their issues. Also, it does that when I have a text message. With my free hand, I fish my cell phone out of my bag. I push the button for text messages.

> *@ regency hotel having many cocktails. You should come.*
> *C U soon??—E.*

I look at the *E* for longer than I look at the rest of it. I try to imagine how different I would feel if the *E* in my message, in my night, in my life, stood for Elliot instead of Evan. In the cell phone of my mind, I start typing, in all capital letters, the letters that I wish came after *E*.

L.L.I.

I stop there, pretending that Elliot and I have skipped ahead, to some parallel future in some parallel reality, where I don't have a boyfriend and he doesn't have a girlfriend, and also, doesn't ignore me. Some future in which we call each other pet names. I'm not quite sure yet what his name for me would be, but my name for him, I'm sure of it, would be Elli. I stop typing there also because there is a small, sensible part of me that stands off to the side, reminding me that pretending Evan's text message is from Elliot is more than a little fucked up. But I try not to think too much about how fucked up it is. Because while, yes, people really do need to confront their issues, I don't necessarily think they need to confront them all at once.

chapter eight

Just Like
Jean-Paul Belmondo,
Albeit Briefly

As I set my keys down, in their proper spot on the mantle, I notice out of the corner of my eye that the answering machine is blinking. *No,* I think, *it really can't be.* And that, pretty much, is not a good thing to think when you see a blinking light and think it is a message from your boyfriend. I hit play.

"It's Kara, just calling to say hi. Um, we're going out tonight, so give a call or send an e tomorrow. Looking forward to seeing you next Saturday. Chloe says hi, too." Kara is my foil-to-Pamela friend, and also my best friend. Having a friend like Kara, who's as wonderful and caring a friend as she is, makes it, I think, okay to also have a friend like Pamela—a friend who while also good, says judgmental things to you, that you of course take to heart, for fear that her insistence on not taking them back could mean that in them there is some kernel of truth. And so to prove her wrong, you mess up your life. And yes, I know that perhaps I'm taking that tangent a bit far.

And I like Pamela a lot, too, really I do, just not as much as Kara. I think that's okay, I think when it comes to your friends, it's just natural to have a favorite. I'm not a person with tons and tons of friends. I think the upkeep, the social whirlwind that surely would be involved in maintaining many, many friends, in the way of someone like Evan, is, to put it nicely, not in my nature; to put it less than nicely, it is really quite beyond me. But given that I do have two very close friends, and they are on the opposite sides of the spectrum in terms of what types of friends they are, I feel sometimes that these two, my two, are so representative of the very different kinds of friendships a woman can have, that in essence it's really like having many more.

I look at the calendar on my desk: there, written in red is Kara's daughter Chloe's second birthday party next Saturday. Evan's not coming with me. Evan has a general rule about not attending baby parties. His logic being that if you go to one, you have to go to all of them so as not to offend, and these days, seeing as we are both in our thirties, that would mean spending a hell of a lot of time at baby birthday parties. The thought of how every moment spent at a child's birthday party would be a moment not taking a long, purposeful walk in the cold prevents me from acknowledging that he does have a very good point.

I sit down at my desk and turn on my laptop. I sit back in my chair for a minute, as the light from the computer screen glows out at me. I hesitate and look around my apartment. Before I can type The New School's Web address into my Internet Explorer, the phone starts ringing. I am sure it is ringing in a way that is hostile.

"Hello," I say, knowing as I do that it is perhaps a bit hostile in itself to answer the phone sounding so tense.

"Hope, it's your mother."

"Hi," I say.

"Are you tense?" she asks.

"No," I say quickly. "I just walked in is all. Hi," I say again, so we can go back to the normal start of a phone call, without the whole are-you-tense segue. Because, really, I am not tense.

"Dad tells me he called and mentioned the speech," she says, and I want encouragement, love, coddling. That is what I want, but this is not the place to get it. Mom doesn't know about my fear of public speaking. As skilled as I am at running from my fears, I am more expert at not owning up to them.

"Yeah, yes," I say too quickly, a bit robotically. "I'm so happy that you asked. I'm really looking forward to it." Mom doesn't say anything for a moment and I wonder for a second if she's about to call me on it, to say that not only am I a big fraidy cat, I am also a liar. *Love thyself,* I think for some reason, as I try to slow the quickening of my pulse.

In with hysteria, I think, taking a deep breath, *out with love.* Or, wait, is that supposed to be the other way around?

"Good," she says, instead of "fraidy cat," or "liar," and then she says, "we're looking forward to it, too." We make small talk for a while; everything, I say, is just fine with me and everything, she says, is just fine with her. And then the topic turns to Evan.

"How's Evan?" she asks, and the very tone of her voice reminds me that even though I have my moments when I am so convinced they are in this together, determined to chip away happily at my self-esteem, they are, in fact, not. The tone of her voice reminds me that Mom is no longer a fan of Evan, hasn't been since I told her recently about how he criticized my hair and said I brushed it too much. I'm sure that when I told her this, there had to have been a part of her that had to hold herself back from jumping in and saying that with everything colorists are doing these days, there is no reason at all that I have to walk around with it red. But I think what won out in the end was the part of her that felt critiquing me was her domain and her domain alone, and that Evan was not invited to join the club.

"He's fine," I say and listen to the silence on the end of the phone. I've been dating for a while now, for quite a long while come to think of it. You'd think somewhere along the way I would have wrapped my head around the concept of not telling my mother bad things about my boyfriends. I haven't. In case you have some trouble with this concept, too, let me try to help you, since clearly, I am beyond help. If you're going to listen to anything I say, listen to this: Do not tell your mother bad things about your boyfriend. Repeat this to yourself a few times; maybe it will help: *Do not tell your mother bad things about your boyfriend. Do not tell your mother bad things about your boyfriend.*

Sure, getting it off your chest and all, it might make you feel better *momentarily*. But what happens inevitably is that you will forget all about whatever it is that upset you in the first place, and continue on in your relationship happy as a lark (or some approximation thereof, adjust as necessary). Your mother, however, if she is anything like my mother, will never forget. Once the bad information is out there, your mother will forever change her once-happy tune about your boyfriend. She will go quite quickly from commenting loudly, whenever his name comes up, on how much he looks like Jean-Paul Belmondo (that you have no idea who Jean-Paul Belmondo is, let alone what he looks like, is clearly beside the point) to commenting repeatedly on the fact that he is a schmuck.

"Has he told you he loves you yet?" she asks. Mom isn't one to beat around the bush. I, on the other hand, have been known to beat around the bush and have even been known to take some solace in that bush. Solace, it seems, is nothing if not fragile.

So, yeah, there's that. Evan has never told me that he loves me. It's one of the problems with the Evan thing. I told him I loved him once. The fact that I was drunk when I said it, that it was midnight on New Year's Eve at that, and the fact that I most likely didn't mean it at all outside of the context of that "Auld Lang Syne" moment, when you just want someone to love and want that someone to love you back, has become severely overshadowed by the fact that Evan didn't say anything back.

If you go by what my mother says is acceptable and not acceptable, six months of dating with nary an *I love you* to bandy about, is six months too long. I consider my answer, consider lying and think how much easier that would be. But I also consider how things would be different for me right now if I hadn't lied by omission so many times about how afraid I am of public speaking.

"No," I say, resigned.

"Schmuck," she says, and to hear her say it, it all seems so simple. I wonder if it really is, even as I simultaneously try to push the thought from my mind.

"No, Mom, he's not a schmuck," I say, my mind kaleidoscoping onto the very first hours of this year.

"No, um, honey, I think that maybe he is."

"He's not," I say, again, letting every tense cadence in my voice loose, free to scurry down the phone line, all the while thinking that maybe he is. Mom doesn't say anything else; it's not a talent you can teach, knowing how to usher a pause into a conversation so that even *silence* sounds disapproving.

"Mom," I tell her, this time more firmly, "Evan isn't a schmuck." What does it say, I wonder, that with all the time I have spent thinking lately that Evan is indeed a schmuck that right now I'm so motivated to jump to his defense? A little voice, one of the dramatic ones, pops into my head. "Oh, what does it mean?" it exclaims, arms theatrically outstretched. I refuse to indulge it. Really, I have too many other things to think about.

"Okay, Mom," I say again, once the screaming silence has become far too much to bear, approximately two and a half seconds later. "I'm going to be late."

"What are you going to be late for?"

I look over at my cell phone, lying forlorn on the table, The New School catalog lying next to it in a way that I want so very badly to believe is hopeful.

"I'm going to meet Evan," I say. I'm going across town, I think, back over to the Upper East Side to have a drink with my boyfriend, even though his drink of choice is Scotch, and I hate the smell of Scotch, even though if *anyone* shuns their Judaism, it's Evan, and even though all his friends are so Biffy, all their girlfriends so Buffy.

chapter nine

Don't Hate the Player, Hate the Game

An hour later, and I am sitting next to Evan on a banquette in the library bar at the Regency Hotel. The squash-playing friends are in a different area of the bar with a group of Junior League–type women, only the occasional *caw-caw* sounds, the intermittent, "Oh, Brandon, really, stop," belie their existence. Evan is crunching on his Scotch-soaked ice cubes, there is such a determination in the way he crunches them so. I am eating M&M's. The Regency has these big glass urns everywhere, filled with M&M's; their very presence makes everything else about the place infinitely more enjoyable. I grab another handful and turn to face Evan. *He is my boyfriend,* I think, *my supporter, my confidant.* I can tell him this. I take a breath.

"I think I'm going to sign up for a public speaking class," I blurt out.

"Yeah?" he says sort of distantly, looking across the room. I wonder if he's thinking about his squash game, or about the next time everyone at The Union Club decides to dress in Lilly Pulitzer just for fun, or about something else entirely. I follow his gaze to the Junior Leaguey women, and I wonder if he wishes one of them were his girlfriend instead of me.

"Yes," I continue. "There's a class starting next week at The New School."

"Uh-huh," he says nonchalantly and I have to remind myself that it isn't his fault; he doesn't realize what a big deal all of this is. Because I haven't told him.

"What night?" he asks absently.

"Thursdays."

"Thursday nights?" he asks, turning his attention to me. "Why that night?" *Why that night,* I repeat to myself. This is what he asks. He asks, "Why that night?" instead of the clearly so much more appropriate, "Why are you taking the class?" I mean generally people don't take a public speaking class just for fun, do they? Generally, there's something there, some sort of back story, some sort of reason why someone would want to take that class. Shouldn't the question here really be, "Why are you taking the class?" Shouldn't that be the question? Wouldn't it *all* be so much better if he cared about the *why,* more than he cared about the *why that night*?

"Because that's the night the class is offered," I say, simultaneously wishing I'd never said anything, and also wondering if this could be one of the instances in which I'm maybe too hard on Evan, if asking, "Why that night?" isn't really as big a deal as I am making it out to be.

"Thursday night is a big going-out night; it'd just be better if the class was a different night." *This* is what he says, and any thoughts, any thoughts at all that I am being unfair, unkind, too hard, they just evaporate, vaporize. I look back at him and say nothing.

"There's not another night?" he asks and I shake my head no, to which he feels compelled to say, "Everything is replaceable, Hope."

Evan likes one-liners; especially likes this one-liner, "Everything is replaceable." He sprinkles it into conversation as often as possible. Once it had been around awhile, bandied about enough to clue me in to the fact that it was a favorite saying, it had struck me as a really sad outlook, and I hoped I'd never be the type of person to say things like "everything is replaceable." Later I began to wonder if it, this saying, was maybe some kind of threat. Right now I only wonder if Evan simply spews one-liners all the time, one-liners that mean absolutely nothing just because he likes to hear himself speak.

"That makes no sense," I snap, and snapping, if you think about it, is better than the alternatives, better than, let's say, standing up and screaming at the top of your lungs, or running, arms flailing, out into the street.

"Everything is replaceable," I mimic, and while mimicking is as ungracious as snapping, it, too, is better than other options. "It's not in the right context," I try to explain. "It's just a dumb thing to say."

"No, *Hope,* it's not," he snaps back, leaning forward in his seat toward me. "I'm just saying that if you wanted to, you could do it another night." I slide back an inch or two on the banquette, away from him.

"And I'm just saying I can't, that is the only night." I try to gather my thoughts, as much as they can, at present, possibly be gathered. "And, I'm not just saying that, I'm also saying that 'everything is replaceable' doesn't fit. I'm saying that, too."

"What do you want me to say?" he says, tilting his glass back, another ice cube sliding to its unhappy end. I just wanted him to say, "Why?" That is what I wanted. Want*ed,* past tense, because I don't want it anymore.

"I just want you to say you think it will help," I tell him, and lean back against a cushion.

"I think it will help," he says, and the fact that he says it, somehow only makes me feel worse.

"Thanks," I say. "Do you want to go home?"

"I want to have another drink." He signals a waitress and first orders a Scotch for himself, and then turns to look at me in a way that I am sure says, "Order something other than a white wine spritzer."

"A white wine spritzer," I say and glare at him and we sit. There would be something to be said for letting this conversation end; this I know. But also, there might be something to be said for explaining how hard this is to Evan. I take another bracing breath and try to explain it to him.

"It's just," I begin, "I've been so scared of it, of public speaking, so scared of it my whole life and now I have to do it, soon. See, my parents want me to make a speech at their anniversary party and I can't say no, but I don't know if for a thing like this, this big, if I can say yes and mean it, and I'm just really freaked out, and really scared." I say it all at once, so quickly. He looks back at me, he cocks his head slightly, in a way that I think could be thoughtful. There is a small, tiny part of me that thinks, *this is it*, this is where Evan actually *gets it,* where everything that I thought was wrong about us turns out not to be such a big deal at all, because the most important thing is that *he gets it*.

"I love public speaking," he says. "I really excel at it." And that small tiny part of me: it dies. I urge the parts of me that are still living to take a deep breath.

"Really?" I say, telling myself that completely freaking out in the middle of the bar at the Regency Hotel might be something I'd look back on later with regret.

"Yeah," he says, "If you Google me, an article from the *Pennsylvania Gazette* comes up. It's from when I went back to Wharton to speak on a panel. I spoke about hedge funds," he explains.

Who Googles themselves? Do people really do this? I stare at him blankly. Evan doesn't care that I'm staring blankly. Evan just keeps talking.

"They say, 'Evan Russell, consummate public speaker.'"

"Consummate, huh?" I say.

"Yeah, consummate," he says. And then, "Thanks," to the waitress as she sets down his new Scotch. He leans forward and takes a first sip and then turns back to look at me. His eyes sparkle; they always do. I wonder if confidence, if appearing to be so sure of yourself, even when there is quite a lot of evidence to suggest that you are not, if that is what makes a person's eyes sparkle. Or if it's something else.

I look over at Evan and take a sip of my spritzer. It's times like this, when I notice the way his eyes sparkle, that I can understand why I ever thought I loved him. Just as it makes it all so clear why I don't think I love him anymore and makes me wonder, actually, if I ever did. He drinks his Scotch and I drink my spritzer. I eat some more M&M's, and we sit in silence for a while.

"Do you want to have another drink?" he asks me, hopeful, once his Scotch glass is once again empty, the ice-cube pillage but moments away.

"I don't care," I say. And I don't, because right this second I know that no matter how hard I try, I won't be able to hang on to that phone call when he said, "All I want in the world is to have another drink with you," and I melted. That was just a phone call. No matter how much I want it to be, it's not going to be more than that. And it's certainly not going to be enough.

"Don't be scared, Hope," he says, and I feel for a moment like he's saying things out of context again. But then, maybe it's not as out of context as I think. It occurs to me, and I'm sure it can't be for the first time, that maybe there are things in this world other than public speaking that scare the hell out of me.

*   *   *

As our taxi speeds through Central Park on the way over to the west side, that very thought is still very much in the forefront of my mind. I have the feeling it's scouting around, looking for a good place to pitch a tent. I have a feeling it wants to stay for a while. I'm not sure I want it there. I turn to Evan.

"Maybe we could get out on Broadway and get a slice of pizza?" I say.

"Why do you want pizza?"

"Well, we've been drinking for sport all night." I let the words hang there between us. The staying-home-versus-going-out war, in which we have for a few months now been engaged, had been the topic of a vigorous argument the week before, one in which I had made him so mad that he threw a microwave pizza (pre-microwaving) at me. I'd been so sure that was going to be the argument to end all arguments, the one to segue into the breakup, but somehow it never did. The fact that I am bringing up pizza again right now should in no way be seen as a coincidence.

"I didn't have dinner," I add on, "and I'm hungry."

"You'd think five million M&M's would have done the trick." He exhales in this way, this aggressive way that ends in a little snort. It reminds me of Pamela. I think this is fitting, as this is all her fault.

The cab pulls up outside of Evan's building. He has not, as it worked out, asked the cab to stop on Broadway. As we walk toward his building, I think of how tonight, how so many nights, I would so much prefer sleeping at my apartment, with the nicer pillows and all my stuff. I exhale myself, and Evan stops in his tracks and says, *"What, Hope?"* He says it meanly, as meanly as you can say, *"What, Hope?"* And then, just like that, I know what comes next.

"Evan." I take another breath, let it out.

"No, Hope, listen," he says. *He's going to say it first*, I think, and I think also that maybe I prefer it this way, that maybe I always have.

"Hope," he says again, and I feel like it's been so many times already tonight that he's said my name. I wonder if maybe he thinks someone else is here, too? "I just don't think this is worth it," he says it softly, not so meanly at all. A line from a song that I don't know the name of pops into my head: *I was the one worth leaving.* I try not to listen to it.

"I-I don't either," I say, instead of anything else. I look away from the sidewalk that up until now I have been staring at so intently. I look up at Evan and I think it's the first time I've ever seen him look sad.

The past six, almost seven, months with Evan flash before my eyes, much in the manner of one Stouffer's microwave pizza. It occurs to me that I could possibly stop this, that maybe I could say something about trying to be better or trying to find compromise. It occurs to me that maybe we could go together, just about ten blocks up Columbus to the Patagonia store and buy some new fleece things and some microfiber, the kind of materials that would wick away the cold. I could wear my fleece and see the meaning behind long, purposeful walks in the cold, and things right away would be better between us.

But I don't say anything at all to Evan, because right now

I know I'm afraid of more than just public speaking, and I want to believe that it's entirely possible that sometimes the only thing to fear is fear itself.

"Sorry," he says. I wait, but he doesn't say my name again. He looks at me. I tell myself it is nothing if not unwise to try to build a foundation with someone who will throw a pizza at you.

"I'm sorry, too," I say, even though I harbor darkness in my heart, even though I'm pretty sure that I'm not. And then for a while neither of us says anything.

"I mean, uh, it's late and all, and do you want to, like, talk about this more, do you want to come inside? I don't want to be a dick or anything."

No, I think, *of course not.*

"It's okay, I think I'm just gonna go," I say and I feel like I've done this already, a million times before.

"Here, I'll hail you a cab," he says and starts walking over to Broadway. I walk with him and I think that it's good, that all he's saying right now to me is that he'll hail me a cab. I think it's so much better than other things he could say, things along the lines of, "Hope, don't you have anything, anything at all, to say?" or, "Hope, I just want you to know I really did care about you," or "Hope, I just want you to know I don't really think your upper arms are fat." Because any of those things, any combination of them or even any of them alone would, I am pretty sure, make me cry. And I don't want to cry.

A taxi stops and we stand for a moment outside of it, and I worry it's going to drive away without me. And then, I want it to.

"You know," I say, "I think I'll walk."

"Are you sure? It's late."

"It's not that late," I tell him, and also, I'm telling myself, too. "It's really not."

Evan leans over to the cab driver's window, waves and

shakes his head no, and the cab drives away. He reaches out right then and touches my arm, just under my elbow, and leaves his hand there for a moment. As our eyes meet, I want to be the type of person who will remember this. I want to be the type of person who remembers that there was softness, tenderness even, in the way he touched my arm and held it for a moment, right under the elbow. But I know I'm not.

I walk up a block and then cut over to Columbus. Columbus feels safer to walk on alone when it's late, even though, as I mentioned already, it's not that late.

chapter ten

There's One, One Pug

I know what I don't need right now. What I don't need right now is to go to Pug Hill and be reminded that the pugs are not always there. But the thought, that if I went there, I would maybe see a pug, overrides any memory of how much worse I felt when there were no pugs at Pug Hill. And anyway, I've never been tremendously skilled at learning from my mistakes. Historically, I've been much more of a fan of trying them out for a second time.

Though I do aspire to be the type of person who learns from her mistakes, or at least from her previous breakups. If you get to thirty-one years old and find yourself single, as I now have, chances are that in order to get here, you've gotten yourself through quite a few breakups, quite a few breakups from which you can learn. Unless, of course, you've had one boyfriend or even a husband for the past, say, ten years and at thirty-one, this is the first breakup you are dealing with. If that is the case, I fear I cannot help you with the knowledge I've spent a while now accumulating.

Granted, as far as breakups go, I know that the Evan breakup is going to be slightly easier, because I really do believe that the leaving of this relationship is such a better thing than staying in it. But even so, there will be things I'll have to hurdle over, concepts I'll have to wrap my head around. The first, and I believe the most important, thing that I will need to understand is that things are going to be different. Clearly.

This morning, for example, when I first woke up, the first thing that popped into my head was no longer a muddled, fuzzy, *What is going on with me and Evan, and why are we even holding on to any of it, and why don't we just break up?* The first thing rather was crisp, clear: *I am single. Here I am.* And that, I'm pretty sure, was as good a place as any to start. And then I thought about Pug Hill and how I'd like to go there before work, just really quickly, and see if maybe any pugs were there.

I get ready for work as quickly as I can. I don't linger over the paper or spend a lot of time figuring out what to wear, because of Elliot and all. Today is not, out of respect mostly for the relationship that just ended, a day to think about Elliot. As I head out the door, I realize something: I have to get my coffee at Starbucks now.

Today is not the day to go to Columbus Bakery, the place where I usually go in the mornings to get coffee. Columbus Bakery, for years, was just Columbus Bakery, a place with excellent coffee—so excellent as to overshadow the stressful clientele and a mind-bogglingly disorganized and really rather senseless ordering system. But then the inevitable association happened. Maybe it was because he liked the coffee there as much as I do, or maybe it was because I'd clued in fairly early on that the suggestion of a trip to Columbus Bakery could sometimes keep us from the never-ending game of Arctic Explorer that Evan always seemed so determined to play. But somewhere along the way, Columbus Bakery went from being just a place to being an *Evan* place. And now, I can't go there.

It isn't the time to get nostalgic. Nostalgic, as everyone who has ever had a breakup knows, is just a stop or two away on the train from Maybe-It-Wasn't-All-That-Bad-ville. I tell myself that no matter how lonely I may feel in the days to come, when the IM's don't pop up on my computer screen, when there isn't anyone there on weekend mornings (even if the person who was there on weekend mornings believed himself to be Nanuk of the North), I know I don't want to go to Maybe-It-Wasn't-All-That-Bad-ville. I've stopped by this town so many times in my past. It's taken me a long time, longer perhaps than most, to figure out that they don't tell you the truth there.

* * *

Starbucks, I am compelled to say, as I cue up behind five or six comparatively less-stressed-out-than-the-Columbus-Bakery types, feels remarkably (or at least comparatively) more serene. How sad really, if you think about it, for Columbus Bakery. To be so disorganized and stressful and chaotic that your very existence can make a Manhattan Starbucks seem peaceful, even serene? I imagine though that the Columbus Bakery people, clearly an oblivious lot if ever there was one, do not care about things like this.

Serenity though, just like solace, can be quite fragile. It's a lesson I seem to be learning and learning again a lot lately. As I approach the counter, in the instant that I make eye contact with the Starbucks person, I get so confused I'm not sure what it is that I want. I just don't know and, on top of that, I have forgotten what everything means.

Is it a *grande* that I want or a *venti*? And then, just like that, regardless of what I've been telling myself all morning, regardless of what I've been telling myself for all the months leading up to this morning, I *miss* Evan. Or maybe I just *think* that I miss him, but, really, I don't know what the difference is. As my eyes start to sting, I think, maybe not for the first time, that I am insane. I tell myself that I don't really miss Evan, that I'm just really bad at change. I forge ahead, I order a tall coffee, and a moment later, when it is handed over to me, it looks so small.

"Can I have a large coffee?" I say. "Please," I add on hastily, because the Starbucks person, the barista (I think barista is what they're supposed to be called) does not look pleased.

"You ordered a tall," she tells me. She points this out in such a way that I do not feel she is inclined, on her own, to simply pour the small coffee into a larger cup and then add some more. Yes, of course the obvious here is that I suggest this to her, but there is, I fear, the looming possibility of a horrible, "that's wasting a cup" scene, or something along those lines.

I stare for a moment at the small coffee in front of me. Starbucks is such a ubiquitous part of normal city life, and I've just completely missed it. It's like working at a place where there are conference rooms and water coolers and clients, where coworkers go out at night for drinks together. It is everything that is normal and everyday about living and working in New York, and I, for the life of me right now, just don't get it. I don't want, after everything else, to be a Starbucks cliché. And this might already be obvious, but to tell you the truth, I have a small (tall?) problem with confrontation.

Instead of anything else, I look up and say, "Okay, then, could I please have another tall, too?" and I kid you not, the Starbucks person, the barista, she rolls her eyes at me, just like Evan. I wonder if maybe it's all so I don't get too overwhelmed with things so suddenly being so different. I wonder if it's all just so I feel a little bit like nothing has really changed. It occurs to me that lately I have been spending a lot of time wanting to believe that everything is a sign. It also occurs to me that, like it or not, I don't think the world actually works that way.

"Thank you," I say, at the arrival of my second coffee. I walk away, two coffees in hand. I stop at the coffee preparation station, add Splenda, skim milk, twice; I look at my watch and I don't have that much time. I hurry out the door, hurry across Central Park, double-fisting coffee and hoping a little bit against hope that there might be some pugs.

* * *

There's one. One pug on her own. I see her owner out of the corner of my eye. He's this guy I recognize from other times; he's got these bright white Tretorns on every single time I see him. It always makes me wonder: where do you even find Tretorns these days? It's not like I wouldn't like a pair for myself. But more than that, I wonder if this guy has like a million pairs of Tretorns at home, and does he wear a new pair each time he comes to Pug Hill? Or does he just have one pair and wash them after every wearing? And, most importantly, does it never occur to him that sometimes, especially when sneakers are involved, that there is some merit to be found in a little scuffing, a little wear and tear? I pull my attention away from the Tretorns. The Tretorns are not important right now, the guy wearing them is not important; what is important, of course, is that here, today, there is a pug. There's a pug at Pug Hill, even on a weekday, and that means something, even if everything isn't a sign.

This pug—her name is Roxy—isn't a black pug like my little friend Kermit, the one I am so sure likes to wait, just for me, by the tree. But Roxy, one of the longer-legged varieties, not much older than a puppy, is right up there in terms of coolness. And that's a pretty great height of coolness, when you consider that all pugs, by sheer virtue of the fact that they are pugs, are quite cool. I know Roxy pretty well, because she's here a lot of the time, because of her owner's footwear decisions, but most of all, because she's one of the pugs who often delights in spinning herself in a circle for long periods of time.

I feel peaceful, let's say, momentarily content, as I watch Roxy run from where she'd been lingering, a yard or two behind the pine tree, quickly over to the spotless Tretorns. I hold my two cups of coffee and think again that one larger coffee would have been better. I think again that I need to be better at confrontation, as much as maybe I need to be better sometimes at just letting things go. One of the coffee cups, after all, can always be put down if need be, if what I want to happen actually happens: if Roxy sprints over to me, eyes wide, tongue lolling out to the side. At which point, once the extra coffee is safely out of the way, I will ask the Tretorn guy, hopefully without even having to make eye contact, if I can pet his pug.

I watch as Roxy spins around, two and half times—pugs, generally, are pretty big fans of spinning themselves around, but Roxy's got it mastered—and takes off again down the hill. She is so fast and runs with such a sense of purpose. If you didn't know any better, you'd think that she were chasing a ball. But I know better, and not only because I didn't see any ball thrown, but because I know enough to know that pugs are not the types to go running after a ball.

"Roxy!" the Tretorn guy yells, and Roxy ignores him. Just as they are not the types to go running after a ball, pugs generally are not the types to trip over themselves in order to please their owners. As clear as it is that Roxy is not planning on obeying her owner at present, it also seems pretty clear that she does not plan on running over to me. I think this is too bad, but also expected; Roxy is not an enchanter like Kermit is, Roxy is much more independent in spirit. But I'm happy for the fact that she was here at all and for the fact that I've been here for about twenty minutes, just standing here watching her, and the shiny new Tretorn guy has not looked over at me suspiciously, accusingly, as if I am a pug stalker. I don't think of myself as a pug stalker. It's different from that, I know, but I also know that standing around so long at Pug Hill without a pug, especially when there's just one other person here, can make you look like one.

"Roxy!" the Tretorn guy calls again, this time with a more assertive tone. She does not go to him, she turns around and regards him coolly from her vantage point atop an incline. A moment passes, and she sits down regally, her head held high. As the Tretorn guy sees the wisdom in going over to her, and does so, Roxy flips over onto her back to display her belly. I watch as Tretorn guy leans down to clip Roxy's leash to her harness, and then I'm not so sure that Roxy flipped over like that just to have her belly rubbed. I think she might be peeing.

From my vantage point, I see Tretorn shake his head at Roxy disapprovingly.

"Oh, Roxy," he says and softly clucks at her. I'm pretty sure she's peeing.

I smile to myself, silently cheering Roxy, cheering her independence. Before I turn to leave Pug Hill, I nod just barely in Roxy's direction, not only a stealthy good-bye but also a thank-you to her, for being here this morning.

As I walk up the cement path, in the direction of the museum, I try to continue on the positive track; I try to think of all I do have, instead of thinking something along the lines of how now I don't have Evan. Really, I have so much more, I remind myself, than a terribly mismatched relationship and a phone call that melted my heart for a moment but really was, in the end, just a phone call. I take a last look over my shoulder and see Roxy spinning around again. That's a good note to leave on, surely as good as any. *I have the pugs,* I think as I walk toward the museum. *I have them.*

* * *

I settle into my desk, only a few minutes late. Elliot is the only one here.

"Hi, Elliot," I say. Really though, I am just saying hi, I am not making a play for him now that one of us is single. The breaking of the traditional morning silence seems to disorient him for a second. He leans back on his stool and looks up at me.

"Hey, Hope," he says, and his eyes are a little glazed-looking, and I wonder how long he has been here, and if he ever leaves. His eyes are also so green, but I have too many other things to think about. I glance at my Rothko, so intimidating, and think optimistically that focusing on it might be easier now, now that I have all this free space in my mind, now that I don't have to think anymore about Evan. Before testing that theory out though, there's something I need to do. I need to sign up for Overcoming Presentation Anxiety. I turn to my computer, stare at it for a minute, and open up my Internet Explorer. Before I can type anything, my eyes are drawn to the bottom of the screen, to where the IM man sits, completely still. I wonder if he's ever going to bounce again. I think probably not. In spite of myself, in spite of all the other things I need to do, I imagine a future scenario in which the IM man could bounce again:

EVAN2020: *Hope, I have all your stuff.*

But that's an IM that won't ever come. Because, as I believe I have mentioned, I didn't have a preponderance of stuff, hardly any, over at Evan's. This is something I now feel was both indicative of, and resulting in, several problems. I tap on the delete key in my mind, rewriting for myself the imaginary IM from Evan.

EVAN2020: *Hope, I have your contact lens case.*

I imagine to myself that even if it were so much more than my contact lens case, even if it were my entire spring wardrobe, or every book I've ever loved and wanted to save, I would type back to him, hastily:

hopemcneill: *Keep it, Evan.*

And then a pause, and then alone, its own IM:

hopemcneill: *everything is replaceable.*

I shudder internally. Certainly, this is not productive, and also, most likely not normal. I turn back to the Internet Explorer, type in what I've needed to type in for far too long: www .newschool.edu. *Okay,* I think, taking another breath, *here goes.*

For an institution devoted to learning, The New School's website is vastly confusing. I look up at Elliot, then notice Sergei across the room settling silently into his workstation;

no one is paying any attention. Stealthily, I pull my spring bulletin out of my bag and flip to the back for directions. It explains there how to register online for classes, what to type in, where to click and hit send. I find the right page, click on the right buttons. I check the time and duration: Thursday nights at 7:30 P.M., for six weeks. *Okay.* I type, I click, I hit send, and then, it's done. Or rather, I think, it's begun. I try very hard not to feel afraid. I remind myself that at the end, the sad egg smiles. *I'm going to do this,* I think. Starting exactly one week from Thursday.

One week, and then it occurs to me that I should make some initial efforts at filling up the week ahead. In Evan's absence, that is not going to be taken care of for me anymore. An image of The Union Club flashes into my mind, and I think how that is very much a good thing. I send Pamela a quick e-mail, seeing if she's free this weekend. I send another to Kara saying I'm looking forward to Chloe's birthday party the weekend after, even though I'm secretly wondering if there is a way to get out of it. I'll tell them about Evan, I think, when I see them. I don't feel inclined at all to e-mail about it now.

Before turning away from the computer, my eyes are drawn again to the bouncing man. The bouncing man who does not bounce. I take one last look at the stillness, the finality. It's just a little yellow cartoon man. I think how Evan told me once that a woman in her thirties had a better chance of getting struck by lightning than she did of getting married. I'd told him I didn't think that could possibly be true. He'd winked at me then, in a way I think he must have thought to be charming, and he'd said, "A girl can dream."

I put my hand on my mouse, click a few clicks, and send the entire IM program to the trash. I forego, for now, the now customary several moments of stealing glances at Elliot, and instead, I swivel my stool around to my easel and reach for my paintbrush. I turn to the task at hand, I turn to the Rothko.

chapter eleven

I Am Jan Brady

"Okay, so I'll be sure to get out of here by six, six-thirty at the latest. I'll pick up the rental car and then come to get you."

Elliot is on the phone with Claire. It's easy enough to know when he is on the phone with Claire because, as far as I can tell, she is the only person he ever talks to. But more than that, whenever he talks to her, his voice gets softer, so considerate, and his posture relaxes. I try not to listen. I stare through my magnifying visor at the lower left section of the red and try not to hear anything.

"See you soon," I hear him say softly, in spite of my best efforts not to. And then, in spite of all my best efforts not to get busted *again* looking over at Elliot, I look up at him right then, just as he's hanging up the phone. He looks up, and the instant I always dread, but also must always secretly want, is upon us. Our eyes meet, and I smile awkwardly. I am, for some reason, perhaps to quell the awkwardness, perhaps more to quell my curiosity, compelled to ask, in a way that I hope is cheerful, merely conversational, "So, you're going on a trip?"

As soon as the words are out of my mouth, I realize that this was, of course, the wrong thing to ask, as asking it simply screams across the Conservation Studio, I WAS LISTEN-ING TO YOUR PERSONAL PHONE CALL BECAUSE, TRY AS I MIGHT, I JUST CAN'T HELP MYSELF!

"Yeah," Elliot says, "just for the weekend, we're going fishing."

Fishing, I think. In March, in the *cold.* It takes a moment for it to settle in, that Elliot may in fact be a cold weather outdoorsy-type person. Thoughts race through my mind: *this could in fact change everything; this could in fact set me free!* But can I, right now, in fact, deal with any more change?

"Cool," I say, and though I know nothing at all about her, mostly because I have steadfastly avoided like the plague asking even the smallest of details about her, I need to know. "Does Claire like fishing?"

"Well," he says, his beautiful green eyes bright, "she likes camping, but she doesn't actually fish. She's getting more into it though. She's really psyched about it; she says this time she wants to learn how to gut fish."

Two thoughts run through my mind. One: *she lies.* And, two: *I could gut fish.*

"Sounds fun," I say and turn, defeated, back to my Rothko. In this past week, this first week of being single, I have learned that it is a hell of a lot harder being unrequitedly in love with Elliot from afar, now that I don't have a boyfriend, a reason why we couldn't be together even if there was no Claire, even if the love for Elliot was not so unrequited.

Also, this past week has gone by very quickly. Apparently, a week goes by much more quickly when there is a class called Overcoming Presentation Anxiety at the end of it. My plan for tonight had been to stop by Pug Hill before going to the first class. Though I know now that there is always the chance that the pugs won't be there, I'm beginning to learn that, just maybe, that's okay. I'm beginning to think that while for me it will always be more about the pugs, just like for Holly Golightly it was always more about the diamonds, the place itself holds some, if not quite a lot, of importance, too. There's a reason *Breakfast at Tiffany's* was not called *Breakfast Anywhere There Happens to Be Lots of Diamonds*. The Tiffany's part, just like the Pug Hill part, is pretty important, too. Just think if it had been *Breakfast in the Diamond District,* think how much poetry, how much symbolism would have been lost.

I thought I'd go to Pug Hill after work, hang out there for a while and just try to chill out. I thought Pug Hill, even without any pugs, would be the best place to try to get ready for class; for the inevitable introducing of ourselves, saying our names and our occupations, all of this while very possibly standing in front of the room. I had it all planned out. I'd even brought along my fleece gloves, in case it was cold. It's important, I often think, to have a plan, and what with the fleece and all, I had mine.

* * *

As I leave the museum, it's a downpour. A downpour I was not at all aware of, having spent the day, as I spend so many of them, in the basement of unrequited love. The Conservation Studio, to protect the vulnerable paintings from light damage, is in the basement; the unrequited love part you know about. There are, to be fair, windows right up at the top, close to the ceiling, and even though it seems like it would be easy to tell if it was raining through basement windows, it's actually never very clear.

I stand in the doorway of the staff entrance of the museum and look out at the rain pounding down on the plaza like darts. On a few different levels, it's not looking so good. The plaza in front of the museum, while a great place to get a coffee, a pretzel, a black-and-white photograph, or even a bus, is not the best place to find an umbrella stand. I head back into the museum but I pass the Conservation Studio, I don't want to go back there again today. I keep walking down the internal hallway, to the end of it, emerging at the far end of the Antiquities Wing. I pull my ID out of my pocket and slip it around my neck, turning right into the Met's gift shop, open late, along with the museum, because it's a Thursday. I stand on line with so many other people, and think how something like this, me being out in the museum rather than always in its background, was how I met Evan. If only that hadn't been a lie.

I buy a bright orange Metropolitan Museum of Art umbrella with my employee discount, wondering how many of these umbrellas I have stashed away at home, and if I always select orange umbrellas because my mother believes with some conviction that redheads should sooner die than be seen carrying or wearing anything orange. It clashes.

I exit through the grand front entrance of the museum. A glance at my watch reveals that in my plan, I had not left much extra time for walking the length of the museum and back, and then waiting on line in the store. There isn't much time left now in which to go to Pug Hill. Even if I had, come to think of it, wanted to go there right after it turned dark. It's the second time in as many weeks that it has been revealed to me that a good plan consists of more than just fleece.

I stand for a moment, up at the top of the great steps, and

look out. It's one of those great New York scenes, the steps of the Metropolitan Museum of Art in the rain. It's a Woody Allen view, standing at the top of the stairs of the Met and looking down at Fifth Avenue. I love that about New York: all the great Woody Allen scenes you can pretend you are part of. I open up my orange umbrella; I walk down the steps and forget for a moment how much I am dreading the rest of the night.

Of course the thing with New York is that as soon as you are the star of your very own Woody Allen film still, you're not. As I approach the entrance to the subway on Eighty-sixth and Lexington, the crowds get thicker and thicker, and the scenery gets vastly less poetic. All it takes in New York is a few blocks, a few minutes, and you've gone right from being Goldie Hawn in the opening scene of *Everyone Says I Love You,* all the way to Best Buy.

I put down my new orange umbrella, forget all about the Woody Allen movie I starred in so briefly, albeit only in my mind, and head down into the subway to catch the downtown train.

* * *

Twenty dread-filled minutes later, I emerge into the hustle and bustle of Union Square, about seventy blocks and a universe away from the uptown New York vista in the basement of which I spend most of my days. The downpour has not subsided at all, quite the opposite really; it's that type of rain that comes sideways at you, that's determined to drench you, no matter what.

I picture myself standing in front of a room full of strangers, saying, "Hi, my name is Hope," maybe saying what my job is, and depending on the brutality of the teacher, maybe saying what brought me to Overcoming Presentation Anxiety class in the first place. And the self that I picture standing up there, in front of the classroom in my mind, she has an extra bit of confidence because she's wearing nice shoes and her hair is straight. *Good-bye to that,* I think, looking down at the suede high-heeled boots that I wished I hadn't worn. *Good-bye,* I feel I have to say again, because as I march on, past University Place and over to Fifth Avenue, I can literally feel my hair frizzing.

I'll admit, I'm a person whose confidence does increase if I feel I'm looking good, and I'll admit that for me that might be a bit of a vicious circle. See, in addition to having spent her career making rooms beautiful, my mother is also a person who has spent a lifetime having people see her from across those rooms and think that she is beautiful. My sister, Darcy, inherited this from her, the beauty along with the accompanying poise, the charm, the charisma, the ability to light up a room, and to always be the center of it. I didn't.

All my life people have felt it necessary to tell me how beautiful my mother is, and how my sister is the spitting image of her, too. People seem to think this is a nice thing to say. People seem to think that your life must be filled with glamour simply because the people around you are so pretty, that everything is as shiny and bright and filled with laughter as a sitcom.

"Your sister, Darcy," people used to say to me, time and time again, "looks just like Marcia Brady."

"*Just like* Marcia Brady," they'd say. And you know what that made me; that made me Jan.

I wonder sometimes about where Jan Brady would be now. Not Eve Plumb the actress, but Jan Brady, the *real* Jan Brady, if her character had actually existed, had actually continued on, lived a life, not just in syndication, but out in the world. I hope she'd be fine and all, but part of me also thinks that maybe she'd be lighting up in a crack den somewhere, and if not that, at the very least, she'd be spending a tremendous amount of time in a therapist's office. And you might think that sounds a bit rash, and you might think that maybe I'm getting a little carried away. I might be, I'll give you that much, but I think what's more likely, I think what makes so much more sense, is that it's just really hard to understand what it does to you, growing up with a sister who is the new Marcia Brady. It gets to you. Really, so much more than you'd think.

* * *

Maybe it was all the thinking about being Jan Brady, something I try most of the time not to think about, but as I look at my watch, even though I thought I was going to be early, I am just barely on time. Finally inside the building, I dig in my dripping wet bag for the registration piece of paper I got in the mail. Everything is wet. I think how I hate the rain. And while that thought for me is so very true, I imagine it also must be so very unoriginal. I worry sometimes that a lot of things that are mine are that way. I locate the piece of paper and pull it out to double-check that my classroom is 502. It is. I dive through the elevator doors right as they close.

chapter twelve

How Awful Would It Be
If This Thing Stopped?

I see room 502. The door is shut. I have that feeling in my
stomach: that feeling that not only have I just done something wrong, but that also, I am about to. It's a very high
school–oriented feeling for me, and I can't help but think,
Why have I done this? But the reasons, I know, they are
many and vast. The only choice I will let myself have is to
turn the handle on the door and walk in.

I pause for a minute, just inside the door, and smile an
apology to the teacher as she stops saying what she was
saying and looks over at me, as does everyone else. The
teacher smiles at me, really pretty nicely and I think that's
good that she did that, so at least I don't instantly hate her.

All the chairs are organized in a horseshoe shape around
the room; I sit down quickly and soggily in an empty chair,
right at the end of the horseshoe. The moment I am situated,

the moment I have wriggled out of my coat as inconspicu-ously as possible (not very), I realize I have chosen poorly. This is a bad chair. I don't like this chair, how it is right on the end, so vulnerable. I stare at the surface of the desk part of my chair. The chairs, they're all the kind of chairs with desks attached to them. Immediately, I start wondering if I've missed all the important stuff and will never quite catch up or (much better) if maybe I'm actually so late that I missed the whole introducing of oneself part. I look at my watch; I am only about four minutes late.

"Okay, so, I'm Beth Anne," the teacher says and what I have just suspected crystallizes into clearness in front of me: I have not missed the introductions, or more importantly, I have not missed mine. I take a breath, I remind myself for what seems like the millionth time that there's not going to be some sort of escape hatch that opens up for me at the last minute, that I'm really here, that I'm in for the long haul. Or at least for the next six weeks. I breathe out and move my head from side to side slightly, trying to relieve the mounting tension in my neck. I wonder how it can feel like it's been such a long night already when it hasn't even really started. I look to the blackboard just to be sure there isn't any math there. There isn't.

Beth Anne Nelson is written largely across the blackboard. Underneath it, slightly smaller, she has written, *Overcoming Presentation Anxiety!* The exclamation point, justifiably so, causes me concern. Yet the writing is so loopy, in such a big, sweeping script that it makes me want a drawing of a flower, or at the very least a smiley face, to follow it. I look to the woman standing before her girlish handwriting on the blackboard. She's wearing a long, flowing skirt and a necklace of large brown shellacked beads. She wears her graying brown hair behind her in a long braid. I think her eyes seem kind. I wonder if what she is going to teach over the next six weeks will indeed unlock the secret of how to be normal. It's a secret that's been kept from me for so long. I tell myself I will pay attention to every word; I tell myself I will try my very best to embrace this.

But first, I have to check out my fellow public speaking–impaired classmates. I am concerned, of course, that there are only eight other people here. I double-check, thinking that maybe there are more. But no, there are only eight, and while you might think that eight is a good number because it's not as hard to get up and speak in front of only eight people, that's not true. If it's hard to get up in front of a room and speak, I don't think it matters if there are eight or eighteen or eighty people in it. It is hard no matter what. Trust me on this. I am nothing if not an expert in the field.

What causes me grave, grave concern is that eight people is actually not enough. The thing about eight is that, including me, it is still only nine. This could mean we all have to get up and make speeches in front of the class a lot more times than if there were, let's say, twenty people, or even twenty-five. Are there not twenty-five people in all of New York City who need help overcoming presentation anxiety?

My inner math whiz, the one I've never come close to letting out, is stretching out inside of me. It's raising its hand, and for some reason that I don't fully understand, it's doing somersaults as it tries to figure out how many people will have to give speeches each week. Two? Three? Four? And if there's six weeks, then what's the maximum amount of time we'll have to spend giving speeches?

My inner math whiz flips over and disappears without answering any of the questions it posed. I think with dread that, worst case scenario, we could each have to stand up and give a speech *every week*. I don't need to have an inner math whiz to figure out that I very well could be making a speech in front of all these people *six times*. Six times seems like an awful lot. I wonder if that's what everyone is thinking. I wonder if they are looking around the room, in a similarly panicked, though much more mathematically organized frame of mind, trying desperately to figure out the same thing as me.

"Why don't we all introduce ourselves?" Beth Anne says, freeing me from my fun with numbers. I snap back to the present, contemplate my position in the room and think, *Oh no, I bet she's going to start with me.*

"Let's start here," she says to the guy right across from me, and really, *thank God.* I relax ever so slightly.

"I'm Lawrence," he says, and I wonder if he hates his chair as much as I, right now, love mine. Lawrence, I'd say, is in his late forties. He lisps a little bit on the end of his name. That, along with the way he's got his legs crossed in a very ladylike way, and the way he's got his arm stretched out across the chair-desk with his wrist hanging off the end, makes me wonder, I hope not stereotypically, if he's gay. I notice there's a gold band on his finger.

"I'm Diana," says a serene and peaceful-seeming woman in a wrap dress. Next to her are two women in pantsuits, their chairs are angled in toward each other, and they seem so similar, their pantsuits both so elegant and tailored. The way they keep looking up at each other makes me think they've come to the class together. I notice how nicely accessorized they are, one has a Marc Jacobs purse slung over the back of her chair.

"I'm Lindsay," "I'm Jessica," they say, just short of in unison. I envy their camaraderie, along with their outfits, as much as I am intimidated by it.

"Amy," says the woman next to them. Her exhausted tone is matched perfectly by the expression of boredom she wears and her tight-fitting black sweater, black skirt, heavy wool tights and clunky boots. She has very short hair; almost white it is so blond. She has black roots, the kind that look deliberate, the kind of hairstyle that makes me feel even more un-hip than I generally do.

"*Je suis*, uh, I am Martine," says a very thin blond woman with a French accent. Maybe it's just the accent but she seems haughty, mean, hostile. And this has nothing to do with the accent, but I wonder if she's anorexic and then, if she seems hostile because she's hungry. Anorexics, I imagine, are generally hostile. I would be.

"I am Rachel," says a woman with black frizzy hair and enormous breasts. Her eyes are very glazed over, a little freaky looking, if you ask me. And I know what you're thinking, you're thinking that maybe I'm being jealous right now because it's pretty much a toss-up as to what I want more, to have enormous breasts or to be really skinny. But I'm not being jealous, I'm really just being descriptive, this is what they look like.

Then finally, right next to me, "I'm Alec."

I turn in my chair to look at him. *Hot guy,* I think, *and really well dressed.* Instinctively, I look to the floor: excellent taste in shoes. It occurs to me that this is very much *not* what I need: to have another crush on someone else, to spend my time in Overcoming Presentation Anxiety class lusting after yet another guy. That'll make it real easy to concentrate, regardless of how much poorly executed practice I have at concentrating on things in the presence of a hot guy. I turn back to face forward and cross my arms in front of me. As I do so, I knock my pen off my desk. It hits the floor and starts rolling, I can feel everyone watching its progress across the floor.

Beth Anne walks over and stops the rolling of my pen with her foot. She picks it up and hands it to me.

"And your name is?" Right, it's my turn.

"Hope," I say quickly, and look away from her.

"Well, welcome everyone," Beth Anne says warmly. "Does anyone have any questions?" I think I have a question or two, but none so pressing that they override my desire not to raise my hand and draw any more attention to myself. Clearly, I'm not off to a brilliant start.

"What's your background?" one of the pantsuit girls asks, I no longer have any idea which one is which.

"Yes," Beth Anne says, standing straight, and looking around at each of us. "I'm an actress slash cranial-sacral therapist slash anthropologist slash social worker slash movement trainer slash public speaking coach." I notice Amy, the punky-looking blond woman, rolling her eyes. I don't think that's altogether called for, but as against eye rolling as I am, it's not that I don't entirely see her point. It really is quite a lot of slashes. I mean, yes, even though Beth Anne is dressed very earth mama chic in her long flowy skirt and a tunic-style shirt, a look I usually find quite comforting, she makes me very uncomfortable. But I think, just by the very nature of my fear, I may be predisposed to dislike her. I endeavor to give her the benefit of the doubt.

"Alright then," Beth Anne says authoritatively, once it's clear there won't be any more questions. "Let's all get up in front of the room and introduce ourselves, and say what we do, when we're not here overcoming our presentation anxiety." She pauses to smile. "Then, if you'd like, why don't you share with the class what brought you here." She smiles again, in a way that I think she means to be soothing.

"Now, concentrate on pausing before you begin speaking. Try looking around the room, making eye contact with each person before you speak. This is what I like to call 'Taking the Room.' It's an excellent exercise to begin with. Hope, let's start with you."

I take back anything I said about giving her the benefit of the doubt. I don't like her.

I get up slowly and walk the few steps to the front of the room. Beth Anne slips off to the side as I take my place in front of the desk. Instantly, my stomach is in knots. I can feel the sweat beginning to break out, behind my knees, under my arms. My turtleneck, it strangles me. I take a breath. Did she say to do that? *Eye contact,* I think, *eye contact.* I look first to Lawrence, his arm still stretched diva-like across his desk, his lips pursed, his eyes bright. That's enough. I can't stand up here and make eye contact with everyone. It'll take forever. *Forever,* I think, *is way too long.*

"My name," I begin, and I can hear my voice betraying me as it cracks, "is Hope McNeill, and I'm a paintings restorer at the Met." And how do I summarize, how do I say, really, what brought me here, when all I'm sure of is that it has been so much? Do I tell them about Mr. Brogrann's tenth grade English class and *The Grapes of Wrath*? Do I tell them I think it might have something to do with the fact that I am Jan Brady, that I've never been slim of thigh, have always been better with dogs than with people and that a long string of bad boyfriends ending with Evan, has only served to cement the fact in my mind that dogs really are so much the better bet? *My God,* I think, in between all the shaking in my mind.

And the thing is, I knew this could have been a question, I knew it was coming. I should have prepared. I realize that I'm standing frozen in front of everyone, so much like a deer in headlights, and right then, before I'm able to do anything about it, I think of the Rothko. I think how the problems of the present can be just as hard, if not harder, than the problems of the past. I take a deep breath. I turn and head right back to my seat, hoping with every part of my being that Beth Anne doesn't say, "You should try again because you hardly came close to taking the room." Thankfully, she doesn't say anything and I am allowed back to my seat. The firestorm has spread from my brain to my chest and stomach.

I wish I were alone, not only because then I'd be alone, but also because then, I could lay my head on the desk part of my chair-desk, just until this feeling goes away. I'm sure that once everyone has gotten up and said what they do—that is, when they're not smack dab in the middle of a nervous breakdown over the fact that they can't speak in public—I will get a special mention as the worst one. I'm sure that Beth Anne will pull me aside and ask if perhaps I'd like to work with her privately.

As I focus on the floor, out of the corner of my eye, I see Alec get up from his seat next to me. He takes his position at the front of the room, in front of the large metal desk that I wish I could crawl underneath, just really stealthily so that no one would notice. I look up at Alec and notice again how strikingly tall, dark, and handsome he is. The tall, dark, handsomeness distracts my heart from its mission of beating right out of my chest. In a reversal of the usual effect of seeing someone so very good-looking, the pace of my pulse begins to slow.

He doesn't look at anyone and begins to speak right away. "Uh, uh, I'm Alec, and I'm an attorney. Uh, I'm here because public speaking gets me very hot under the collar." He smiles wanly and looks to Beth Anne, who nods a stoic approval. He heads back to his seat, and I think he did so much better than me, and I have to remind myself that this is not a contest. And, even if this is in fact a contest, it isn't a fair one, because Alec isn't as hindered as I am by frizzing hair.

Rachel, with the very frizzing hair, walks quickly to the front, stares out at us with her freaky eyes. Really, so blank and so glazed. She opens her mouth to speak, and a long, slow gurgle comes out. I think a little bit of validity has just been added to my frizzing-hair/poor-public-speaking-ability theory. Perhaps all either of us needs is a good blow-out. The gurgle ends, and she returns to her seat. Beth Anne, to her credit, does not ask her if she'd like to try again. The thin French woman glides gracefully to the front.

"I am Martine. I am director of New York City Board of Le Lait. We work very hard to get *le* message out about the importance of, how do you say, how do you say, breast-feeding. I must work on speaking public." Martine, out of everyone, I feel has done very well.

Amy, blond and punky, stands up with an exaggerated exhale, and clomps to the front of the room. "I'm Amy. I'm a *novelist*," she says and pauses, and exhales again. She seems to me so much less nervous than just really put out. I wonder what her last name is, what she wrote. "I'm here to practice for readings," she tells us with a huff and trudges back to her seat.

"I'm Lindsay," the first pantsuit girl says softly, her hands clasped together. "I'm an accountant, I work at a big account-ing firm. This *thing* happened a few years back, this *e-mail thing,* and I'd rather not talk about it, but ever since then, I've had a really hard time, um, um"—she reaches up and tucks her hair behind her ears, one side and then the other—"I've had a really hard time with presentations." I wonder what happened. I am amazed by her endurance because rather than returning to her seat, she continues. "Jessica, here"—she ges-tures to her pantsuited twin—"is doing this with me because she knows how hard this is for me, and she's a really great friend." She smiles over sweetly at Jessica, who in turn gives her a sorority girl thumbs-up as she heads back to her seat.

Jessica walks up to the desk and as she does so I'm sure she'll be the best speaker, the best at introducing herself, as she's not here because of any deep-seated distress, but more in a friendship/moral support type of way.

Jessica turns bright red and runs from the room.

"Uh, I should go see," Lindsay says softly, a few moments later, and walks out the door with her head down.

"I'm Diana, I work in insurance," the wrap-dress woman says quickly, not nearly as serenely as she seemed initially. I wonder if it's cheating that she got up there so quickly, before everyone's attention was back from the door.

Lawrence, the guy who said his name first in the last round, gets up and all but skips to the front of the room.

He stands upright, his lips in a tight, prim smile, his eyes traveling slowly around the room. With each person he sees, he stops and gives a small nod. He spreads his hands wide out to the side, such an open and welcoming gesture, for anyone, let alone the public speaking impaired.

"Hello, everyone. I'm in real estate by day, but my true calling is *poetry*. I'm a poet, yes," he says and smiles widely, more like grinning, and nods his head. "I'm so looking forward to getting to know everyone, and working together, and sharing my poetry with you. I thought, if you'd like, I could read right now." He looks to Beth Anne who is still darting concerned glances in the direction of the door.

"Yes, Lawrence, that sounds like a lovely idea," she tells him, "but we've got some more to cover tonight, so let's look forward to your poem at presentation time." Lawrence's proud posture changes, becomes deflated as he returns to his desk very slowly, as if at any moment Beth Anne's mind will be changed, and she will call on him to read.

"Thank you, Lawrence," she says in the direction of his head, which is now laid down upon his desk. "And thank you, class. I'm sure we are all looking forward to working together and getting to know each other, and helping each other in the weeks to come." Everyone present, except of course for Lawrence whose face is still hidden from view, darts their eyes around.

"Okay then, so before we continue, I'm wondering if we should wait for Lindsay and Jessica." Beth Anne's voice sounds the slightest bit flustered; for several reasons, I don't think it should. First of all, the public speaking class teacher's voice shouldn't waiver, it's more than a little unsettling. And also, you'd think Beth Anne, being a public speaking teacher, among other things, would be used to things like people running red-faced from rooms. You'd think it might be a little bit par for the course.

"Would anyone like to go look for them?" she asks. I, for one, wouldn't know where to look, though in my experience the bathroom would be a good start. I stare at the floor, and no one else ventures a response.

"Okay then," she continues, smoothing down her skirt in front of her, "it's interesting that Lawrence has brought up his poetry. One of our assignments will be to select, and then read a favorite poem to the class." *Two roads,* I think, *diverged in a yellow wood.*

Beth Anne continues speaking, "Public speaking can be very, very difficult. It is something many people fear. The human body's response to fear is often an adrenaline rush, in preparation of flight. Since often the option of flight is not the best one," she says as her eyes dart once again to the door, "the result is that we get sweaty, nauseated, our hearts and pulses race, among other symptoms." I hear someone exhaling, and look up to see Amy rolling her eyes as she lets out an exasperated breath.

"Most people would rather be in a casket than delivering the eulogy," Beth Anne says and smiles. I guess that's pretty true, but I doubt this can be news to anyone here, even if it is a pretty good one-liner. And who doesn't like a good one-liner? Well, me, for starters.

"In the weeks to come, we'll learn many techniques for being an effective public speaker. We're going to work on different relaxation techniques. We're going to work, of course, on practicing, and we're going to work on some different exercises that will help take you out of the moment, help you forget that what you're doing is frightening and scary. We'll do certain things that will hopefully make you forget you are public speaking." Beth Anne smiles approvingly, individually at each of us, slowly making her way around the horseshoe.

"It's important to remember though," she adds on now in an extra soothing tone, "that what will help you will be very personal. Maybe it's counting to ten, maybe it's picturing the audience in their underwear. Think about what will work for you."

Amy raises her hand.

"Yes?"

"I don't think that's really fair. Aren't you supposed to tell us what works?" Amy asks, her tone a bit snappish, aggressive.

While there is a small part of me that agrees with her, I don't want to subscribe to the hostility. I'm sure it's wrong to feel so hostile to Beth Anne, so early in the process. So, instead, I picture Alec in his underwear.

"Practice works, getting out of the moment works," Beth Anne says, not missing a soothing beat. "It will be an individual journey, but one we'll all take together. Next time we'll work on relaxation techniques, and then we'll talk more about the assignments.

"So," she says brightly, glancing toward the clock and then the door. "Until next time. Should anyone wish to address any matters privately, I'll stay for a few minutes after class."

Lawrence at last raises his head from the desk. Everyone begins to gather their things and put on their coats. There are a few murmured thank-yous as we all head out to the hall. As we wait for the elevator, no one speaks. Everyone stares straight ahead. Instinctively, I cross my arms in front of me. The elevator door opens and we all pile on. I think the same thing I always think when I'm on a crowded elevator. *How awful really would it be if this thing stopped?*

chapter thirteen

I Should Tell You
About the Commune

"Hope, it's your mother."

"Hi, Mom."

"Are you still sleeping at this hour?" I look at the clock, nine-fifteen. I usually don't sleep this late, even on Sundays. I'm usually more awake by now. I wonder if I am depressed and that is why, at nine-fifteen, even though that's not *that* late, I am still asleep. I could be depressed.

"No," I tell her.

"It sounds like you were."

"I'm not," I say getting out of bed and heading to the kitchen. I want to say I'll call back, after I've run downstairs to the new intimidating Starbucks that now must be part of my life, to get a coffee. Yet there are possibilities: possibilities that such a statement could possibly result in an entire conversation devoted to why, at the age of thirty-two,* I do not have an ounce of domesticity in me and do not even make coffee in my apartment. Rather than admit that I've just woken up, rather than explain that I did make coffee, just last week, I pour myself a glass of water and think of a latte, one from Columbus Bakery. I listen to my mother as she exhales heavily through the phone.

"How's everything?" I venture, trying to infuse my voice with as much cheeriness, as little sleepiness, as possible.

"Well, you know the party is on May seventh," she says, matter-of-factly. I can picture my mother looking at her desk calendar, various party-related tasks and organizational feats written out from March to May.

"Yes, I know."

"What are you doing the week leading up to it?"

"Uh, I imagine working?"

"I'm hoping that for the week leading up to the party, you might be able to take some time off and come out to help Dad."

"What's wrong with Dad?" I ask, alarmed now. Mom sounds tense and angry, over something more than the color of my hair or my inability to match my foundation to my skin tone. Something is wrong. I reach out for the kitchen counter, hold on to it; I need support.

"No, your father's fine, but I'll be traveling."

"Oh, okay," I say, and take a moment to regroup, relax. "Um." I hesitate for another moment, think of my vacation time for this year. We get three weeks a year at the museum, and to date, I have taken none. I think of the romantic Caribbean vacation that Evan took with his girlfriend before me.

---

*I am, by the way, thirty-one. In Mom's book, however, I am thirty-two. Mom's a fan of rounding people's ages up. As soon as your thirty-first birthday has passed, you are, in her book, thirty-two. She has always done this, in a way I have come to believe is hostile.

He told me all about it once. The mentioning of how he and I should take a trip that I was sure would follow on the heels of such information never came. I shouldn't think like this.

"Sure," I say, "I don't see why not. But you sound weird. Is everything okay? Are you sure Dad's okay?" It's important to double-check things.

"It's nothing like that, Dad's fine. It's just a lot for him out here with the dogs and all, if I'm not here to help." My parents currently have three dogs, less than they've had at other times, but granted, Mom does have a point. These particular three dogs, Betsy, a neurotic-to-the point-of-possibly-insane Jack Russell terrier; Captain, a half-blind, diabetic Pembroke Welsh corgi, who very sadly was just diagnosed with cancer; and Annabelle, the French bulldog of whom we have spoken, are a bit of a production.

"So you can come?"

"Um, yes, I'm sure I can come, let me just check at work tomorrow. I'm sure it's fine. Where are you going?" I ask. "Just out of curiosity," I add on, because even though she has said that everything is fine, to me she sounds pretty much on the verge.

"I'm going to Canyon Ranch for the week."

"Oh," I say, "that'll be nice."

"Well, yes," she says, and exhales again.

"Mom?"

"Yes?"

"You sound a little bummed for someone who's just planned a trip to Canyon Ranch."

"Yes, well, I guess, everything isn't okay," she sighs. "It's Darcy." It is *always* Darcy.

"The commune again?" I ask.

"Yes, the commune. And, you know, C.P. in general."

"Well, the commune thing is hard," I say, "but I don't think she'll ever really go." Neither of us says anything for a while as I, and I imagine my mother, too, picture Darcy, beautiful, golden, and rather materialistic the last time I checked, giving up all of her worldly possessions and joining a commune with the much-loathed C.P.

And you might be wondering what we're talking about, now that all of a sudden, seemingly out of nowhere, we're talking about a commune, and someone, much-loathed, with the name C.P. Yes, I can see now that I probably should have mentioned this before. Let me try to catch you up.

For every guy who hasn't liked me, or hasn't loved me, or who has loved me but just in a really unproductive way, and for every guy who has left me, there are five guys whom Darcy has had to beat off with sticks. Darcy, at this point, has pretty much made a career, and a very successful career at that, out of having boyfriends who are head-over-heels in love with her; boyfriends who, in turn, make careers of their own out of pledging their undying devotion to Darcy. And Darcy, entrepreneur of love that she is, has started up a side business of selecting, out of all these men who vie for her heart, the most annoying and insufferable of the lot. And steadfastly shoving them down everyone's throat.

My theory has always been that all the attention she's always received for being so pretty, somewhere along the way got old, so she had to find other ways to get attention. For the last decade or so, she seems to go about this by selecting truly weird, bizarre and awful boyfriends, embracing them wholeheartedly and insisting dramatically that everyone else embrace them, too.

For the last two years, it's been C.P. C.P., by the way, is short for Crested Possum. Before you infer from my tone that I'm not being open-minded, or that I'm being prejudiced or something because Crested Possum is a Native American, I'd like to point out that Crested Possum's real name is Bradley Klein, and he's from Short Hills, New Jersey. But apparently in a past life, or it's in this life, deep in his soul—I can never quite get it straight—he's sure he was/is a Native American. And Buddhist. Jewish-Buddhist I think, and also Zen. And so, C.P. decided recently that what his Inner Guide wanted to do was to live on a commune outside of Albuquerque.

"I really thought once the commune thing came up, it would be the end of this whole nonsense with C.P." Mom exhales again.

"I know," I agree. No one ever thought that Darcy would actually consider packing up and moving to a commune outside of Albuquerque. But lately Darcy has taken to calling up my parents and telling them that if C.P. moves to the commune, she's moving, too. And, as you might imagine, my parents think this is absolutely terrible, and if you so much as mention the word *Darcy* these days, the whole atmosphere just instantly changes.

"So, I'm taking Darcy with me to Canyon Ranch. I think it'll help," Mom announces after another pause. My mother is a person who believes pretty solidly that there aren't many wrongs in the world that can't be righted by a spa week, so this should not take me by surprise, but it does.

"Okay," I say.

"Clearly, you can see how it will help," Mom announces more than asks. "If nothing else, just some time away from C.P. will be a help. That C.P. is such a schmuck."

"Yes," I agree, "he is." I listen to my mother exhale again. She is not finished yet, I can tell.

"Both my girls date schmucks, and for the life of me, I don't know where you get it from. I never dated schmucks. I dated your father."

"Well," I say, and I do not know what to say. I want to say, I date a schmuck and the only thing that happens is you call me up and tell me he's a schmuck and revoke his

Jean-Paul Belmondo status. Darcy, simply because she dates a schmuck in a far more extravagant fashion than I do, just because Darcy, by her very nature, is more extravagant and over the top than I ever am, gets a SPA VACATION! I say nothing though because to get noticed in the background of *all that is Darcy* is a battle I've fought my entire life and lost. And also, if she does really join a commune, I don't want to be the one who complained about a week at Canyon Ranch. I realize at this point that I may sound unsympathetic. At this point, I think maybe I am.

"Speaking of schmucks," Mom adds, "is Evan coming to the party?"

"Evan and I broke up," I say and wait, just for a beat. I wait for, "Oh, that's too bad, you must be upset being thirty-two and single." I wait for, "I'm sorry, dear, you should come to Canyon Ranch, too."

"Well, that's certainly for the best."

"Yes," I say, "it really is."

"You're okay?" she asks.

"I am, I'm fine," I say. And then, "Can I say hi to Dad?"

"He's upstairs in his office." Relinquishing the phone to my father is a constant issue for Mom. We do not know why.

"Okay," I say slowly, "would you like to yell to him, or would you like to hang up, and I'll call back, and we can let it ring until he answers?"

"No, I'll get him. But, Hope?"

"Yes?"

"I do not want you bringing up the commune with your father. Your father is very upset about the commune. Under no circumstances are you to discuss the commune with your father."

"No problem," I tell her, "no commune."

"Okay, talk to you soon, and thanks for coming out."

"No problem," I say again.

"Write it in your calendar, so you don't forget."

"Sure thing."

"Henry!" I hear Mom shouting, more or less directly into the phone. I move it slightly away from my ear. A moment later Dad is on the line.

"Hi, sweetheart," he says, and though I can still hear my mother breathing on her end of the phone, the stress that is a phone conversation with my mother begins, ever so slightly, to dissipate.

"Hi, Daddy."

"Okay, Caroline, you can hang up now," Dad says.

"I was just waiting to be sure everyone was on," she informs us with a slight harrumph, and we listen to the click as her phone is returned to its charger.

"How are you, Dad?"

"I'm good, good, you? How's work, Evan?"

"I'm good, work's good, but Evan and I broke up," I say, adding on quickly, "I'm fine though, really, it's all for the best."

"Oh, well, sweetie, I'm sorry to hear that, but I'm glad to hear you sound okay. You let me know if there is anything at all that you need."

"Thanks, but I'm fine, really."

"Great, then, while I have you on the phone, I have a question for you. Do you know much about this Google? On the Internet?"

"Sure, what do you want to know?"

"I want to know what I do? I want to search."

I start from the beginning, explain opening up the Internet browser, keying in www.google.com, and typing what you want to find out about into the blank space. "Okay, okay," Dad says softly, methodically as he goes, signaling the completion of each step.

"And now I just type *communes*?"

"Communes?" I say and hold my breath. I wait for my mother, surely listening with supersonic hearing downstairs, to pick up her phone, and admonish, "Hope, I told you *not* to talk about the commune!"

"Yes, I want to do a search on communes, on why people join them," Dad explains, and I know it might say terrible things about me, might reveal the fact that somewhere along the way, I lost any sisterly instinct, but I worry so much less about Darcy than I do about how everything she does, all the drama, affects my parents, takes up so much space in their lives.

"Right," I say, taking a breath, "you could type just *communes,* or *communes people joining.* Play around with it for a while until you find what you're looking for," I explain. "But, Dad?"

"Yes, dear?" he says and I think his voice sounds tired, and in all the time I've been speaking to my dad on the phone—how long has it been since I left home, fourteen years?—I've never heard him sound so tired.

"I don't think Darcy's really going to join a commune. I wouldn't just say that either; I really believe it. We know Darcy; she's not the type—she just likes saying it, she just likes causing a stir. I think it'll all be okay."

"Yes," he says, and I listen to him exhale, feel how hard it must be for him when he's always been the type of dad to fix everything, and he can't fix this. "But I guess I just want to learn a little more."

"I understand," I say, "and, look, we've got a whole week together coming up, that's really great."

"Yes, yes, I'm looking forward to it," he tells me, but he sounds so far away. We say things next about love and good-bye and seeing each other soon, and by the time I put down the phone, object of endless anxiety that it always is, it's been one of those mornings that has been so long. It makes me nervous about the rest of the day.

chapter fourteen

Man!

A few hours later, I find myself at Mary Arnold Toys on Lexington Avenue and Seventy-third Street, buying a Groovy Girls doll for Kara's daughter, Chloe. I did not, as it turns out, quite make it to Chloe's second birthday party yesterday. I had all the best intentions. No, really, I did. It was just that the closer the party got, I just couldn't bear the thought of being the only single woman at a baby birthday party. I have done this before, and it is far from fun. Have you ever been the only single woman at a baby birthday? The best thing I can liken it to is to being a two-headed monster with a terminal disease. Really, I'm pretty sure I'm not imagining it. People see you there, childless, *alone,* and look at you first as if you are a very strange specimen indeed and then, pretty much, they feel very sorry for you. The closer I got to the party, the more I envisioned the secret conversations, so very "Lorelai-on-*The-Gilmore-Girls*-before-it-all-worked-out-with-Luke" in theme I imagined them to be:

"Kara's friend, the one who works in a museum, she's *still* single?"

"I think it's more like, she's single *again*."

"Poor girl."

"I know. It's sad."

"It really is."

Luckily, Kara is the type of friend—perfect, as I may have mentioned—who once I called to say I couldn't make it, did not counter with guilt, did not counter with telling me how much Chloe was looking forward to seeing me, even though it's entirely possible that Chloe has no idea who I am. She simply said she understood. By way of further explanation, I told her via phone and not in person as I'd planned, that Evan and I were no more, and she'd said she understood that, too, and then she said, just like me, and oh my God, *just like my mother,* that she thought it was for the best.

Then, as soon as I was off the hook in terms of the party, in celebration of it being the second Saturday in a row of not having to go outside at all if I didn't want to, I didn't. But as it turned out, I felt guilty, and kind of sad, for not being at Chloe's party. I tried to tell myself that guilty, and even a little sad, was better than the two-headed and terminally ill monster alternative. And I can admit it: I watched the Zoloft commercial. Twice.

I pull a Sandra Boynton book from a shelf and bring that, along with the Groovy Girls doll, to the cash register. Now that I'm here, I really have no idea if a Groovy Girls doll is age-appropriate for a two-year-old. *Maybe it's too advanced? Maybe two-year-olds are still all wrapped up in Elmo?* I grab an Elmo marker set. "This, too," I say, putting everything all together in a pile on the counter. "Could you wrap them, please?" I hand over my credit card, knowing on some level that if I am ever a grandmother, I might not be the grandmother who visits all the time, I might be more the kind of grandmother who stays down in Florida and compensates for her absence with gifts.

I walk up Lexington to Seventy-fourth Street and into Kara's beautiful lobby. Kara and Todd's apartment is pretty fantastic, pretty perfect actually. But of Kara you'd expect that, because she's one of those people who's always together and whose clothes are always stylish and always match, but she's very cool even though she seems so perfect. And maybe she's a little tightly wound about certain things but you'd have to be, wouldn't you, to keep everything so perfect?

"Eleven-C please," I tell the doorman.

"Your name?"

"Hope," I say, and he buzzes up to what I am pretty sure is the domestic bliss epicenter of the universe.

* * *

As I step off of the elevator, Kara's husband, Todd, is standing in the doorway. In front of him is Chloe. Chloe is redfaced, shaking her tiny clenched fists in the air, dressed only in her diaper.

"Maaaaaaan!" she screams the second she sees me.

"Hi, Chloe," I say, even though I have this feeling that "Hi, Chloe," might not be what she wants to hear.

"Maaaaaaan!" she wails again, and again, "Maaaaaaan!"

"No, honey, that's not the man. Hi, Hope," Todd says looking over at me, a brief flash of what I think might be desperation in his eyes.

"Hi, Todd," I say, standing there a bit dumbly between the elevator and the doorway. I wonder if Chloe actually knew it was her birthday last week, and now she misses it?

"Maaaaaaaaaaaan!" *Man*. I try my best to push the thought from my mind that Chloe is speaking directly to me.

"Uh, sorry," Todd says, picking up the screeching Chloe and moving aside.

"Man!" she says sharply, defiantly, *right at me,* as I walk past.

"She wanted rice," Todd says to me, and I look back at him and say, "Right," as if all this makes a tremendous amount of sense. And I ask, "Is, uh, Kara in the living room?"

"No, kitchen."

"Right," I say again and head in the direction of their kitchen. Todd and Chloe, who is still screaming, just nothing so legible as *man* anymore, follow me.

As the three of us walk into the kitchen, Kara looks up from the banquette where she's sitting. Kara and Todd have a sitting area in their kitchen, a little banquette right by a window. I love their banquette. If I lived here I think I'd do exactly what Kara is doing right this very second, sit with a magazine and look out the window from my kitchen sitting area; it seems so much more civilized, *so* much more grown-up than my apartment where everything from magazine reading, to watching television, to meal time, to computer time, takes place in the corner of my couch.

Kara is in a light purple cable-knit sweater, her very thick, very straight dark brown hair is pulled back in a flaw-less ponytail. I notice how tired she looks. Chloe has gone beyond language at this point to convey her feelings on this whole thing about the *man*. She's transitioned into this sort of screeching that I've noticed all the babies like to do, the kind that gets so high pitched that it sort of disappears into silence, and then starts again, only louder, and more pierc-ing. The level of piercing is such that it could make a person pretty sure the *entire* reason they haven't met the right guy yet isn't actually because they are unlovable (as they often suspect) but because maybe, deep down, they are just not cut out for motherhood.

Kara looks past me, at Todd, and blinks. Kara's a good blinker. I believe that there are actually really good blinkers in the world, and that Kara is one of them; she can convey a lot with her blinking and if I'm not mistaken, right now the blinking at Todd, it seems to be saying, *What the fuck?*

"She wanted rice," Todd says, a little defensive.

Kara blinks again, the meaning this time unmistakable, and we wait as Chloe finds language again and goes back to screaming, *"Maaaaaaan,"* and Todd exhales.

"There *is* no rice, *Kara,* and so I ordered Chinese food, and told her the man was going to bring her rice."

"You know you can't tell her that. You know she has a hard time with patience and with the concept of time," Kara snaps, getting up from the banquette and crossing over to where Todd and Chloe are standing behind me. "Hi, Hope," she says to me as she passes.

I say, "Hi," but what I really want to say instead is, "Um, great then, here are some things for Chloe, and I'll just be going," because this is so unsettling. And it's not that anything so bad is going on, except for Kara looking tired and snapping, and Todd looking something close to desperate, and Chloe not wearing any clothes. It's just that I'm not used to Todd and Kara's prewar classic six, not right on Park Avenue but pretty close to it, with all the fabric, and the decorating, and the linens from Schweitzer Linens, being anything less than perfect.

And it's not that I can't handle a little less-than-perfect (believe me, I'm pretty accustomed to the less-than-perfect) it's just that Todd and Kara, *this,* right now, seems to go against the proper order of the universe. Ever since I realized that the pugs aren't always at Pug Hill, I feel like that's happening more and more often.

Kara reaches over to Todd who hands off Chloe. I'm still wondering what all of this has to do with Chloe only wearing her diaper, but decide it's best not to ask, best to assume that not wanting to get dressed is just one of those things babies sometimes do.

Todd and I both watch silently as Kara sets Chloe down on the floor and squats down next to her, speaking slowly and softly. "Honey, the man isn't here yet. The man might not get here for a while so you need to try and be patient."

And, really, that's it. Chloe takes this news startlingly well and puts her arms around Kara's neck and sighs. It's all so beautiful, and it all makes up for the screeching. The mysterious reason of why Chloe's wearing only her diaper doesn't seem to really matter at all anymore. Even though there's still the tension, and even though I think Kara's now rolling her eyes at Todd, who's slipping into this office room they have, I feel very emotional over the fact that even when their apartment is really far from domestic bliss, it's still pretty close. I'm about to tell Chloe that I have some birthday presents for her, but she looks at me first, quite solemnly for a two-year-old, and says, "The man may not be here for while."

And I think, *I know this, I really do.* I nod back to her, and tell her, "I know."

The buzzer goes off and Chloe yelps with delight.

"Thank God," Kara says as she picks up the phone that connects to her doorman. "Please send him up, thanks."

Chloe squeals, and claps her hands, and heads to the front door with Kara.

I go to the bathroom, the one in the hall with the red toile wallpaper, and cry.

chapter fifteen

We Should Really All
Just Go Get a Drink

Before I know it, it's Thursday, the end of Thursday; the little bit of light that comes through the basement windows is diminishing, the conservation room is getting darker, and it's time again for Overcoming Presentation Anxiety class.

I very slowly and meticulously press my paintbrush in the Naphtha Solvent that we all use now instead of turpentine, because it's so much safer. I roll back a bit on my stool and stare at the corner of the red section. I've added some of my mixture of red restoration paints in, and I'm waiting now to be sure it's a match. I don't want to say for certain yet, but I think it might be. I stare at it more until my eyes get a little blurry and I know I've looked at this one spot as much as I can for one day. I know that at this point I'm just still staring at it because there's a part of me, a big part of me actually, that would rather stay here tonight.

As I head in the direction of the sink, I try to give off an air of only the utmost normalcy as I walk by Elliot. And then, of course, I'm done with washing my brushes and my hands and done with drying them, too, and I have to walk past him again. I wonder how long, how inhumanely, can this go on. And I know, from past experience, all too well, the viciousness of the circle that is unrequited love for me. I know how long these kinds of circles tend to keep me trapped inside them. I try not to think so long about the answer, because in the end, I'm pretty sure I don't want to know.

"Good night, Elliot," I say on the way back past him, pausing before I say it just to be sure something else doesn't slip out, something along the lines of, "Are you quite certain then that you aren't in love with me, and are you quite certain then that all this time I've spent, and continue to spend, mooning over you is really all for nothing? And do you maybe want to tell me that Claire really isn't your girlfriend? Do you maybe want to tell me that Claire doesn't really exist at all?"

And then, just like every other night, instead of "Hope, let's you and me run away together and leave this crazy Conservation Studio that's really just a basement behind," he looks up from his easel only slightly, smiles even more slightly and says, "Good night, Hope."

* * *

I enter room 502 a few minutes before class is scheduled to start: an improvement on last time. I take a far less vulnerable seat: not on either end, nor right in the middle (which I feel could be dangerous, too) but a few seats into the horse-shoe, on the side closest to the door, you know, in case of an emergency. I can't help thinking it will surely be another improvement. I look around and notice there seem to be fewer people here than last time. The serene girl who wore a wrap dress isn't here, which I think is too bad, because I liked her, or at least I thought she lent a calming influence to the room. One of the two pantsuit-girls, the one who was supposedly here for her friend, but then ran from the room, isn't here. Alec, so tall, so well-dressed, so good-looking isn't here either. That's too bad, too. I mean what are the odds of there being a completely attractive man, who is also public speaking impaired and not only that, in *your* public speaking class? To beat all those odds and then have him show up only once doesn't seem fair. It makes the absence of the serene woman in the wrap dress seem like nothing. I picture Alec, think of how he said he gets hot under the collar. *Hot under the collar,* I think, *I'll say.* And then as soon as I think that, it's pretty clear, seeing as my goal here is to embrace class and pay attention, that Alec's absence might be for the best. Then Alec walks in.

"Uh, sorry," he says, even though we haven't started. Amy looks up from a notebook she's been writing in and scowls at him. He sits down directly across from me. That makes me smile, in spite of the voice in my head that keeps reminding me that I don't need to lust after any more guys, that Elliot, really, until I somehow manage to get over that, is enough. I have to agree. The voice in my head is right; I simply cannot spend my time in public speaking class the way I spend too much of it at work, staring across the room at a cute guy. As it is, even without Alec, I've been starting to wonder if somewhere along the way I have become a stalker. It's not a nice thing to contemplate. I drag my attention, as completely as possible, away from Alec.

I re-scan the room, recount my classmates, noticing Lawrence especially because he sits up so straight in his chair. Everyone else from last time is here. We're only down two people. I consider that this makes me braver than two people. Beth Anne gets up from where she's been sitting in the back of the room and takes her spot in the front of the classroom, right in front of the big metal desk.

"Welcome, class," she says beaming, fanning her arms out to the side and holding them there outstretched. She is covered head to toe, shoulder to wrist, in a giant bright orange caftan. "Welcome back." *Two down,* I think again, and consider that this possibly makes me not as smart as two people. Beth Anne refers to a clipboard on her desk and looks out at us.

"Lindsay," Beth Anne asks, "will your friend Jessica be joining us tonight?"

"Uh, no," Lindsay says, looking decidedly more hunched over in her chair than last time, and I think it's too bad for her that her friend, whom she made the point of saying was such a true friend, seems to have left Lindsay, the victim of some bad accounting scandal, in the lurch.

"Uh, no," Lindsay says again, a little bit sadly, "I don't think she thought it was the best use of her time." Just like true love, it seems the course of true friendship sometimes doesn't run smooth either.

"Well," answers Beth Anne, with one last look to the door, "let's get started then, shall we?" She walks to the door, and seals us in, an airless grouping of anxiety, nerves, and deep-seated fear. I look around the room at this group I am part of, a group of people whose relationship to public speaking being described as merely "anxious" is an understatement at best. I can't breathe.

I remember how last time Beth Anne had her name written across the blackboard, so many loops and swirls, and how comforting I found that to be at the time. I look to the blackboard again. The blackboard, I'm sure, is a good place.

to look right now. Or is it? There, Beth Anne has written, from top to bottom, in big, capital letters, no loops, no swirls anywhere:

ONE NOSTRIL
LION
DEITY

Oh, I think, *no,* because I just don't think there's any way to look at a list so cryptic, and so surely boding of ill, as this one, and think anything else. I look quickly around at the remaining classmates. I want to see that everyone else looks just like how I feel: nervous and closed-in, like a rat trapped in a corner. Lawrence looks ecstatic; Amy looks pissed; and Martine, the hostile French woman, the very thin one with the need to make speeches about breast-feeding, looks haughty. Everyone else looks a little scared. There's that.

But even still, even with the fear camaraderie, I dread the thought of the next step. It's like an emotional minefield in here. Every step can bring disaster or at the very least despair. It is extremely discomforting to see words like that, words I don't understand, just written across the blackboard so menacingly. I read the lines again: *One Nostril. Lion. Deity.* I decide, for certain, there is something quite ominous about them.

"The most important thing is . . ." Beth Anne pauses in a way that can only be described as meaningfully. I forget instantly about being a trapped rat and lean forward a bit in my seat. I, for one, am quite interested to hear what the most important thing is. Maybe I should get out my notebook.

"Relaxing," Beth Anne says next, and I, for one, am a little bit let down. "Relaaaaxing," she repeats, saying it slowly, stretching it all out, all the emphasis on the *aaaaaax.* She points to the first line on the blackboard: ONE NOSTRIL.

We all watch silently as Beth Anne begins to demonstrate the somewhat—now that I think about it—less cryptic, possibly even self-explanatory, One Nostril Breathing. She holds her thumb over one nostril and breathes in deeply, then she uses her index finger to pinch both nostrils closed for a moment before she releases her thumb and exhales. After each exaggerated step she pauses to nod eagerly at us, eyebrows high, like a mime that wants so much to say, "Yes, class. Yes, yes." From what I can see out of the corner of my eye, a few people are nodding in agreement with her.

"Why doesn't everyone give it a try?" she says encouragingly, and suddenly, I feel better than I have felt since I first set foot in this classroom. I feel a way I never imagined I would feel, not for the duration of Overcoming Presentation Anxiety at least. I feel advanced. Quite advanced, at least for this particular second, and I am, for the briefest of brief moments, at peace.

See, now that I've seen it demonstrated, I remember that, believe it or not (well actually you should just believe it) I have actually done One Nostril Breathing. Once, in yoga class when the Asthanga-influenced and very hot (my God, is there anyone I don't lust after?) yoga teacher was in India learning more, I assume, about Asthanga, there was a sub, a follower of what must apparently have been a more breathing-based yoga practice. The sub—who seemed to lack any understanding that seeing as we were at a gym, everyone in the class wanted their yoga to be more athletic and calorie-burning in spirit—had us do One Nostril Breathing. He called it something else though, hence my delay in recognizing it. He had us all do it for half an hour once. Then I think someone complained to the management, and he didn't come back again. I confidently take a few alternating breaths, quite proficiently, adeptly, if I do say so myself.

Out of the corner of my eye I see Martine. Martine is

clearly not someone who has spent a tremendous amount of time in yoga class; she is scowling at her thumb and index finger as she holds them a few inches away from her nostrils. Next to her, Lindsay seems to be having some struggles with coordination. I think how very possibly I am the best in the room at the One Nostril Breathing. It's sort of sad, I know, that this makes me as happy as it does. But it does.

And then it doesn't anymore, because Beth Anne is now saying something how Kalabati helps, too. Kalabati isn't even written on the board. Kalabati definitely sounds like it might have something to do with yoga-breathing, too, but, as you know, the time I had with the breathing yoga teacher was brief, perhaps too brief, and I'm no longer leaps and bounds ahead of my classmates. I am no longer the star, if, come to think of it, I ever really was. Now I am just one of the many people in the room who has no idea what is going on. I'm back to thinking that around any corner there could be danger, and if not that, at the very least, despair.

"Kalabati," Beth Anne explains to us slowly, "is also called Breath of Fire." Amy raises her hand.

"Yes, Amy?" Beth Anne smiles at her brightly, clearly Beth Anne is a big, big fan of class participation.

"How come *Kalabati*, or *Breath of Fire,* isn't written on the board?" Beth Anne furrows her eyebrows as Amy continues, "I mean, why just write One Nostril? If this is like a whole separate category of relaxation, then why not write it down, too?"

"Well, I would say it's a subset," Beth Anne says, in a way that makes me think she's slightly thrown.

"If it's a subset why not write it, but indent?" I wonder if Amy is going to be the one who wants, more than she wants to overcome her presentation anxiety, to ruin it for everyone else. There's usually one in every group, the one who just likes to hear herself talk out loud. I'd been thinking though that this group would be exempt from that since the people in this group, by the very nature of their fear, might tend to not like talking out loud in a group, let alone being heard talking. I look over at Amy: regardless of any public speaking impairment she may suffer from, she does indeed look like a good candidate to be one of those people who just likes to hear herself talk. It could be an occupational hazard for her, since she's a *novelist* and all. If you think about it, her job might provide her with even less of an opportunity to talk to people than mine.

Beth Anne seems to be opting for not answering Amy. Amy scowls slightly, but then snaps to attention, as we all do.

"Okay," Beth Anne says, clapping her hands together sharply, quickly, twice. "KALABATI!"

Beth Anne bares her teeth and begins breathing in and out through her nose really quickly. I can see her stomach pumping through the thin material of her caftan.

"Now everyone try," she says, and obediently, we all do. Everyone bares their teeth and snorts in and out. "Remember your abdominals, pull in your abdominals with every short, sharp intake of breath," she explains, beginning to clap softly, rhythmically, along with our very overheated—very puglike, come to think of it—breathing. Lawrence jumps up from his chair and fans his hands out to the side: jazz hands. He stays there and continues his Kalabati, waving his jazz hands around. The rest of us continue practicing from our seats, nudged along by Beth Anne's clapping, encouraged to continue via her enthusiastic nods. I look over at Lawrence—how can I not?—and I have to admit that I see his point.

The happy-hubris-inner-me, the one who proudly wears her own orange caftan and waves her own hands in the air, and shouts ecstatically, *I am one step ahead!* is back. It's been a big night for her. As you might guess, I don't let her out very often. But here she is again, standing right next to Lawrence with her own jazz hands, exclaiming, *I know Kalabati, too!*

Then of course, the part of me for whom every moment is *not* a celebration of self, the part of me that would *never* be caught dead in an orange caftan, the part of me who I imagine prefers black clothing and moody vintage overcoats, puts down one of the cigarettes she's always smoking. She exhales and reminds me what a big loser I have the propensity to be. I actually see that the dark, brooding, cigarette-smoking inner me might have just made a valid point, so I try to temper the excitement. I'm actually pretty successful at chilling myself out, vanquishing the orange caftan version of my inner self away again, but still, I am nothing if not relieved that I have mastery of all these techniques. *I can relax,* I think, *I really can.*

"Great, class," Beth Anne announces the end of our breathing. Lawrence takes his seat. "Try to practice these breathing exercises right before any presentations. They'll truly help you to relax."

I think about my speech: my speech will be made at a party, most likely somewhat spontaneously. It will be delivered, I imagine, from the middle of a dance floor. I think how very likely I won't even know when it is ten, or even five, minutes before it is time to make my speech. I think how, as is so characteristic of all big scary things, I won't have any warning at all. I picture some clearly nefarious DJ/wedding singer/leader-of-the-band-type holding his microphone. He has a mullet. He's taken the microphone off the stand and is walking around with a swagger, holding the mike in one hand, holding the wire to the mike in the other, twirling it, trailing it along with him, like a hideous pet snake.

"And now Caroline and Henry's daughter, Hope, would like to make a speech," he will say. I think about how that will happen and how everyone, *all the people,* will turn to look at me and I'll have to get right up from whatever chair I've been sitting in, holding onto white-knuckled. There won't be any time, any place, to practice One Nostril Breathing, and certainly not Kalabati breathing, unless of course I want to have another reason to be embarrassed in front of people. And again, so quickly, all is lost.

"The Lion is another technique that's wonderful, just wonderful for relaxation," Beth Anne says, signaling that we're moving on from the breathing exercises, and I think how this is a good thing, as clearly the breathing has really done nothing to relax me so much as it has brought me to the bad place. I'm ready to move on.

"First, close your eyes *tightly, tightly, tightly,*" she says, closing her eyes, as you can probably guess, tightly. "And scrunch your face up *tightly, tightly, tightly,* too," she says and follows suit, both puckering her lips and raising them up to touch her nose while keeping her eyes still tightly shut. We wait.

It appears she is going to stay that way. The classroom is all awkward moment enmeshed in strained silence as Beth Anne continues to stand at the front of it with her face like that, with her clenched fists. I look down at my desk. Around me I can hear the rustling, I can feel the movements of my classmates; I imagine them looking away from Beth Anne and trying, as I am, not to look at anyone else. I stare harder at my desk. I try, even though I know it is hopeless, to zone out, to disengage, to do anything to make this moment pass.

And then, the second I think that what I want most in the world is to get as far away from this moment as I can, I am inexorably drawn, right into the center of it, by the hissing.

Beth Anne has unclenched her fists to the other extreme, fanning her hands out, stretching them out in front of her. Her eyes are unscrunched, they are the polar opposite of unscrunched, to say the least; they are open wide, bulging right out of her head. The other features of her face are just as assaulting; her mouth is as wide open as I've ever seen any mouth, her tongue is flattened out and protruding, wiggling around. Little bits of spittle are flying from her mouth, and with this, through all of this, is all the hissing. Hissing, I don't even know if that's the right word. It reminds me of a much exaggerated, grotesque version of the sound people sometimes like to make when they've just had a sip of soda, that sort of *ach* sound, but stretched out.

The rustling around from before is gone; everyone is now perfectly still, the silence that just moments before was so awkward, has now morphed into shock.

"That, class, is The Lion," Beth Anne says, wiping a bit of spit from her chin. "Let's try it all together."

And as much as I want there to be, it still doesn't seem like there is any escape. I look around at the rest of the class, and everyone is scrunching their face up. I picture them all at some point in the future: brilliant public speakers. I picture myself in the future: still seeing public speaking as a slow, painful, excruciating death. The reason for this future difference between my classmates and myself is that I wouldn't do The Lion. I scrunch up my face and wait for the sound of everyone else hissing. And then, there it is.

I open my eyes wide. I stick out my tongue. I splay my hands out in front of me. I hiss right along with everyone else and as I do so, I cannot say that I feel I have learned a great lesson about how to be a better public speaker, but what I can say is that people do not look well when they are doing The Lion. People, in fact, look quite disgusting.

And if there is any advice I can give anyone, I would like

that advice to be that if you find yourself in an Overcoming Presentation Anxiety class, and in that class you happen to find yourself doing The Lion, just look at the floor, or out the window while you're doing it. Whatever you do, don't look around at your fellow classmates, eyes wide, tongue thrusting and wagging, spit flying all over the place, so that you are repulsed by your classmates as surely you are to them repulsive. And if you just can't listen to me, if you just *have* to look around, at the very least don't look right up and into the eyes of the really good-looking and well-dressed guy in your class while you are both in full-extended Lion so that you pretty much kill any (admittedly quite slim) chance you ever had of sleeping with him.

"Okay, class," Beth Anne begins again, and The Lion it seems, thankfully, has come to an end. "Let's talk about our Deities."

I look at my watch. At this point I'm thinking it's a pretty safe bet that I'm in the type of situation where things, if they change at all, are only going to change for the worse. I look across at Martine and I think she is exhaling very heavily, but then I think also that I might be projecting, so I steal a quick look at some of the others. I look at Rachel, so frizz-haired and freaky, staring blankly, robotically ahead; Lawrence is still actually practicing The Lion. Alec just looks hot. Oh, right, I'm not supposed to look at Alec. Amy looks pissed, and really, to tell you the truth, at this point I have no idea whether or not I am projecting. How on earth am I supposed to tell?

"A Deity is a god or a goddess," Beth Anne goes on to explain, and I'm pretty sure I knew that and I can't help thinking, *Come on, we're just afraid of speaking in public, we're not idiots, we know what a Deity is.* I look around at everyone staring blankly at Beth Anne. Or at least, I *think* we know.

"Think about your Deities over the week, but don't pick them until next week, right before class, before you speak. When it comes to Deity selection, the best thing you can do, the way you can get the most power is to pick one at the very last moment," Beth Anne explains, beaming, and though I have no idea about what, triumphant. I look around at my classmates. It seems no one else has much of an idea as to what she is really talking about, or why she is suddenly looking so triumphant. For this very moment we are not swimming in a vast sea of anxiety, we swim instead in a sea of blank stares. I imagine that in spite of the confusion, everyone welcomes the change.

"Though you mustn't pick one yet, you can indeed think about them," Beth Anne adds on assuredly. I steal another quick glance around the room. A few of them, Lindsay, and Lawrence in particular, do look like they are thinking about Deities. Everyone else's expression seems to be as close an approximation as you can get to, *You have got to be kidding me*. Then, with the mysteries of the blackboard safely solved, Beth Anne reminds us that we should each pick a poem to present next time in class.

"It's important, class, that you feel comfortable. Should you not feel comfortable reading a poem, please feel free to read a passage from your favorite book."

Options are nice, I think, as Lawrence shakes his head from left to right and back again.

Beth Anne explains that if we start right away next time, we'll all be able to fit in our poems. Then for the following two classes, we'll need to split into groups to deliver our longer presentations.

"I'll give the assignment for your longer presentations after we've completed our poems. I don't want you to think about that yet, I don't want to distract you from your first assignment," she tells us as if we are all ADD children who simply can't bear the thought of thinking of two things at once. Everyone looks happy though, and I wonder if maybe we are.

"Okay, but for the groups," Beth Anne adds, "let's figure that out now."

We spend a lot longer than you would think would be necessary figuring out when everyone will present his or her longer speech in front of class. Everyone has ideas about whether they think going first is better, or last, or somewhere innocuous right in the middle.

"Such decisions," Beth Anne explains, "cause anxiety, and we are all here to overcome anxiety rather than create more." So, because of that I guess, I can't think of another reason, we watch as Beth Anne rips a piece of Xerox paper into seven strips and writes something on each strip. She rolls each strip into a tight ball and places them all on the center of her desk. We take almost as long as that going up to her desk one by one and selecting one of the tightly crumpled balls of paper, all the while I still have the sensation that I have somehow gone back to childhood.

Once we are each back at our desks with our pieces of paper, Beth Anne says we can open them. Mine has a tiny 2 written in the center. I'll go in the second group, not next class, or even the next one, but the one after that. I recrumple my piece of paper, thinking that there had to have been an easier way, and thinking also that I already know what poem I'll read next time, my favorite one. I try not to think of the longer presentation, since for one thing, we're not supposed to, and for another, we don't know what it is anyway.

I look at my watch again, and it's not like this class flew by the way time does when you're having fun, but I'm actually surprised, and more than a little relieved, to see that it's time to go.

"Well, I think this has been a great class. I think we really learned and accomplished a lot," Beth Anne says, nodding again to us, smiling at us warmly, telling us that, like last week, she'll remain after class for a while to answer any questions.

"Great class!" Beth Anne calls out again after us as we shuffle out the door and stand in front of the elevator, leaving her alone in the room, questionless.

"Do you feel relaxed?" Amy says, to no one in particular, as we all stand, each of us with our arms crossed in front of us, staring at the lights on top of the elevator, waiting for the "five" to light up, waiting for the doors to open. The communication has startled me, and I stare ahead harder, not wanting to engage.

"I am not feeling so much relaxed," Martine says in a way I think sounds ever so slightly contemptuous, or maybe, just French.

"Me, neither," says Lawrence very loudly.

Alec chuckles, much more a *huh-huh* than a *caw-caw*, I notice, and says, "We should really all just go get a drink."

He says this, remember, to a group of seven people about whom it is questionable as to whether or not we are actually socially ept. We all take a moment to look around cagily at our group. I notice some people even uncross their arms, and then, almost shockingly, six of us agree to go for a drink. It is only Rachel who says, "I cannot. I need to get home," so much like the robot I secretly think she is, and disappears through the stairwell door.

chapter sixteen

The Encyclopedia of Dogs

"Cedar Tavern is just a few blocks down on University," Alec offers as we walk out onto the street. Everyone nods in agreement. "Great, maybe we can get one of those big tables in the back," he adds in as we head down the street. Alec and Lindsay walk in front, the well-dressed leaders of our strange group. I walk behind them, Lawrence, Amy, and Martine, silent behind me. Alec strides purposefully, Lindsay not quite as proficient in the posture department, keeps pace with him, but is slightly hunched over.

He turns to her. "So, dude, are you that girl from that accounting firm whose pretty raunchy e-mail got sent *everywhere*?"

My initial thought is that I'm surprised, and yes, a little disappointed, that Alec is the type of guy to address people as "dude." Though I don't want to have a crush on Alec (clearly), I hope in spite of myself that his addressing Lindsay as "dude" was a one-time slip. Then, as Lindsay hunches inward a little bit more and mutters, "No," I think, *Oh my God, I remember that story!*

Six, maybe seven years ago, a woman at some big accounting firm forwarded to her friend an e-mail, one from a guy asking her if she'd like to go out with him. She included in the forward some fairly X-rated, and actually now that I think about it, pretty awful commentary about how the guy who'd just e-mailed would buy her and all of her friends drinks because she hadn't slept with him yet. She then went into *way* too much detail about someone she *had* slept with the night before (she used a far less G-rated term for it) and how he'd fallen asleep during the, uh, act. Her big, or rather *biggest* mistake, one she must regret really a whole lot, is that rather than hitting the forward button, she somehow hit *reply.* The guy then forwarded her e-mail to his entire address book, and it traveled around from there. I must have received it ten times, once from a college friend who lived in London.

I looked up at her, and even though she'd said no, I guessed it was she. *Wow,* I think, remembering even more of the e-mail, *Her* Grapes of Wrath *is so much worse than mine.* We all stop in front of Cedar Tavern. Lindsay looks up. I remember after that e-mail scandal, I read how she had to work from home, how her company's e-mail servers had crashed. I'd wondered a few times what it must be like to be her. And here we are: so completely different, but in exactly the same place.

"You know, I have a conference call. If you guys go out after the next class, I'll try to make it then," she says to the group.

"Aw, come on, I didn't mean anything by it," Alec protests. "Come on, one drink. I mean, you kind of brought it up last time, right?"

"Next time, really. Have fun, you guys," she says quickly and rushes away. I can't help thinking that unless he pulls a complete one-eighty, all the cuteness and fashion sense is wasted on Alec, because Alec just might be a bit of an idiot. I imagine that's probably for the best, reminding myself that I just don't have it in me to love anyone else from afar, or come to think of it, even from up close right at this juncture in time.

"What was that all about?" Amy asks heavily as she clomps just as heavily behind me as we climb the stairs and head to the back of the second floor of the Cedar Tavern.

"I'm not sure," I say, because as intriguing as the tale of the slutty accountant whose e-mail was read around the world is, I want to do something nice for Lindsay, and that's the only thing I can think of.

"Dude," Alec calls from in front of us, "she's the girl who sent some e-mail about nailing this guy who fell asleep and not nailing someone else so he'd buy all her friends drinks but she sent it by mistake to the guy who wasn't, uh, getting nailed, and then it got forwarded, I mean *everywhere*. A celebrity in our midst." He flashes a grin over his shoulder. Such a boyish, handsome grin, I think, and wish he'd stop using the word *dude*.

"Wow," Amy says, "I absolutely remember that. That's intense."

There's a round table in the back, we circle around it, take our seats as a waitress appears to take our drink orders. A bourbon for Amy, just ice water for Martine, a Manhattan for Lawrence, and whatever you've got on tap for Alec. And then it's my turn, and I want it to be a friendly night, a nice night, I want people to like me and I wonder if it's really true what Evan always said about white wine spritzers.

"I'll have an Amstel Light," I say, and as soon as I say it, I wonder if maybe that's the next worst thing to a spritzer.

"So," Lawrence says brightly, "where does everyone live?" No one answers, I take a sip of my beer, gather any reserve that is left after all that has been spent in class, and say, "Upper West Side."

"I hate ze Upper West Side," says Martine.

"Why do you hate the Upper West Side?" Lawrence asks. "I live there, too."

"Zare are so many mothers on ze Upper West Side, so many of zem bottle-feed. I think ze people on ze Upper West Side, zey think zey are so great with zare proximity to ze park and zare decorative fireplaces but so few of zem breast-feed."

Lawrence purses his lips. Amy curls a lip at her, I imagine more over the breast-feeding than over any defense of the Upper West Side. I decide that, as in many situations, it might just be better not to say anything.

"I live in Brooklyn," Amy says and I'm happy we're moving on, and I wonder if she lives near Elliot.

"My coworker lives in Carroll Gardens," I offer and she nods. Alec tells us he lives in Tribeca. I've long had a theory that all the cutest guys in New York live in Tribeca; everything looks good about this guy, except it seems for his personality.

"So, why does it make you so angry when people don't breast-feed?" Lawrence asks, really rather provocatively if you ask me. Martine takes a deep breath, it seems she is preparing to launch into a tremendous tirade. Lawrence leans into her, stage whispering so that everyone can hear, "My wife didn't breast-feed."

Wife? I think, and Martine's tirade begins. Luckily, she and Lawrence are at one side of the table, and the group seamlessly, naturally separates at this point: Lawrence hunkers down to listen to what I'm sure will be a long speech, and Alec and I turn in our chairs toward Amy. Alec leans in to Amy. "So, you're a novelist, that's totally cool. What have you written?"

She exhales and says, "My first novel came out about two years ago, *Black*."

"Oh, I think I've heard of it," Alec says in a way that reveals he hasn't heard of it. I can't really fault him too much on that though, because I haven't heard of it either.

"It's very *literary*," Amy offers. "You may not have." And I think, *Well, okay, Amy,* but feel also that I should contribute to the conversation in some way.

"Are you working on another novel now?" I ask.

"Yes"—big exhale—"I *was* about halfway through my second novel, *No Yellow,* and it was really fucking brilliant, but . . ." She trails off and stares into her bourbon.

"But, what, it didn't sell or whatever?" Alec pipes in.

"No, uh, it sold. It sold on a proposal," she answers back quickly, haughtily. "It's just, I, uh . . . I lost it. It got erased."

"Dude," Alec says. Amy looks at her hands.

"Yeah, so I have to write it again. I mean I have parts of it that I e-mailed to myself for safekeeping, it's just, the majority of it was on my laptop and I spilled, uh, a glass of water on my laptop." Her eyes tear up. "Accidentally, of course."

Alec says, "Dude, that's fucked up."

"Yeah," she says, nodding her head slowly.

"Didn't you have it backed up anywhere?" I ask, and the way she looks at me says, really succinctly, "No," and also, "Do you have any idea how many people have asked me that?"

"Do you have any idea how many people have asked me that?" she says, just in case I missed the point.

"I'm sorry," I say, "that was a dumb thing to say," and Amy looks like she might start yelling.

"Dude, it was a dumb thing to do. Uh, no offense, Amy."

She looks at me with squinty eyes, turns in her chair a bit to look at Alec, she takes another deep breath, lets it out.

"It was really fucking brilliant, and now it's just really fucking depressing," she explains again, and though everything about her seems so utterly pessimistic in tone and in feel, I can't help thinking that somewhere at least, she must be really optimistic in spirit, to come to a public speaking class to prepare for reading a book out loud that hasn't yet been written.

"So are you just working on the second book now?" I ask.

"Yeah, mostly, it's just, you know, it's hard. I write for magazines, too."

"Dude, no way, I love magazines, what sort of things do you write about?

"*Trends,* mostly. In New York," Amy says, haughty again, and again I think I don't really like her. I contemplate angling my chair the other way, joining into the other conversation, happy the chair I am in has left me with some options. I look across the table: Martine is speaking quickly, making quick circles in the air in front of her breasts; Lawrence is smiling brightly, looking not so much at her as off into the distance. Amy, I think, is better than the alternative.

"Did you ever want to be anything other than a novelist?" Alec asks her. It seems it has yet to occur to Amy that she could, and probably should, ask us some questions, too.

"What?" She hisses.

"Did you ever want to be anything other than a novelist?" Alec repeats.

"Yeah," she says wistfully, "thin." I think that I may have more in common with Amy than I'd care to acknowledge, and that is most definitely a bad thing. I also think that maybe I should jump in here, that maybe we need to change the subject, before any further similarities reveal themselves to me.

"Well, what are you guys going to read next week?" I ask.

Amy answers first, "I'm going to read a haiku I wrote, it's about despair."

Right, right, I think.

"I don't know, maybe I'll just read a paragraph or two from *The Da Vinci Code,* that's my favorite book of all time. How great was that book?" Alec asks us, bursting with enthusiasm.

"They never went to the bathroom," I say. "Every minute was accounted for, every second, and they never went to the bathroom."

Amy puts her face in her hands, rubs vigorously for a moment up and down. She tilts her head back, leaving her hands on her throat and says, loudly, to the ceiling, "I cannot believe it has come to this. I cannot believe I am part of a conversation that is debating the merits of that commercial piece of crap, *The Da Vinci Code.*" Amy spits a little as she says this, and then reaches quickly for her bourbon, taking a big sip and turning away from Alec, to me, "That's not *your* favorite book also, is it?"

"No," I say, and really, it wasn't. I liked it and all, it was just, I spent a lot of the book waiting for someone to go to the bathroom. You'd think that if every single second of time was accounted for, and the course of the book was at least three days long, then someone would have to go to the bathroom, or at least at some point say they'd be right back. That bothered me, and a favorite book, in my mind at least, should be one that doesn't bother you at all.

"What *is* your favorite book?" she asks. Questions one

and two for Amy: why do they have to be hostile ones, directed at me?

"My favorite book," I say in all honesty, "is *The Encyclopedia of Dogs*."

"*The Encyclopedia of Dogs*?" she says, very much in the manner of someone whose favorite book is probably by Proust. I am inclined to explain, as much as I am inclined to never ask her what her favorite book is.

"Let me explain," I say, because this is important, I think, so much more so than the deleting of novels or the search for the Holy Grail, at least to me. "See, I've always really loved dogs, and *The Encyclopedia of Dogs* has every single one of them in there. It was the first book I ever loved. I can remember how big it was, I can remember pulling it down from the bookcase and looking at it for hours." I notice they are both paying complete attention to me, but still, I continue.

"I had this game I played with myself, where I would turn to a page and slap my hand down, and whichever dog my fingers landed on would be my imaginary dog for the day. I used to love playing it, I called it, 'That's My Dog.'"

I leave out the part about how Darcy wanted to be involved in my game of "That's My Dog," how she then changed the name to "That's Me," and how the dog your fingers landed on would be the dog that you *were* for the day.

I leave out the part about how Darcy, more coordinated and quicker at slapping her hand down onto the page, and not averse to resorting to hair pulling to get her way, always got first choice of the dog she wanted. I leave out that Darcy was always the collie, just like Lassie; the elegant French poodle; the mysterious and sleek Weimaraner; the beautiful Doberman; the all-American golden retriever. I leave out that I was always the bulldog; the squat longhaired dachshund; the sad-looking, peculiar Clumber spaniel; the pug.

I think the story is better without those facts, and then I think, *Oh my God, I was the pug.*

"You can't really read from a book like that," Amy says, and, just like that, I'm back in the present.

"I know, Amy. I'm going to read a poem."

"Dude," Alec says, turning to me and grinning, "you're cute."

I look down at the floor, at Alec's square-toe loafers. *Prada,* I think. And once I'm done with this class, once I've made my speech, and finished the Rothko, and somehow gotten free of the crush on Elliot, once I've done all the things I need so desperately to do, I think I might need to rethink the amount of importance I place on footwear.

"It is an outrage! An absolute outrage!" Martine yells from across the table, slamming her palm down for emphasis.

"Okay, then," Lawrence says, remarkably still in good cheer, "well, I think I'm gonna call it a night. Go home and work on my poem." He winks.

We survey the empty glasses in front of us. No one jumps in to suggest another round.

"Maybe next time we'll all go to dinner," Alec suggests as we head down the stairs. He taps the breast pocket of his jacket as he says this, as if something important is in there. "I've got the private number to Balthy."

"Balthy, what's that?" I ask, assuming, the moment the words are out of my mouth, that Balthy is some new, trendy, hip place that just about everyone knows about and I have once again revealed my complete and utter dorkiness by speaking at all.

"Balthazar," he says proudly.

"Oh, I'm sorry," Amy says without turning around to face him, "I didn't realize we were in a time warp and all of a sudden it's 1999. Balthy, *please.*"

"What? It's hard to get into!"

We head out into the street and say quick good-byes, heading this way and that, spreading out into the night. I walk a block or two toward Union Square and then stop. I reach out my arm and hail a cab; it is, conveniently for me, I think, too late for the train.

chapter seventeen

Under No Circumstances Are You to Mention the Tent

The phone is ringing.

As I may have mentioned, I am not quite the fan of the ringing phone. I am even less of a fan of the ringing phone when it rings and wakes me up on a Saturday morning. I open one eye, look over at the clock: nine-fifteen again, exactly. Definitely there is the possibility of being depressed, even though, strangely, for much of Friday I felt buoyant at work. Perhaps all the relaxation exercises that I may have prematurely counted as useless, have somehow, secretly, seeped into my psyche.

The phone keeps ringing. It could be Pamela calling to see if I minded that she left me alone at the bar at 'Cesca last night, on one of my first nights out on the town as a newly single woman. Actually, I kind of did mind that she left me there, left with the guy dressed all in black, the guy who I thought, with the black shirt and the black pants and the black belt and the black shoes, reminded me so much of the old Mike Myers skit on *Saturday Night Live,* "Sprockets."

"Now is the time on Sprockets ven ve dahnce!" is what I'd said to Pamela when she said she thought he was looking our way. She hadn't laughed. Instead, she'd gone to talk to him on her own, and they had left together a short while later. She had waved coquettishly to me on her way out, and I'd wished that being single didn't mean you had to have single girls' nights out with friends like Pamela.

Rather than pick up the phone to hear Pamela tell me that being single can be fantastic if only I'd embrace it and not call potential suitors Sprockets, I let the machine pick up. I picture Pamela and the Sprocket, hear Mike Myers saying, "Do you want to touch my monkey? Touch him!" in my mind. I always prefer to screen, right now is no exception.

I listen as my machine clicks over to record mode, and then, through the speaker, "Hope, it's your mother. Are you there?"

I stare at the phone, right there. I weigh my options. I sink down deeper into my pillow.

"Okay," she continues. "I'm just calling to tell you, under no circumstances are you to mention the tent to your father. Your father is very upset about the tent, and I really don't want it discussed," she says sternly, and then brighter, much more full of cheer, "Talk to you soon, look forward to seeing you."

I have no idea, no idea at all, what she is talking about with the tent. I assume it is, as so many things are, Darcy-related. I sit up in bed.

"Hello! Hello! Hello!" I say a few times, to no one, to be sure there is no sleeping sound in my voice. I want to know what this is about: the tent. As I turn to grab the phone, begin dialing my parents' number, I think it's a good thing that I'm such a dog person—the way curiosity always kills cats and all. Mom doesn't answer, Dad does.

"Hi, Hopey," he says. "What's up?"

"Oh nothing, just calling to say hi," I say. We exchange pleasantries, work is good, arrangements for the party are good, everyone's looking forward to the party, and then, just as I am about to switch gears, to ask to talk to Mom, Dad says, "While I have you on the phone, do you know anything about L.L. Bean donating money to pro-life causes?"

"Uh, no, I don't." I don't ask why. I may have arrived at my ripe age of thirty-one (or thirty-two depending on whom you ask) with the feeling that I have not learned as much as I should have along the way, but I have learned enough to know that if Mom just called and said not to talk about a tent, then a sentence that includes L.L. Bean could very well lead to a conversation I was just told to not have.

"Well, see . . ." I listen to Dad exhale, get ready to explain something. "C.P. doesn't want to sleep in the house when they come for the party, he wants to sleep outside in a tent."

Oh, I think, *no.*

"A tent?"

"Yes, and I was going to buy them a tent to sleep in."

"You're *buying them a tent*?"

"Yes, but Darcy says C.P. will only sleep in tents whose manufacturers he doesn't find objectionable."

I want to say, then C.P. shouldn't come at all. I want to say that Darcy isn't really going to join a commune, and that even though Dad is the type of dad who strives to see the good in everything, who strives to fix everything that isn't good, buying Darcy and C.P. a tent isn't going to fix anything.

"Um, you could try REI," I say instead of anything else.

"REI? They sell tents?" Right after the word *sell,* I hear another connection pick up somewhere else in the house.

"Hope!" my mother shouts, aghast.

"What?!" I shout back.

"I thought we talked about not talking about the tent!"

"Uh," I stutter and while it indeed would be logical to say that we haven't *technically* discussed not talking about the tent, I know it will not help. "Uh, yes, but—"

"Caroline, why did you tell Hope not to talk about the tent?"

"Because it upsets you and it upsets Hope!" my mother shoots back, and I guess, yes, she's right. It does upset me, all of it, and I'm kind of touched right now actually that she sees it this way.

"Well, Caroline, it's upsetting!" Dad yells through the phone. "But we have to deal with it! We have to deal with it as a family! We need to address it! We need to FIND A SOLUTION!"

"I'M TAKING HER TO CANYON RANCH! THAT IS A SOLUTION! INDULGING *C.P.* IN A NON-OBJECTIONABLE TENT IS NOT A SOLUTION!"

"CAROLINE! STOP SHOUTING!"

"I'M NOT SHOUTING!"

"Uh, Mom? Dad?"

"WHAT?" they both shout at me simultaneously, in sync at least on something.

"I have to go actually, I'm going to be late for work."

"But it's Saturday," my mom offers. It is now, I'm sure of it, her deepest desire to keep me on the phone to discuss with me why I felt it was necessary to bring up the tent when she specifically told me not to. Her second deepest desire is to not listen to me at all when I explain that I didn't.

"I know, but I'm actually behind on a few things and need to catch up. But I'll call you both later."

"Okay, then, bye Hope," says my father, remarkably mellowed.

"Bye!" I say as breezily, and as quickly as possible, and hang up.

I stare at the phone in its charger, and for a moment, I contemplate calling Darcy up in California and talking to her myself about the commune. I just want to tell her that all she has to do is say it's not true. But Darcy and I don't really jive ever, not in any way that is productive, and if she does wind up going to a commune, I don't want to be the one who called and pushed her over the edge. I want so many things, but what I want right now is not to feel like the whole world is only an exercise in powerlessness.

"I hope everything is okay, at least as okay as I want to believe that it is," I say this out loud. I'm saying this, I know, to Darcy. I wonder if C.P. is really as Zen, as connected with the universe, as he says he is. I want to believe that if he is, maybe somewhere, in a tent whose manufacturers he does not find objectionable, he hears me. I hope he does. I hope he gives Darcy my message.

I look at my pillow, I want to sink back into it, pull the covers up high over my head. I wonder if the *Law & Order* I saved—the one with the Zoloft commercial—is still on my list of saved programs, or if it's shuffled off yet. I think of the day stretching out in front of me. Not surprisingly, going to paint pottery at the place on Amsterdam loses a significant amount of appeal when its suggestion is not merely a way to antagonize Evan. I head for the shower and realize it's true what I said: there are some things I need to catch up on. And some of those things even have to do with work. Going to work, I decide, dealing with the Rothko's problems, and not my own, is nothing right now, if not a very good idea.

* * *

I walk slowly through the silent hallways of the Met, and just for a moment everything is so peaceful, like it used to be, before there was Elliot, before Patsy Cline kept piping up, belting out "Crazy" in the background.

I walk into the Conservation Studio, and while the silence is still there, the peace is gone. Elliot is here. Annoyance flares inside me, but there is, in certain situations—in this situation in particular—some merit in being annoyed. Being annoyed at the sight of Elliot could be a very good sign; it is an improvement to say the least on the usual rendered speechless, melting of my heart that takes place.

"Hi, Elliot," I say, as I walk to my station and begin sorting immediately through my can of brushes, looking for the one I was using at the end of yesterday; it was working so well.

"Hey, Hope," Elliot says, he even looks up halfway and smiles, which of course makes my stomach flip over.

Patsy Cline isn't playing in the background anymore. Suddenly, the song has changed. The Red Hot Chili Peppers are singing now, singing the first lines of the song, "Otherside." *How long? How long?* I've always liked to believe that the music that always plays in my mind has a point, and I think: *How long, indeed.* I mean, really, how long can this go on? And worse than that, with me being single and all, how long, if it doesn't get better, until it just gets worse? How long until I'm not just staring across the room at Elliot, how long until I'm more desperate, brazen even? How long until I am up and off my stool, charging across the Conservation Studio and lunging at his penis? *My God.* I shake my head, it is the only way I can think of to make the Red Hot Chili Peppers song stop playing. It works. The music stops. I angle my easel and my stool away, and find the brush that I want.

Thankfully an hour, maybe longer, goes by, and I'm able to concentrate only on the picking, the tiny painting of red dots onto the red section of the Rothko.

"Hello, Elliot, and hello, Hope." Sergei's deep voice bounces off the ceiling, off the walls, as he strides purposefully into the room, past us, and over to the canvas stretchers. *Why is Sergei here? Is Sergei here all the time on Saturdays with Elliot?* Am I the only one who generally does not come in on the weekends? I always thought no one ever came in on the weekends; well, I guess I assumed Elliot did, because on top of being the object of my endless fascination, he also does seem to have a bit of an obsessive-compulsive disorder lately when it comes to whipping through his Old Master landscapes. Landscapes, though, they are so much easier to restore. You can hide so much among trees and leaves and blades of grass. You can't hide anything on a Rothko. With a Rothko, with the broad areas of color, everything you do is out there for the world to see. You can't make any mistakes; you can't hide anything at all.

I remind myself that Paintings Conservation is very much *not* a race, and that it doesn't matter one bit that Elliot must have finished three Old Master landscapes in the time that I've been laboring over the red section of my Rothko. *Unless, of course, it does?* How sad really would it be if one of the great prides of my life, that I am diligent and studious and hardworking in my career, turns out not to be true?

They can't be here all the time; there must be something special going on. I put down my brush. Then I pick it up and decide to carry it with me. Perhaps I'm just going to wash my brush and not really on a stealth fact-finding mission. I walk over to Sergei. He's much farther away than Elliot, but he is safer. If any of my fears in fact turn out to be true, there isn't any chance at all I will lunge and grab at Sergei's penis. *My God,* I think again. *Has it really come to this?*

"Sergei?" I say, sidling over. Generally, just so you know, I don't usually sidle.

"Yes?" he says looking up from the back of a canvas he has just laid out across the large table.

"Why is everyone here?" It sounds stupid as I say it, and I am glad I chose Sergei rather than Elliot as an informational source. "I mean, I know why I'm here. I'm having trouble with the Rothko, but are you and Elliot always here on Saturdays?"

"Elliot," he says with a nod in Elliot's direction, "who knows about him? That one loves to work. No, I am not usually here on Saturday. I'm here," he says a little sheepishly, "because of the news about May."

"What news about May?"

"You haven't heard?"

"No."

"It is hunch, she has not told us anything officially, of course, and, well, I guess that's clear because then you would have heard, of course." *Yeah,* I think, *of course,* and Sergei continues. "But the word is that she is taking a sabbatical for a year. While she's gone, one would think she will put one of us in charge."

"A promotion?" I ask softly.

"Yes," he says, and we both nod seriously. *Promotion* isn't a word often heard in Paintings Conservation at the Met. It takes so long to get here, and it's such a good job to have, that no one ever leaves. Even if it would be just for a year, a promotion would be a pretty big deal.

"Wow, well thanks for telling me." I turn and slink slowly back to my desk to let the news sink in. I'm upset, of course, that I didn't know. I bemoan ever so briefly the pitfalls that inevitably pop up when you spend so much time in the background, the background even of your own life.

I think about the promotion and I think how each one of us is a contender. This morning it appears, pretty blatantly, that maybe Elliot is bucking for a promotion. He is always the first person here, and he is always the last person to leave. It occurs to me again how that even though Paintings Conservation isn't a race, he *has* gotten through three Old Master landscapes in the time it has taken me to basically just get started on the Rothko. But, on that, I've said it before and I'll say it again: going over the contemporary problems, the problems of today, can be a lot harder than the problems of the past. I flip through my brushes until I find the smallest one. I sit back and stare, and try again to focus. I try to remember where I was when I left off.

It's no use. I sit back and instead of focusing on the Rothko, I think about this new element of competition in our workplace. I look up suspiciously at Elliot, then over at Sergei. Both Sergei and Elliot could be given May's job while she is gone. Sergei's been here longer than I have, and even though Elliot hasn't even been here for a year, he used to be Head Restorer at the Brooklyn Museum. And also, to get a promotion after only being here for, what, five months: such is the way of Elliot.

I think of May, the nicest boss I think anyone has ever had. She's always fostered an environment so free of competition and office politics—not that paintings restoration is such a hotbed of office politics or anything—that this new feeling of competition in the workplace is very strange, very foreign indeed. I think a bit dramatically, even for me, that everyone is the enemy. But then, of course, they're really not, because May is so great to work for, and learn from, and the whole earth-mama-flowy-dress-dangly-earring look really appears so much more genuine on her, like it's the way it should be, than it does on someone like Beth Anne who, dressed all flowy like that, in my mind, winds up looking somewhat fraudulent. And Sergei is not really the enemy because he is, well, he's just lovely. And Elliot isn't the enemy because, as I might have mentioned, I love him.

I put my paintbrush away and look over at Elliot.

"Did you know that May might be leaving?" I say across the room to Elliot. He pauses, stares at his canvas for a moment, making some sort of conscientious Elliot-type mental note before looking up and squinting at me.

"Of course I knew," he says, and the way he says it, it's just so matter-of-factly that you could almost miss the slight condescending tone. But I choose not to, and I think, in this case, that's a good thing.

"Whatever happens though," he continues and the "whatever," it sounds so ominous to me, "the good news is that we'll get another restorer in here, someone with more time to actually restore than May has. We might even catch up one day." He nods in the direction of the paintings lining the eastern wall of the room. I think it is a very good thing he didn't just nod in the direction of the Rothko.

Suddenly, Elliot doesn't look quite as perfect, quite as ideal, quite as, "Let's you and me, babe, run off into the sunset and leave this crazy Conservation Studio behind us" hot as he usually does. This is, I realize, because he's over there, so studious, intense, and dedicated not only because of his inherent *Elliotness* but because he is bucking for a promotion. Elliot is bucking for what could very well be *my* promotion. I lean back, as much as you can lean back in a stool, and I wait for something to happen, for something to change. Nothing happens.

Then I think something dreadful, something horrid, something that goes against every effort I've ever made to have a successful career. Something that goes against every hope I've ever had of being an independent, career-minded, successful woman. I think that if Elliot gets the promotion, I'll be really pissed off, I'll be really bitter, and because of all that, because he has a promotion, even if it is just for a year, that could have been mine, I won't pine away for him anymore. As I pull my magnifying visor down over my eyes, I think that if Elliot gets the promotion, it'll be the one thing I can think of that will set me free.

chapter eighteen

Be My Boswell

"Are you sure you're not mad?" Pamela asks again.

"Really, I'm sure. I'm not mad," I tell her again. There's a pause; I wait. I have an idea what is coming next, now that I am not mad: a pep talk. Even though historically it hasn't worked out well with Pamela and me when she administers her form of a pep talk, I feel a bit this morning like maybe I could use one. I just hope the phrase "eHarmony.com" doesn't factor into it.

"I just think that you could have more fun than you actually aspire to have," she begins, "you know, like at 'Cesca. It doesn't have to be a bummer being single."

"I'm not bummed about being single, I swear, I'm not. I don't think it's a bad thing and to tell you the truth, after Evan, it's kind of nice."

"Right."

"Look," I say, and I try to think how to say this, try to think how to put into words that being like Pamela, being gregarious, and outgoing, and extremely confident about everything (and not to mention long-limbed and completely fatless) makes for a far different experience being single at places like 'Cesca, a trendy pickup place. And, come to think of it, everywhere else. I take a deep breath and try.

"It's not that I didn't want to have fun on Friday at 'Cesca," I explain, "it's just not my ideal environment."

"Nothing is an ideal environment, Hope. And also, and don't get mad, no one is an ideal guy." I think that also not everyone is a Sprocket, but I don't say that because Pamela, I hate to admit, has a point.

"I know," I say.

"Sometimes I'm not so sure if you do."

"What does that mean?" I ask, the beginnings of annoyance sprouting up inside of me.

"I just think, and really, don't take this the wrong way, that you might be a little too quick to make judgments about people, and that sometimes those judgments are, uh, innacurate."

Judgments?! Judgments that are inaccurate?!

"I think that you make judgments that are inaccurate, too," I say, trying my best not to bring up the whole shunning of my Judaism, because to tell you the truth I am pretty far from being over that one.

"Maybe I do, but we're not talking about me right now. Look, I'm just saying this because I care about you," Pamela explains, and actually, at the end of the day, I know that she does.

"I know you do," I tell her and then, I feel again like I want to explain, even though it's hard to explain things you don't really understand yourself, and also aren't entirely sure you believe. I decide to go for it anyway.

"It's just, you know, it's very different for me, I'm much more of a solitary person than you. I'm not so sure being single is something I want to run away from."

"Oh, please, Hope," she scoffs, "being single is something *everyone* wants to run away from." And at this point, I think I am completely and utterly confused.

"But you're the one always saying to embrace it!"

"The only reason to embrace being single is so that you don't have to be it anymore," she explains.

I wonder if she might be right about this, and if maybe, I want her to be.

"Yeah," I say, deflecting any invitation for further debate. Happily, Pamela seems to have said all she needs to say on the now vastly confusing topic of how being single is so great that everyone on earth wants to run away from it, and she moves on.

"Well, what are you doing today? Do you want to go to lunch?" I look outside, at the two chairs on my balcony, sitting side by side, looking out onto a late Sunday morning. There's something else I want to do much more than have lunch with Pamela.

"How about coffee at, like, four? Want to meet at Café Edgar?"

"What are you doing until then?"

"Um, I just want to work on this assignment I have for the public speaking class," I lie.

"You want to go to Pug Hill, don't you?"

"Um, yeah," I say, "actually I do," and hope that she doesn't want to come. Probably she doesn't. Kara and Chloe see the beauty of Pug Hill and they come with me sometimes. Chloe loves the pugs, even though admittedly I don't think the pugs love it when she screeches and runs after them. Pamela is not as interested in Pug Hill, mostly, I think, because she thinks only married guys and dorky guys actually own pugs. I think of the Tretorn guy, and of how I have to learn that footwear is unimportant.

"Okay, four o'clock. Café Edgar," she announces, and that's good. "Hope?" she asks, "if you like pugs so much, why don't you just get one?" Pamela again has a point.

"Not right now," I say, "not just yet."

"Yeah," she says, "that's probably good. I think having a dog would make dating harder."

"Absolutely," I agree, even though I really don't.

* * *

I walk across the park, down a hill, up another incline, and I'm almost there. I don't really expect there to be many pugs because it's not all that warm out. I mean, it's not like I expect there to be no pugs like *that* day, it is Sunday, after all. Can you imagine no pugs at Pug Hill on a Sunday of all days, a day I believe to be the day of all days for pugs coming to Pug Hill? Saturdays are up there, too, but *the* day for coming to Pug Hill, if you are in fact a pug, or, like me, just an admirer of pugs, is Sunday. I step through the row of benches and across the cement path. I'm here.

There aren't too many pugs, but there are actually more than I thought there would be. That's one of the benefits of being cautiously optimistic rather than just brazenly optimistic: you get disappointed a lot less than if you were brazen. I look around at the pugs who are here, and they all seem especially jaunty and proud. The way they march around, spinning, snorting, darting off at nothing in particular (definitely not at a thrown object of any sort), makes me sure that these pugs know just as well as I do, maybe more, that Pug Hill is the place to be.

I take a seat on the bench. The ground by the tree that I like, the ground anywhere, actually, is looking a little too cold and uninviting. I glance hopefully toward the pine tree, but unfortunately, Kermit is not waiting for me there. Actually, I don't recognize so many of the pugs today. They're all bundled up in their coats and sweaters, and it's hard to know them as well when they're all so bundled up. I lean back on the bench and take in all the pugs, pugs that I don't quite recognize but still adore, all prancing around like so many secret agents.

"Eustice!" someone yells from a few feet to my right. An extremely, let's say, girthy pug, in a gray turtleneck sweater, comes bounding up the hill. His tongue hangs out to the side, the way so many tongues of so many pugs seem to like to do, and he's panting very loudly; I can hear the panting, accompanied by some intermittent snorting even before he gets close, even before he heads in a beeline right past his owner and right toward me.

"Well, hello, Eustice," I say very encouragingly and very enthusiastically at his arrival. He looks up at me, and very politely hoists his tongue up and licks the foam from his pug nose. And the way he does it, everything about him, makes me smile so completely. I say next what makes the most sense, "Thank you, Eustice." With a jerking motion, he moves his whole body to the side, throws back his head and turns around, and just like that, he's off. He runs toward his owner and I feel, for right now at least, that everything is going to be okay. Everything is going to be just fine.

I settle back into the bench and look out in front of me to see who else is out there. Over there, by the tree, there's another fawn pug. He's very tall for a pug, rather spindly actually, and he's dressed in what looks like less of a sweater and more of a green Mexican blanket with a belt. The spindly pug is hovering over a much smaller and rounder pug, who isn't wearing any pug accoutrement at all. I lean forward a little bit because the spindly Mexican-blanketed pug really does seem to be breathing down the little unadorned one's neck. But then it seems that the Mexican-blanketed spindly pug bores easily; he trots off. A woman comes over to put a red harness on the little pug. He snorts up at her and reaches out his tongue to kiss her. I wonder if she has any idea how lucky she is, how much I envy her.

I stare out at the frolicking pugs, there must be ten of them here. Each one to me is love, each one is unconditional friendship, each one is happiness and each one is freedom.

"Is this seat taken?" says a British accent from above me.

Startled, I look up and I see that attached to the British accent is a very cute guy, who, I kid you not, looks exactly like David Duchovny. Maybe, I think, just for a second, it *is* David Duchovny. That is if David Duchovny had a British accent.

"No, please," I say, gesturing to the rest of the bench, and I'm pretty sure as he sits down, that he's not actually David Duchovny, but, *still.* He leans back against the bench and looks out with me at the pugs spread out all around the hill in front of us.

"Which one is yours?"

"I don't have one," I answer. I feel him turn toward me. I look over at him and he's looking at me quizzically.

"I just like to see them," I say by way of explanation.

"Oh, a pug voyeur, then? A bit like myself today . . ." he says, trailing off, his eyes following as a pug in a hot pink jacket with a bright green hood charges past us.

"You don't have a pug either?" I ask, stunned.

"No, can't say I do." He says *can't* like *cahnt,* and it occurs to me that I just might have read one too many chick-lit novels in my day. I have, somewhere along the way, lost the ability to hear an English accent and not think that it so surely implies that somewhere within earshot is the man with whom I am to live happily ever after.

I look over at him and he's smiling; a really cute, really

boyish smile, by the way, and his teeth aren't banged up at all, the way I tend to sometimes think British teeth might be. I try not to think how in so many of the books I've read, how the love interest is *always* British, how the happy ending *always* involves a cute British guy. But I do.

I smile back at him and then I *cahnt* really think of what to say, which isn't so unusual because I can't think of what to say a lot of the time. And so I just smile again, and he smiles back, and I can't help wondering if maybe this is how it happens, if maybe this is how my search ends. I think how cinematic it would be, what a great ending this would make to the movie I would so prefer my life to be. Imagine: if after all my years of coming to Pug Hill, I meet someone, who by virtue of being British is, of course, happy-ending preapproved, and who also likes to just come to Pug Hill to sit here and see the pugs.

"Do you quite like pugs then?" he asks.

"I do," I say and smile again, still. I feel a little funny and I wonder if this is how a person feels when she knows that her search for love is over, when she knows that everything is going to turn out okay. I'm not sure how, but I think I always imagined that it would have felt somewhat different from this.

"Pugs were quite a big thing for the duke and duchess of Windsor, you know," he says.

"Indeed," I say. And I know that *indeed* is sort of a British thing to say and that, as you know, I am not British. I am just caught up in the moment, in the so-close-to-perfect-ness of the moment.

"My wife misses England a lot and I thought a proper pug might do the trick, because of the duke and duchess," he says and smiles at me so sweetly. I think, *Of course he has a wife,* and then I think how I wish it weren't true. I stare out at the hill and I think that there is a reason people should wear wedding rings, so that people like me will know that while they are handsome and David Duchovny–like and have a nice accent along with the bonus of nice teeth and are admiring of pugs and talking to me, they are also FUCKING TAKEN!

"Yeah," I say, "that's a good idea," and that's a good thing to say. It works out well because I imagine to him, it sounds like I am talking about the procuring of a pug for his home-sick British wife, even though I'm not.

I smile somewhat feebly and we both go back to looking at the pugs. After about five uncomfortable minutes—minutes that I imagine are probably more uncomfortable for me than they are for him—he turns back toward me and says, "I don't think I could *stahnd* the exposed arsehole day after bloody day."

Apparently, my thinking for that one brief, exhilarating moment that he was my soul mate and then finding out that he was, of course, not, was not enough in terms of disappointment for one afternoon.

I look at him even though I don't want to anymore, and he is actually *sneering,* disdainfully I might add, at all the beautiful pugs. And even as prone to jumping to conclusions as I am, I just can't believe that I thought, for even the fleetingest of fleeting moments, that he might have been my British chick-lit happy-ending soul mate. Whoever my soul mate may be, I know that at the very least, he has to like pugs. Even if only dorky guys like pugs, like Pamela says. I'm wondering if it would be rude if I stood up right now. I wonder where'd I go though because I don't want to leave Pug Hill on this note. But I also would really *rahther* not stay here with him anymore.

He sighs. "I think I'll have to find a proper British breed. Maybe a mastiff," he says after he's given it a moment of thought. And even though I don't want to talk to this man anymore, even though I kind of hate him, I feel, for the sake of English mastiffs everywhere, that I need to jump in.

"Don't pick an English mastiff," I say. "The city isn't good for them."

He cocks his head to the side, looks at me quizzically. "Because they're so large?"

"Well, that," I say.

"I see plenty of large dogs in the city," he counters.

"No, the thing you don't know is that besides it being hard to be such a large dog in the city, English mastiffs scare easily."

"How do you know?" he asks. I do not in fact know if English mastiffs really do scare easily, I only know that Boswell did.

"We had one, my family, when I was growing up," I explain.

"And she scared easily?"

"Oh, she really did," I say. "Let me tell you about Boswell." I turn more fully toward him, sit up a little straighter on the bench. I take a breath and make eye contact. Somewhere in the background it occurs to me that I am, in fact, about to make a speech, but that's overshadowed by the fact that I need to tell him about Boswell.

"Fine name, by the way," he says and I think, but don't say, "Let's try not to interrupt." I think back to the time in my life that was all about Boswell.

Boswell came from New Hope. New Hope, Pennsylvania, that is, not New Hope, me. I was only four years old at that point, not so much had happened to awaken me to the long-ings to be a new person. Something flashes in the British guy's eyes, I think it might be impatience.

I begin. "My mom found Boswell in New Hope, Penn-sylvania. She went antiquing there one weekend and the antique dealers were dog breeders, too. We already had dogs: Morgan, a Saint Bernard; Adelaide, a bulldog, an English bulldog"—I hate to get off track but hope he takes note of the English part because maybe a bulldog would be a better idea for him—"and Mischief, a French poodle. When my mom called to try to get my dad to see the light about how a fourth dog, a soon-to-be-two-hundred-pound dog, was indeed a very good idea, she just kept repeating again and again how Boswell was magnificent. 'She's magnificent,' my mom said again and again. 'Such a regal quality to her gait, such a soulfulness to her eyes.'"

I want to close my eyes for a minute. I know that if I did, I'd be able to hear my mom's voice, the mom of my childhood so many years ago, and I want to hear that. But the British guy doesn't look quite as wrapped up in the story as I am. I figure an important part of public speaking, of a lot of things, actually, might be knowing when to get to the point.

"So, right, Boswell came home," I continue, "and she *was* magnificent, she really was, but everything scared her and even though she'd been touted, in New Hope, as a wonderful watchdog, once Mom got her home, she spent the majority of her time underneath the kitchen table, chattering her teeth. And this was in the *suburbs*."

I talk more about Boswell, about how magnificent everyone thought she was—how breathtaking, everyone agreed—but so much more than that, how sweet to everyone she was, how loving she was, although she was perhaps not the sharpest tool in the shed. As I talk about Boswell, as the British guy listens rather attentively, I forget that I just decided that I hate him, and then decide that I don't. I change my mind in honor of Boswell, because even though she may not have understood all that much, if Boswell understood anything, I like to believe she understood love.

"I see."

"And I think it was hard on Boswell, harder still when,

because of the magnificence and all, Mom decided to show her. She literally had to be carried out of the show ring, and we think it was a long time after that until she was the same."

"They are quite handsome dogs," he says, and I agree that mastiffs are indeed quite handsome dogs, but I worry that even with my speech, I may not have changed his mind. Still though, I am inclined to give credit where credit is due.

"Boswell was very pursued by the neighborhood dogs," I say this because it was true, and also, I throw it in as a deterrent. "That might get kind of difficult at the dog run." Though tempted, I leave out the long part about the year and a half that Boswell spent pursued by Cosgrove, a ne'er-do-well mutt who lived down the street. I leave out the part about how Boswell had a hysterical pregnancy and went into hysterical labor on Christmas morning.

"Just like the baby Jesus!" Grammy McNeill had exclaimed, before we realized the puppies weren't coming.

"Oh, Jesus," Nana had said.

"Ah." He smiles, indulging me. "Maybe it's not the best city dog." I smile back and I think it's nice that he said that. I think also that there must be something in the air at Pug Hill. Here, you can be a bit crazy about dogs and their memories, and people won't necessarily run from you as if you are insane.

"Well, it was a pleasure meeting you." He pauses, and it occurs to me for the first time that I don't know his name.

"Hope." I reach out my hand.

He shakes it and says, "Marcus."

"Nice to meet you, too. Good luck with the dog search."

He stands and puts his hands into his pockets. We say good-bye and he turns to go, without a last glance at the pugs. I watch him for a while as he walks west, over another hill. I turn back to the pugs and pull my coat tighter around me. I think of love, not because of the British guy, of course not because of the British guy, but because of Boswell and her star-crossed love with Cosgrove, because if Boswell believed in anything I like to think she believed in love.

I take one last look at the pugs and get up myself and walk back toward home. I'll meet Pamela soon for coffee, and then I'll go home and get ready for the week. I'll practice reading out loud for class on Thursday. I'll stand very straight in front of my mirror, I'll take deep breaths. I'll make eye contact, even if it's only with myself. I'll Take the Room even if I'm the only one in it, because like so many things, it's a start.

chapter nineteen

Haiku Is a
Seventeen-Syllable
Verse Form

All week, I've gotten into work early each day and stayed late each night. I have not out-clocked Elliot, but I have put in many respectable hours on the Rothko. I've been here more than Sergei has. I've told myself that I'm spending all this time at work because I am diligent and dedicated, not because I am bucking for a promotion, because I don't want to, all of a sudden, be competitive in the midst of all these things—good at being single, good at public speaking—that I now must endeavor to be. I have told myself that I have spent so much extra time in the Conservation Studio this week because I need to finish the red part of my Rothko, not because Elliot is here and so nice to look at across a room. I have told myself that I am here for all these reasons, but not because I suspect Pamela may have been trying to tell me that as solitary as I like to be, I might just be no good at being single.

* * *

As the Express 4 train hurtles from Eighty-sixth Street to Union Square, as I walk down lower Fifth Avenue, I think of how much I have practiced, of how many times I have read my poem over and over again. I feel like I've done my home-work, and that's always been a feeling I've enjoyed. I walk, almost confidently, into room 502. I'm ready.

I head for my seat, and I notice that there is a video camera set up in the back of the room.

There is a video camera. I take a deep breath. I wonder if it would be simultaneously overzealous and kind of embarrassing to do The Lion in an attempt to calm myself. I decide that it would be. I sit down and turn around halfway in my chair-desk. I stare transfixed at the video camera, letting the gravity of the situation sink in.

There is a video camera in the back of the classroom. It's on a professional stand. It's hooked up by a bunch of wires to a VCR that's sitting on a cart behind it. There is a man with a goatee wearing a short sleeve T-shirt over a long sleeve T-shirt. He is looking through the video camera and fiddling with the lens. There is a video camera in the back of the classroom and it is freaking me the fuck out.

Beth Anne closes the door and I turn the right way in my chair, looking quickly around at the rest of the class as I do. Martine is not here. I wonder if it might be because of the complete absence of lactating women in the class. Lawrence has moved in closer in the horseshoe and has taken her seat. This makes me think she's not possibly late but that she's really not coming back. I have no idea why, but I think it's too bad that she's gone. Lawrence is wearing a bright white sweater; it makes me think immediately of nothing else but Clorox. Amy is here looking angry as always, and next to her is Lindsay, looking meek. With his legs stretched out in front of him, looking as handsome as he did before his frat-boy, dude-filled personality was revealed, is Alec. Rachel is back again, too, looking a little freaky.

"Claaaaaass," Beth Anne says, stretching the word all out, making it sound grander and bigger and more important a word than it actually is. I can't help thinking that maybe she is saying it like that because our class, once much larger than this, is now quite small.

"It looks . . ." She pauses to glance at the clock and then stares back at us. "It seems that some of our friends might not be joining us tonight." She turns to her desk and peruses a list on her clipboard. There is something in the angle of her neck, the bowing motion of her head as she studies the list that puts me in mind of a moment of silence.

"Let's give them another minute or two, and then let's get started."

We all sit in silence; it's a silence so anticipatory, it's almost painful. I distract myself from all the anxiety, floating like bubbles all around us, by looking sideways over at Alec and thinking that he's hot. *Super hot,* I think in spite of myself, and then I think, *Really, Hope, how far away can penis-lunging actually be?*

I hold on to the edges of my desk, less because I am concerned about the penis-lunging and much more because I am afraid of the video camera guy situated directly behind me. I wonder if everyone is afraid of the video camera guy, and if the video camera guy is secretly laughing at us.

"Who wants to go first?" Beth Anne asks after a moment. No one says anything. I stare at the floor, tighten my grip on the surface of my desk.

"Anyone?"

"I will go first," Rachel says. I look up at her; she is blinking, quite quickly, over and over again.

"Wonderful, wonderful," Beth Anne says in her best you-are-all-little-children-of-mine voice. "We'll be picking partners to step outside with us, to help us with our relaxation exercises and preparations. A sort of coach, if you will. Rachel, why don't you pick someone to be your coach," Beth Anne instructs. I look quickly back down at the floor—*eye contact is bad, very bad*—and think how very much I don't want her to pick me.

"I pick Lawrence," Rachel says. Loosening my grip on my chair, I relax ever so slightly. I squeeze one hand over the other, because now my hands hurt. A slight wave of guilt washes over me for wanting, so vehemently, not to be Rachel's coach. But it wasn't, I assure myself, just because I think Rachel is very freaky, but also because, come on, clearly I am in no position to be anyone's coach.

"Okay, then. Let's begin."

Beth Anne walks toward the door, motioning for Rachel and Lawrence to follow her. The three leave, closing the door behind them. The four of us remaining sit in silence, everyone staring at the floor until the door opens again. Everyone looks up, but only Beth Anne has returned, Rachel and Lawrence are still out in the hall. Beth Anne smiles at us sweetly and takes a seat among us in one of the chair-desks, daintily smoothing her purple peasant skirt down behind her before she sits. We all continue sitting in silence together, and we all continue staring at the floor.

I look across the room quickly at Alec. He looks up at me and our eyes meet for a second, and I think it's in a good way; in fact I'm pretty sure it is. I don't know what on earth comes over me, but rather than spazzing out a little bit and looking away quickly, I keep looking at him, and I smile. Alec smiles back at me and we're the only ones here; there's

no Beth Anne, no Amy, no Lindsay. Actually, we're not even
here, we're far away from here, and we're not learning how
to overcome our presentation anxiety, presentation anxiety
is so very far from our minds. We're on a couch somewhere,
making out. Then I remind myself I don't want to make out
with someone who uses the word "dude" so frequently in
conversation, and look away.

The door opens and Lawrence and Rachel walk in. Lawrence takes his seat and opens his notebook and picks up a
pen. Rachel walks up to the front of the room. The video
camera guy comes out from behind the camera and shows
Rachel how to hook the lavaliere microphone onto the collar
of her T-shirt. As the video camera guy heads back to his
post, and Rachel says, "Testing, testing," into the mike and
it comes out loud and clear and amplified, I notice how the
wire of the microphone rests on the giant shelf of her chest,
how it's almost parallel to the floor.

Rachel stands at the front of the room, very straight and
very still. She looks slowly around the room, stopping to
lock eyes with each of us. Taking the Room: how you're
supposed to pause before you make a speech, how you're
supposed to look around calmly, confidently making eye
contact with a bunch of people in the audience. It did not,
the first time I heard the phrase, sound at all like something
I'd like to do. And, watching Rachel as she does it, I'm still
not sure about the Taking of the Room. There's something
about it, an awkwardness, a neediness in it even, that makes
me wonder again if this is something that's really done. It
seems then that maybe the video camera guy doesn't know
about Taking the Room (which in itself makes you wonder)
because Rachel's not quite done with her journey of eye
contact around the room when he interrupts to say, "Whenever you're ready."

Rachel looks momentarily flustered. Beth Anne, who is

sitting right next to where the video camera guy is standing, looks up at him and whispers something, and he nods.

Rachel looks down at an index card she is holding in her hands, pauses, takes a breath, and looks back at us. "I'm here to talk to you about remote viewing," she says. "Remote viewing is the ability to watch other people from inside your own mind."

And I know that poems don't have to rhyme, but this is sounding very un-poem-like to me. I wonder if it matters. I wonder if maybe all that matters is that she's up there.

"Remote viewing is a very powerful tool if used correctly," she says slowly, enunciating, pausing after every word. "But you need to be sure to use it only for good and not for evil."

Lawrence shoots his hand up in the air, waves it at Beth Anne. She shakes her head sternly at him, puts a finger to her lips. Rachel looks directly at Lawrence, her eyes fiery, her cheeks beginning to redden as she says, "A lot of people use it for evil."

It's definitely not a poem. But still, she's up there, she's up there in front of a video camera, and she hasn't thrown up, or gurgled, or simply stood there staring in a daze, or run screaming from the room. All things, by the way, that I do not rule out for myself. I imagine Beth Anne agrees that it doesn't have to be a poem, because she doesn't interrupt Rachel to tell her, "That is not a poem, dear." And for the next five minutes, we learn all about Rachel's belief in the ability we all have to watch people telekinetically. We learn how so many people are actually watching us right now and how even more people are using their telekinetic powers for evil, and terrorism, and, of course, devil worship. And the "of course," just so you know, that was Rachel's "of course," not mine.

What makes it even weirder, even creepier than it already is, simply by virtue of its subject matter, is this: at the end of her non-poem speech, Rachel looks up, over her left shoulder and says, quite calmly, "Scratch that."

I'm trying not to, but I'm feeling a little scared. I've changed my mind, I've decided that it does matter, that a poem would have been so much nicer, since that, after all, is what was assigned.

Rachel looks out at us, and says, "Scratch that," again. After a stunned silence-filled moment or two, everyone starts clapping; a polite, cautious clapping, and so I do, too.

"Um, yes, thank you, Rachel," Beth Anne says, smoothing down her skirt again as she says it.

"You are welcome."

"On a scale of one to ten, what was your anxiety level?" Beth Anne asks. Rachel's eyes, and I'm not making this up, they are all ablaze. I want to raise my hand and say that my anxiety level is pretty freaking high right now, but I try to be respectful of the fact that Beth Anne, right now, is not speaking to me. I wait for the theme from *The Twilight Zone* to start up in the background.

"About a seven," Rachel says, and looks up over her left shoulder, and walks to her seat.

"Well," Beth Anne says, exhaling. "I think Rachel did an excellent job of, uh, of, uh, Taking the Room and making eye contact."

Lawrence's hand shoots up again.

"Yes, Lawrence?"

"We're supposed to read a poem, though, right?"

"Yes, uh, right," Beth Anne says, nodding her head sagely, though with the stammering it seems that she, like me, like everyone else I would venture to guess, is stuck somewhere between slightly and extremely disturbed. "But if you're not comfortable with a poem, remember we discussed you could read a passage from a book?"

"I thought this was more important," Rachel offers and everyone looks at the floor.

"Yes, well, interesting topic and good job, Rachel," Beth Anne says, standing and smoothing down the front of her skirt again, and then smoothing it down one more time.

"Lawrence, who would you like to be your coach?"

I tense up again, because while you'd think Lawrence would pick Rachel because she picked him, you'd also think that maybe he doesn't want to be remotely viewed and that, along with everyone else, he's now a little afraid of Rachel.

"Lindsay," he says, and I relax ever so slightly. Beth Anne ushers Lawrence and Lindsay out into the hall, and the rest of us stare at the floor, and you can almost feel the way everyone is focusing on it now, so intently, much more so than before.

Beth Anne comes back and a few minutes later, Lindsay walks serenely in. After a moment, Lawrence enters the room, and he takes it, too. He perches on the edge of the desk and attempts to maneuver himself so his elbow is bent and his chin is resting in his hand. The angles don't quite work because of the way he's perched on the desk, and after a few moments he sits up straight. He tosses his head as if he were shaking a long mane about him, and once again, Takes the Room.

"I'm going to read a little poem I wrote myself," he tells us as he hooks on the microphone, then spreads his hands out wide to the side again, less jazz hands this time, and more open and welcoming gesture.

"I once saw a little birdie," he begins. "A flirty birdie that flew right into a puddle and got all dirty."

Lawrence pauses, staring blankly into the video camera, for what seems to me like a very long time, and then looks over at Beth Anne, blinking several times very quickly, and asks, "Can I start again?"

"Certainly," says Beth Anne, and then to all of us, "Class, never be afraid to ask if you'd like to start again."

"I once saw a little birdie," Lawrence begins again, and continues speaking confidently all the way through to the end. Except for the actual poem, of course, I think he does excellently.

Afterward, when Beth Anne asks him, he tells us all that his anxiety level was a five.

Lindsay chooses Lawrence as her partner, and that makes sense to me, and I think how I will not know him any longer as Most-Likely-Gay-Even-Though-He-Wears-a-Wedding-Band-and-Talks-About-His-Wife Lawrence but from now on only as Very-Good-at-Public-Speaking Lawrence. Strangely, I feel like I need to take a moment to say good-bye to Most-Likely-Gay-Even-Though-He-Wears-a-Wedding-Band-and-Talks-About-His-Wife Lawrence, and so, silently, I do.

After another round of exiting, and waiting, and staring at the floor, and looking back up, and watching everyone file back into the room, Lindsay walks slowly in and up to the front of the room, She seems slightly less meek, actually rather calm, cool, and collected. Her hands don't even shake as she attaches the lavaliere to the collar of her jacket. She takes a few steps forward from the desk, and clasps her hands behind her back. Her feet are planted firmly as she looks around and Takes the Room in a way that makes me almost understand why rooms should be taken. And then she runs right out of it.

"Okay," Beth Anne says, walking to the front of the class, to where Lindsay, so calm, so cool, so collected, and so apparently none of those things at all, had just been standing. "We'll just give Lindsay a moment, see if she comes back.

"Sometimes, class," she adds on, "people just need a moment."

I need a moment, I think. The chain-smoking, moody-black-vintage-overcoat-wearing part of my inner self—the one I try my best not to listen to—is back. She tells me I need a lot more than that.

I stare at Lindsay's beautiful Marc Jacobs purse and her notebook, over there on her chair-desk, and I wonder if she's somewhere in the building—in the bathroom throwing up, or in the stairwell desperately practicing The Lion over and over again in the hope that somehow, some way, it might help. Or is she out on the street, having decided that her purse and her notebook are not nearly as high on her priority list as is never having to come back into this room again?

When it's clear that Lindsay isn't coming back, Beth Anne turns to Amy. Amy picks Alec as her coach and trudges out the door. It begins to dawn on me that while going last seemed so appealing in the beginning, in the end, it's more than a little anxiety-provoking. In the end, it seems actually so much worse than having gone already because then at least the whole thing would be over with.

Amy doesn't stand up straight, but she does Take the Room in a way that I'd have to say is more threatening than it is confidence-displaying.

"I-I . . ." She falters for a moment, and it's obvious she is scared, and for some reason this surprises me. I never think that people who clearly spend such a great deal of time thinking that they are so cool, actually get scared of the same things that I get scared of. Though I guess I could have been clued in, maybe by the fact that she's in an Overcoming Presentation Anxiety class with me, that sometimes they do.

"I'm going to read a haiku I wrote," Amy says.

Oh, right, I remember, about despair.

"I am a hot, dark . . ." She pauses, stares at the floor.

"Vagina and the world is . . ." She pauses again for a little longer, still staring at the floor.

"My yeast infection." She looks back up, runs a hand through her spiky hair, the index card in her other hand shakes slightly. She doesn't say anything else, and now it's even more uncomfortable in the room than it has been before.

Beth Anne speaks up at last. "Well, that's very evocative, Amy." Amy nods. "But do you think you could read for a bit longer?"

"A haiku is a seventeen-syllable verse form," Amy says, speaking with quite a bit more authority than she had while reading her haiku. "Five, seven, and five syllables; it can't be longer," she explains defiantly, condescendingly.

"Yes, yes, would you like to read one of my poems, then? I have some mimeographed." Beth Anne reaches into her vinyl folder that doubles as a clipboard and begins shuffling through a stack of papers.

"No," Amy says and crosses her arms in front of her. "I'd like to sit down now."

"Okay, maybe for your next assignment it could be longer?" Beth Anne asks hopefully as Amy clomps to her seat and hunches down in it with her head bowed.

"Oh, yes," Beth Anne remembers to ask, "What was your anxiety level?"

"A ten," Amy snaps, and Beth Anne tells her, really rather nicely, "Well, you wouldn't have known." I think that it's nice of Beth Anne that she doesn't point out to Amy that she spent the entire one-minute duration of her haiku staring at the floor. I'm pretty sure I would not have been as nice.

"Okay, Alec, you're up and then Hope."

And then Hope.

Alec picks Amy and they leave. I can't even dedicate my thoughts to the fact that (even though, as I've said, I don't lust after Alec) I don't like that he picked Amy to be his partner, especially after her awful haiku. I am too busy trying to stave off an anxiety attack. I am too busy lamenting the fact that not one of the relaxation exercises we've learned can be done without drawing quite a lot of attention to oneself. Alec returns and reads something out of *The New Yorker*. I do manage to wonder if selecting poetry out of *The New Yorker* somehow trumps saying, "dude," all the time or, more likely, if someone just told him he could find poems there. Other than that, I hear nothing. I sit and feel the torrent of activity in my stomach. I sweat. I seriously, *seriously* contemplate running out the door. And then, like a death knell, I hear, "Hope, who would you like your partner to be?"

And all I can think is *OH MY GOD, it's time!* I try to get a grip, try not to think like that, because I'm pretty sure that is a hysterical way of thinking, and I'm pretty sure that a hysterical way of thinking is only going to make everything worse. I look up, around at my classmates. I want to know where it's been hiding all this time, I'd just like to know: *Where is my normal?*

Right at this moment, Lindsay returns. While, understandably, right now she may not be the best choice for a partner, I blurt out, "Lindsay!" She looks up at me as if she's going to run away again, just like I want to. But instead she stands there calmly at the doorway, waits for Beth Anne to pass, and then for me, and follows us into the hall.

In the hall, Beth Anne smiles and touches each of our arms.

"Practice your exercises," she instructs, "and select a Deity, and talk about the things you might want to overcome." She smiles at us again, so much like a den mother, and then she turns on her heel and is gone. As soon as she is back in the classroom, all I can think is, *Why did she have to go? Why couldn't she stay?*

"Are you okay?" I ask Lindsay.

"Yeah, you?"

"Not really," I say, because a lot of the time I think what

I really want is just to be understood. And at this very moment, if anyone can understand, I think Lindsay might be able to.

"Do you want to do The Lion together?" she asks.

The shakiness has started. I'm not even up there yet in front of all the many people, but that horrible sensation from my adrenaline kicking in has already started. I think about the video camera. I think about all the people. Although there are only seven other people in the room, it seems an amount so vast it can only be qualified as *all*. I think about the video camera. I clutch my book of poetry and think, how on earth am I going to make it through the next ten minutes? Lindsay is staring at me patiently, waiting for me to say something, and so I take a deep breath, and say, "Okay."

I close my eyes and scrunch up my face tightly, tightly, tightly, and I wait until I hear the hissing sound coming from Lindsay. I open up my eyes and stick out my tongue and make the hideous sound, too.

Next, we each do a few rounds of One Nostril Breathing and there is, I have to say, a part of me that is relaxing, until Lindsay leans in a little closer and says, "Which Deity do you want to represent you?"

And I don't know what to say, because I didn't think about the Deities, because even though I don't understand why, the Deities upset me. I want to ask Lindsay where she went when she ran out of class. She's just looking at me now so serenely, waiting for me to answer, and I can't believe I thought just a minute ago that I was relaxing.

"I don't know," I tell her.

"You have green dangly earrings," she says, reaching over to touch one, and then she adds on, "Why not Diana?" and I'm nothing if not a little bit lost.

"Okay, uh, Diana," I say slowly, and she smiles at me. By now I'm too nauseous to smile back. I wonder if I might just throw up right here. I stare at her blankly and she stares back. She's standing too close to me now. Once she stepped forward to get close enough to touch my earrings, afterward, she never took a step back. You'd think most people would have taken a step back.

"Do you want to do The Lion again?" she asks.

"Okay," I say and then I turn my back on her, because it's not nice to look at someone and to have someone look at you while you are doing The Lion. I screw my face up as tight as I can and then I thrust my tongue out and hiss. Then the door opens, signaling it's time for us to come back.

Lindsay gives me a thumbs-up sign, turns, and I follow her slowly, back into the room.

chapter twenty

Cornered

I walk slowly to the front of the room. I manage to clip my lavaliere mike onto the collar of my sweater without dropping it, and without too blatantly revealing my shaking hands to the rest of the class. I take a breath, and smile, and try as best as I can to Take the Room. I imagine I'm a celebrity standing poised on the red carpet, allowing the throngs and throngs of crazed paparazzi to take my picture. *Hope! Hope! Over here! This way!* I take another breath. I picture Alec in his underwear. I picture Lawrence reading his poem, and I remember how very good he was, and I try to think how I could be just as good. And I know I won't be.

"I'm reading a poem by Stephen Dunn," I say.

" 'Corner's,' " I say, looking up. Even though a moment ago I saw all these faces, now that I've started speaking in front of everyone, it's not so much as if I am seeing everyone for the first time, but as if I'm seeing them all again after we had a big fight and didn't talk for years. And that fight? It was completely my fault.

Beth Anne is smiling at me, soothingly and encouragingly, but it doesn't help because the sweating has started. I take one hand from the book for a moment, and rest it on my stomach, trying futilely to quell the millions of little centipede feet running hard and fast across it.

"I've sought out corner bars, lived in corner houses," I say and it comes out so shaky, so timid, that the only way I feel I can remedy it is to speed it up.

I begin to speak very quickly and I can't look up, I can only look at the book. The book, and my hands, are shaking so much that I am really quite sure that I'm about to drop the book. Part of me wants to stop it all and say, "Can I start over from the beginning?" just like Jennifer Beals in *Flashdance,* only nowhere near as coordinated and definitely not as sexy. And I know that if I did ask to start over again, as Beth Anne said we should not be afraid to do, that it would all come out sounding much less like Jennifer Beals in *Flashdance* than like Lawrence when he messed up his birdie poem. But mostly, what keeps me from asking if I could start over, is that if I asked to start over, I would have to *actually start over,* and then I would be up here even longer.

"Hope," Beth Anne says and I look up, and everyone looks very concerned. It occurs to me that it may have been a while since I said the last line. It occurs to me that I've been standing here for a while just staring at the shaking book in my hands, trying not to listen to the voices in my head, the ones I haven't mentioned yet: the ones who have just come in from a bar where they'd been happily drinking margaritas, the ones who, when they walked in and saw what was happening, started jumping up and down and screaming, "Run! Run! Run, run out of this room! Run far away from it! Run from all of these people as fast as you can!"

At the top of the video camera there's a blinking red light, and now that I've noticed it, I can't seem to stop looking at it. I really might throw up. I really don't want to leave the room but I might have to. I think I should pray. But I don't know who to pray to, I never have. If I did, I would promise to do a million things, I would promise to volunteer and be a better person and all that, if I could just get through the rest of my poem.

"Hope," I hear again, and still, I'm standing, and not speaking and the only difference is that now I've stopped staring at the book because I've been staring right into the vast abyss that is the video camera's lens and, *Oh for the love of God, how long has it been?* I squeeze the book as hard as I can to stop it from shaking. I try to speak again, "Corner." But it doesn't come out sounding anything like "corner" at all; it comes out sounding much more like a croak, and I am at a loss. I don't really know what to do. I reach up to tuck my hair behind my ears, but I can't because it's already in a ponytail. I put it in a ponytail before I came to class so that I wouldn't be able to keep tucking it behind my ears, because that was going to make this so much frickin' easier.

"Why don't we step outside for a minute?" Beth Anne asks. I feel myself making the motion to tuck my already secured hair behind my ears, yet again. I notice that my hair is a little damp right by my ear, from all the sweating. Beth Anne gets up and walks through the door. I follow her.

Once we are in the hallway, Beth Anne reaches around and pulls the door shut behind us. We walk a few feet farther into the hallway.

She looks up at me; I never realized she was so small. The feeling that I am going to be sick has subsided. The sour, seasick feeling has been replaced by the feeling that I might, at any moment, start to cry. Beth Anne reaches up to me and puts a hand on my shoulder. I'm sure she's about to tell me that I might be better suited for private lessons.

"Sometimes it helps if you just take a step back, if you just catch your breath for a minute." I nod my head, and I wonder how long I've been needing to hear that.

"Thank you," I say.

"I think we should do The Lion," she suggests.

* * *

And when we get back inside, somehow I make it to the front of the room, and somehow I begin to read my poem.

I get all the way through the poem, and absolutely, I'm a little shaky, and definitely, I read a little fast. But, it all gets said, and it all gets finished. And the fact that I actually finished, when it seemed there for a while like I never would, it gives me a little pause, it makes me think, just for a second, how maybe people are right when they say things like the only thing to fear is fear itself.

When asked about my anxiety level, I say, "Nine," because as bad as it was, I know it could have been worse.

"Lindsay," Beth Anne asks, "would you like to try again?"

"No!" she blurts out, her leg jerking out in front of her. "Not really."

"Okay, class," Beth Anne says, standing up very straight and Taking the Room, leading it by example, "I'm impressed with all of you. Everyone stood up very straight, which is so important, and everyone at least tried to Take the Room. I hope you all found that practicing the relaxation techniques outside helped to lessen the anxiety." I see Lawrence nodding happily, vigorously. I have yet to believe that Lawrence, in fact, has any anxiety.

"I hope you've all seen that not only was tonight an opportunity to practice and to be taped"—she nods in the direction of the camera—"but also an opportunity to take ourselves out of the moment. Because you were busy thinking of your poems or, uh, your remote viewing." She pauses, angles her body slightly away from Rachel. "You allowed yourself to forget a little about the actual public speaking." I'm not altogether sure that happened for me, but I'm glad I was able to finish my poem.

"The next assignment is one that many students have found a great deal of success with, one that they get engaged with, and have found works really well to distract them from their anxiety." Everyone waits. "For the next two classes, I want each of you to prepare a fifteen- to twenty-minute speech on this subject: The One That Got Away."

Amy's hand shoots up.

"Yes, Amy?"

"The One That Got Away? That seems a bit personal."

"Well, yes, that's part of the idea, to really put yourself out there, and also to come up with something on your own. Interpret the subject matter however you see fit." She turns away from Amy and scans the room. "Any other questions? No? Okay, class, remember your groups, and when you're preparing your speech, really let go, really get into it and come back willing to share. I know it's a bit unorthodox but it indeed helps!" Beth Anne seems so excited. I almost feel bad for what I've been thinking: that the assignment makes no sense at all.

"What about pretending we're underwater, didn't you talk about that, what about an exercise like that?" Amy asks.

"Yes, sometimes students find success in getting out of the moment by pretending they are underwater. That might be something productive for you to all try at home. You could even read your poems as if you are underwater." Beth

Anne nods enthusiastically, and continues, "Unfortunately, due to the relatively short length of this class and the fact that I want us to all be able to watch our videotapes, we're not going to have time for that."

"Can we vote on doing the underwater thing instead? I just think that getting up here and talking about something so, well, *vague* and *abstract* isn't really going to help me as much, and I think it's very personal."

"Well, Amy," Beth Anne begins after taking in a soothing, cleansing-type breath, "I'd like that you try this assignment." She pauses for a moment before explaining, "Part of this class, this journey that we are all taking together, is that we trust each other, trust each other enough to share. It all helps. I really believe that thinking about and sharing something personal helps more than anything else in taking oneself out of the fearful moment."

Beth Anne turns away from Amy and Amy sneers at her. I can't help thinking that this assignment should be really easy for Amy, that if she's a writer, and from what I can gather, a depressing writer at that, she can just whip out an essay and read it. And I can't help thinking that such an assignment might be really hard for me.

chapter twenty-one

All the Ones Who Went the Way My Boyfriends Tend to Go

Alec's hand reaches around me to open the door.

"Thanks," I say, and we all walk up the stairs of the Cedar Tavern and head to the back. Lindsay, Amy, and Lawrence are right behind me. Only Rachel declined Alec's invitation, and so far he hasn't said anything offensive to Lindsay, so we're a group of five again. With the absence of Martine, a certain aggressive energy is also absent from our group. For right now it seems the only negative energy is the hostile one that pulses off Amy. I feel like I have no energy; no electric currents are coming off me at all. I just feel drained. And I have a pit in my stomach, because of the assignment.

See, I've been single for a long time, for thirty-one years in fact. During this time I have spent a fair amount of it dating, and I've had my fair share of boyfriends. And maybe, by virtue of the fact that none of them are presently here, you could indeed say that all of them are "The One That Got Away." And when you look at it that way, while sure, yes, it could take your mind off public speaking and speeches for a while, it could also get pretty depressing. I think I've been making a fair-to-pretty-good effort at staying away from depressing, so why—even if it is in the name of getting away from the scariness of the moment that is public speaking—start now?

"What are you thinking about there, Hope?" Alec asks, and I tell him, "The assignment."

What I don't tell him is that I'm trying to narrow down the definition. Lindsay and Amy both nod, at what I'm not sure, and Alec waves an arm at a passing waitress.

Now maybe, and I know I'm rambling here, maybe The One That Got Away, by definition, is someone who broke up with you. Unfortunately, that wouldn't do a lot to shorten my list. A lot of my boyfriends have broken up with me. I realize this might be less due to the fact that I am possibly unloveable, as it is due to the fact that I am pretty bad at confrontation. Often with boyfriends, rather than pull the trigger myself, I've been generally more inclined to become a bad version of myself, to spend a fair amount of time loading up bullets before handing off the gun. But maybe what I'm supposed to do is pick the best one out of all the many boyfriends who went the way my boyfriends tend to go.

Maybe I'm supposed to pick the one I wish had stayed?

Or maybe I'm interpreting it all wrong, too literally, as I have been known to do. Maybe I can talk about a dog instead?

"Dude, that Rachel chick is totally freaky, huh?" Alec leans over and says to Lindsay. She doesn't answer him.

The waitress arrives and we all order drinks. I go with

Amstel Light again. After my poem, after having to go out-side for a private chat in the middle of it, I've already wor-ried enough for one night that I am a giant source of shame.

The moment our drinks are delivered, Amy takes a long sip of bourbon, a longer sip than I could ever take, returns her glass loudly to the table, and speaks for me. "I just really don't like the assignment."

"It's a little weird," Lindsay says, and then Lawrence adds, "I like it. I'm going to write a poem, 'The One That Got Away.'"

"I think it's too personal." Amy waves her hand in the air, waves Lawrence's positive statement away.

"I think that's the point," I say. *The unfortunate point.* "Ideally, we're supposed to get so wrapped up in telling the story that we forget we're standing in a room in front of peo-ple." As I say it, even though I've already heard Beth Anne say it a few times, now it suddenly makes a little more sense to me.

"Yeah, it'll help us see the forest through the trees," Alec says a bit triumphantly.

"I think you're using the expression wrong," I say.

"In what way?" he asks, and now I'm not sure.

"No, I see what you mean," says Lindsay.

"I just don't want to talk about my personal life, talk about some guy I loved and who's gone now," Amy adds in.

"It doesn't have to be a lover," says Lawrence.

"No?" I ask.

"I agree. That doesn't have to be the way you interpret it all, I don't think. It could be a job, a friend, a pet," Lindsay explains.

A pet, I think again, *that would be so much easier.* I remember all the dogs I had growing up, before I moved to the city, so much more fondly than I remember all the "dogs" I've dated since I got here. I worry, of course I worry, what that says about me, as much as I worry that I interpreted the assignment in the same way as Amy.

"Well, good," says Amy a little embarrassed, and I'm glad I didn't advertise my man-centered interpretation, an interpretation I imagine only Pamela could be proud of. "Because I don't want to get up and talk at all, and I certainly don't want to talk about the men I've dated."

"Yeah, I mean I think it's supposed to be about something we've lost, so that's individual, and I think coming up with your own individual thing is part of the getting out of the moment," adds Alec in a rare moment of insight. It's been a while now actually since he's last said, "dude." Maybe the "dudes" just come out when he's nervous or something, in which case I'd feel safe saying that *The New Yorker* trumps "dude."

Amy bangs her glass around on the table. "I mean I don't even date."

"Dude, you don't date? But you're hot."

"I just think it's always the same old story," she says, exhaling heavily, and I know *exactly* what she means. I wonder if perhaps Amy is my long-lost comrade in not necessarily wanting to run away from being single; if maybe she and I will forge a great single-girl friendship because our dating experiences are exactly the same.

"I agree," I say wholeheartedly, and envision Amy and I, our bourbons in hand (I'll switch over to bourbon) fighting the Pamelas of the world, because when it comes to dating our experiences are like one; when it comes to dating, we see eye to eye.

"Right, right," she says, her eyes brightening just the slightest bit. "You go out on a date, you drink yourself into a complete stupor, you throw up in the bathroom of whatever restaurant or bar you are in, which of course leads to looking in the bathroom mirror at your mascara-stained reflection, asking the inevitable questions, What am I really doing here? What is it all for? over and over again. And then, the next day you're so hung over and depressed that all you can do is lie in bed and cry and listen to Coldplay and eat pickles. I mean," and she stops to snort, "it's the same thing *every* time."

Or perhaps, I think as I rearrange every thought in my mind, *Amy and I don't quite see eye to eye on dating.* For a while, no one says anything. For a while, we all just stare at the drinks in our hands.

Lindsay says across the table to Lawrence, "You did really well tonight." Lindsay, I realize, is a really nice person. It's surprising in only the best way, something like that, when someone who seemed so dreadful years ago, as her e-mail was forwarded around the world, is actually nothing like that at all.

"Thank you!" Lawrence says grandly, beaming.

"Uh, what's your secret?" she asks. He leans forward, puts his elbow up on the table and lets his hand flop there loosely at the end of his wrist. He stage-whispers conspiratorially. "Once I'm up there," he pauses dramatically, purses his lips, and nods, "I just pretend I'm someone else."

Lindsay nods silently. I do, too.

"Have you ever just wanted to be someone else?" he asks her.

"Uh-huh, sure," Lindsay answers.

My whole life, I think, and take a bigger than perhaps necessary sip of my beer.

chapter twenty-two

To All the Dogs I've Loved Before

Sunday morning, rain is falling.

Those are the first words of this Maroon 5 song that's been playing constantly on the radio these days. The alarm just went off and I'm lying in bed, wondering if it's just me, or does everyone feel lately that no matter where they are, Maroon 5 seems to be there, too, playing mysteriously out of some hidden speaker. I listen to the lyrics, they're about this guy who hopes some road somewhere will lead him back to the girl he's singing to. I think for a moment how I'm not sure there is *anyone* in my past who I hope I'll be lead back to. But I guess, if you think about all the someones who actually make up my past, that's not such a bad thing. Maybe it says something about how I'm really good at closure. But that would be pretty inaccurate because closure, I'm quite sure, is not one of my stronger points. Also, though outside my window, rain is indeed falling, sadly it isn't Sunday morning, but rather Monday. The only road I'm taking this morning is Eighty-sixth Street, and the only person I'm going to be led to is Elliot, the person who's still in my present.

I hit the stop button on the clock radio with as much force as I can muster, wonder if maybe an alarm that simply beeped would be a better choice for someone like me, and head for the shower.

*   *   *

Work is the same as it's been in this last week or so, the same with its new competitive feeling in the air, the same in that everything about it now is so different. I think May has had this look on her face, this look like she's excited about something, and about to tell us something else, too. But I could just be imagining that. I have a feeling also that maybe Sergei knows something that I don't, and that this something might be something bad, or at least bad for him. He's been slamming things around a bit lately. Well, not slamming them around exactly, but generally handling his canvases and panel paintings with slightly less care than you'd think should be applied to priceless masterpieces of art.

I manage to work well on the Rothko throughout the morning, though yes, I am still on the red. I'm not sure but I think that might be a different Old Master landscape on Elliot's easel. It's getting so hard to keep track.

Right at lunchtime, the phone rings, breaking the morning silence, signaling the shift in the day.

"Hope," Sergei says loudly from his side of the room, "it's for you." *Oh, for the love of God.*

"Hello," I say cautiously, as I pick up my extension.

"Hey, Hope, it's Pamela, and guess where I am."

"I give up," I say once I have guessed incorrectly, Paris, and 'Cesca.

"I'm at the Boat House in Central Park, right near you. Can you get out for lunch?" I picture the Boat House in my mind: it is so close, just right across the road from Pug Hill. I think how maybe just being there, even if there aren't any pugs, might help me figure out what to say for my speech.

"Hope?" Pamela says, sounding slightly less than patient.

"Stay right where you are," I tell her. "I'll be there in ten minutes. I'll meet you right in front of the Boat House." In truth, even at a quick pace, it'll take me closer to fifteen minutes, but I fear if I say that, Pamela will suggest coming up toward the Met and meeting me halfway, which will inevitably mean Serafina on the corner of Seventy-ninth and Madison. And it's not that I don't like Serafina—I quite do; you can get an excellent pizza there—it's just that now that I've thought of it, I *really* want to go to Pug Hill.

"Okay," Pamela says, not suspicious of me at all, I don't think.

"Great," I say, and then, after a futile look up at the basement windows, "is it still raining?" Thankfully, it's not.

As I put down the phone, I glance over at the big table on the far side of the room. Sergei has just taken a seat, May is nowhere to be seen, and Elliot is still over here, all but making out with his easel. Stealthily, I slide out the door. I quickly buy two pretzels from a street vendor, carrying them with me as I hurry through the park toward Pamela.

As I approach her, standing right outside the entrance to the Boat House, Pamela eyes my pretzels suspiciously.

"Hi, Pamela," I say brightly so as to foster the feeling that my next idea will surely be a good one. "What do you say to going right over there and sitting for a while at Pug Hill?" I ask, motioning with my pretzels, and adding on what is obvious, "I've brought pretzels."

"Really?" she looks at me quizzically. "I mean, uh, isn't Pug Hill just a weekend thing? Won't dogs not even be

there?" Pamela looks like she regrets not suggesting Serafina, and worse than that, she looks like she's no more than
two seconds away from saying, "I figured we'd just eat at
the Boat House Café once you got here. The only reason I
wasn't already sitting down at a table inside was because
you said you'd meet me out here." Really, that's exactly what
she looks like.

"Pleeease," I say, stretching it all out, waving my pretzel
in the direction of Pug Hill.

"Alright," she says, shrugging, "but I just don't see what
it is with you and pugs."

Together we cross over the drive that loops through the
park, and when we get to Pug Hill, we sit on a bench. I notice
that the ground looks wet, but then, the next thing I notice
is that there are two, quite stunning if you ask me, pugs right
over by the pine tree.

"Oh, wow, Pamela," I say, "right over there, see? Pugs."

"Yeah?"

"I just always think it's a good sign when they're here on
weekdays," I say.

"Cool," Pamela says, noncommittal, and as if on cue, one
of the pugs (this one's name is Lucerne) runs over and looks
up at us, panting. I reach down to pet him, listen to his
snorting, and take in the look of utter sweetness in his eyes.

"They look like fruit bats," Pamela announces. "I just
think that if you want a fruit bat, why don't you simply get
a fruit bat?" *Oh,* I think, *Pamela.*

"I think you just have to give the pugs more of a chance,"
I suggest, even though I don't think that's quite true. Pretty
much, I think there are pug people in the world, and then
there are not-pug people. And I've learned that there isn't a
lot you can do with not-pug people.

"Hey!" Pamela yells loudly in the direction of the two

well-dressed older women sitting a few benches over. "Can I pick up your dog?"

I shudder at Pamela's brazenness, shake my head. But then, as one of the women nods her approval and Pamela reaches down and gingerly picks up the pug, I wish I were a little more like her. I mean, think of all the pugs I would have held on my lap by now. Pamela holds her arms out straight in front of her, and the inspected pug Lucerne squirms gingerly, suspended as he is, in midair.

"His name is Lucerne," I tell her.

"How do you know?"

"I just know," I offer by way of explanation. Pamela shakes her head; I think it is in disbelief. Lucerne looks at me lovingly.

"I don't know," she says, bringing him in closer. "I still think he looks like a fruit bat."

Lucerne sneezes triumphantly in Pamela's face.

After much squealing and gagging (Pamela's) and snorting and then even some ever-elusive barking (Lucerne's), I manage to get Lucerne away from Pamela, tell him he is simply gorgeous (with the hope that this unfortunate encounter with Pamela has not left him with any self-esteem issues) and watch as he charges over to his person. Once things have settled down, Pamela and I sit for a while in silence, eating our pretzels; Pamela continually wipes at her face. She doesn't look very happy. Pug Hill, one realizes at times like this, means different things to different people.

"So," I say eventually, banishing the fruit bat comments from my mind as much as I possibly can. "I have this assignment for my public speaking class, and I'm hoping you might be able to help."

"Oh, sure, shoot," Pamela says, leaning forward on the bench, her eyes widening a bit. Whatever bad thoughts I may secretly harbor about Pamela, she really is always willing to help.

"Well, we have to give a speech titled, 'The One That Got Away,' and I don't really know what my speech should be about. And the thing is, looking back, I'm not so sure if *anyone* could be called 'The One That Got Away.'"

"I see," Pamela says, and I can tell she's doing a quick calculation in her mind, thinking back, as I have, over the boyfriends I've had, all of whom are now, well, away. "Interesting," she adds and nods.

"Also I think that maybe I haven't been able to dive into figuring out exactly what I will talk about when I talk about 'The One That Got Away,' because I'm still caught up in the interpretation." Pamela furrows her brow in concentration. I think I'm confusing her. Understandably so; this is nothing, if not confusing. I try to explain, "See, we talked about it and someone pointed out that 'The One That Got Away,' it didn't have to be a boyfriend. It could be like a pet or something."

"Oh," Pamela says, nodding slowly. "I would have thought it would have had to be a boyfriend." *Yes,* I think, *I know that.*

"Yeah, I did, too, initially, but it actually doesn't. So I have to decide first if I'm going to talk about a dog, a dog from my childhood who is no longer with me, or if I'm going to talk about a boyfriend, who has gone the way they all seem to go." I laugh even though, really, it's not all that funny.

"Dogs or 'dogs,'" Pamela says, making quotation marks in the air with her fingers after the second "dogs." She smiles, and I smile, too, as that is the exact phrase I've thought to myself, quite a few times since last Thursday, since I remember so many of my boyfriends as being dogs, too, just a very different kind.

"Right, so, if I talk about dogs, dogs without quotation marks around them," I continue, "of course I could talk about Morgan. You know about Morgan, right? The Saint Bernard?"

"The one who was always running away to swim in swimming pools?" Pamela asks, a flicker of recognition in her eyes.

"Yes, that's the one."

"I like that story," Pamela says, and I agree, I do, too.

"In many ways," Pamela says thoughtfully, "it seems that the very purpose of Morgan's life might have been to get away."

I agree. "If anyone could be 'The One That Got Away,' Morgan could be." And I think again of Morgan's story, so full of drama and intrigue as it is, it could make for a very good speech.

"Okay, that's a good start, but we should cover more bases. What else ya got?"

"Hmmm," I think, flipping back in my mind through all the dogs I've loved before.

"Or I could talk about Brentwood," I continue. "The wheaten terrier we had."

"Oh, I remember Brentwood!"

Brentwood, in a most literal and also in a most figurative sense, got away. He dug a hole in the backyard, underneath the fence, and ran off down to the beach. We looked for days and couldn't find him. Two months later a strange man, who looked very much to be homeless, rang our doorbell, returned him to us, and turned away without a word. We wondered a lot what had happened to Brentwood during those two months, if he'd spent it just wandering, being homeless himself, or if he had been abducted. Something bad had happened; we suspected that strongly. We also suspected strongly that he blamed us. Brentwood spent the remaining five years of his life peeing on all of our pillows, every chance he got.

"He was the only dog we ever had who was relegated to the laundry room," I say and we both look into the distance at the pugs, remembering the beleaguered Brentwood with a collective sigh.

After a moment, Pamela says, "I think the Brentwood story is a little depressing," and she is right. I remember, perhaps a bit late, that I've been endeavoring lately to make a good effort at staying away from depressing.

"Yes," I agree, "you're right. And, anyway, if I'm going to talk about a dog, really, I should talk about Spanky."

"Sure," Pamela says, and I think maybe she's a bit bored now, and I'm feeling a little self-centered talking only about my speech, but I'm also feeling happy because I've just thought of Spanky, and Spanky, out of all the dogs I've loved before, is by far my favorite.

"Which one was Spanky?" she asks. Even though Pamela has known me since childhood, has known all the dogs I grew up with, and it's understandable that she could get confused, it seems so unreal to me that anyone could hear the name Spanky and not know instantly of which dog I am speaking.

"Spanky was the shar-pei," I remind her, "the third shar-pei we had." And then, for a few minutes it's just me, sitting at Pug Hill remembering Spanky. Let me fill you in.

Spanky came to us at the end of the shar-pei years, a time I remember as a bit stressful, because the two shar-peis who came before him, Sasha and Margaret, were extremely high-strung. Why my mother continued to acquire shar-pei puppies on a yearly basis, when the first two were such behavioral nightmares, is really a little bit beyond me.

But I'm so happy that she did because Spanky, beautiful Spanky, was so good and so loving and loyal and true, and at first we almost didn't notice it, since he was the third shar-pei, and everything was pretty crazy by the time he got there.

Spanky was a loving dog, as loving as the day is long, and he talked. One of my parents' current dogs, Betsy, does this, too: the gurgling notes from the back of the throat that sound so conversational. Only Betsy does it all the time. Spanky saved his talking mostly for Chinese Takeout Nights. All the shar-peis, being Chinese and all, loved Chinese Takeout Night, most every Sunday, but Spanky loved it especially, talking loudly and agreeably when my father would look down at him, up over his glasses, and read to him, in all seriousness, his fortune.

"Spanky's the one who bit your nana?" Pamela asks, at last remembering the greatest dog ever.

"Right," I say, and, even though I shouldn't, I smile at the memory.

When he was alive, I always had this really strong sense that Spanky watched over me. Like when Nana came over once and gave Darcy a figurine of a fox and gave me a figurine of an owl.

"Darcy," Nana explained, "you have a fox because you're so pretty, which in my day, we called foxy."

"And Hope," she said to me, "you have an owl, because you're so smart. But let's face it, you're not going to win any beauty contests." Spanky snuck up behind her, so stealthily, and bit her on the backside.

"Spanky, no," I can remember saying really unenthusiastically, and I always believed he did it as a personal favor.

I'm about to tell Pamela how I still feel like Spanky watches over me, but decide, I imagine wisely, against it. But just so you know, I was at a yacht club once in Naples, Florida, on a trip with a boyfriend, shortly after Spanky died. I will always remember it, how I felt certain that

Spanky was there, how his presence was unmistakable. And I still feel like he's around sometimes. Sometimes, when I'm falling asleep, I feel something, somewhere, in a corner of the room, and I'm sure it's Spanky. But, never has it been so apparent as it was in Naples, where I was sure I actually saw him on a lounge chair, so sure that I told my then-boyfriend. He said, "No, Hope, it's just a pile of towels," but I knew it wasn't.

"Spanky's a good idea," Pamela says after a while, a while in which I'm pretty sure I've just been sitting here staring completely into space.

"Yes," I agree. "Thanks for listening," I tell her, and then ask, "Tell me, what's new with you?"

Pamela and I sit together for a while and she tells me about a recent date she went on and how she still likes the Sprocket from 'Cesca, even though he could be prompter with the phone. I marvel at Pamela, how she's so optimistic, how she really does take her own advice and embraces being single, embraces it all. I never think this, really I don't, and maybe it has something to do with the spirit of Pug Hill, but I think it wouldn't be the worst thing to be a bit more like Pamela in life.

"This was fun, having lunch," Pamela points out, and then announces that she has to head back to her office. I look down at my watch, and already, it's time for me to head back to work, too.

"It *was* fun," I say, "and thanks again for helping me with my speech."

"No problem. I'm glad you're all set about The One That Got Away."

"Me, too," I tell her, even though as we say our good-byes, and Pamela turns and heads south, I'm not so sure I'm as all set as I might have just made myself out to be.

Because thinking about Spanky so much just now, thinking about how he's always been with me, has pointed something out to me. No matter what anyone says, the thing is, I realize, is that a dog (of the four-legged variety) can't ever be called The One That Got Away. Because once you love them, and they love you, they're always with you. They never really go away.

I turn away from Pug Hill and walk quickly back toward the museum.

chapter twenty-three

What If I'd Just
Laughed?

"Welcome, class. I hope everyone had time to think about their presentations, and I hope you'll all continue to concentrate on them tonight, before you go, and as you go, so that . . ." Beth Anne pauses dramatically, even though I'm pretty sure it's been a while now since we've all gotten the point. "You can get out of the moment, and yet"—another wide-eyed pause—"truly be in it!"

Everyone stares at her, expressionless.

"Okaaaay." She looks down at her clipboard. "We have Alec, Rachel, and Amy up tonight. Who would like to go first?" Everyone stares at the floor.

"Claaaass, someone has to go first, and I would rather someone volunteer than I pick someone. I feel quite strongly that it is far less anxiety producing if you volunteer yourself rather than being assigned." She stares out at us, wide-eyed.

I look down at the floor, too, even though this has nothing to do with me. You can never be too safe.

"I will go first," Rachel says at last. As she gets out of her chair, she looks over her left shoulder again, and swats at the air behind her.

"Wonderful, whom would you like to be your partner?"

"I would rather not work with a partner," she says, looking over her shoulder again, this time nodding. "I would rather go out into the hall and practice the relaxation exercises on my own, please."

"Okaaay," Beth Anne says, "if that's what will make you more comfortable."

"It is." Rachel walks to the door and through it, pulls it closed behind her. Right before it shuts completely, we hear, sharply, "Scratch that!"

A moment later, Rachel comes back in, walks right up to Beth Anne, literally inches from her, and announces, "I cannot go now. I cannot go tonight. I would like to go next time."

"Oh, Rachel, are you sure you don't want to try?"

"I do not." Rachel walks back to her seat, sits down, and bows her head. She doesn't look over her shoulder again. Lawrence has shot his hand in the air and is waving it around frantically. Beth Anne ignores him and continues to do so even after he has stomped his foot.

"Okay," says Beth Anne, seeming slightly flustered. "Amy, why don't you go next?" Apparently she's forgotten about wanting to provoke as little anxiety as possible. That, or maybe she's getting back at Amy for all the annoying questions, though something like that doesn't seem very Beth Anne.

Amy exhales heavily and stands up. "I pick Alec as my partner," she announces, which surprises me because she doesn't seem to like Alec very much and then I remember they were partners once before. I wonder if maybe they're having some mad, passionate, albeit secret, affair where they seem like they hate each other, but behind closed doors they just can't keep their hands off each other. I wonder if maybe I'm a little jealous.

"Uh, dude?" Alec says to Amy. She sneers in revulsion as she looks over at him.

"Yeah," she says with a curled lip.

"Would you mind if I went first? I'm kinda feeling like I'd like to get it over with." Amy somehow manages to sigh, snort, and exhale, all at once. This is something, I'm sure of it, that can't come naturally to anyone, even someone like Amy. It's something I think you'd have to practice a lot to get quite right.

"Yeah, fine, whatever," she says and sits back down heavily. Alec stands up, straightens his tie. "Thanks, dude, I appreciate it. Do you still want to be partners?"

"Uh, not really," she says and rolls her eyes. I think maybe I'm wrong about the passionate affair.

"Uh, Hope? Do you want to be my partner?" he says, startling me. I haven't been asked to be anyone's partner yet. I'd kind of thought no one wanted to partner up with me, with me on the coaching side, because I pretty much suck. I'm kind of happy to have been asked.

"Oh, sure," I say, and I tell myself I'm happy right now just because someone has asked me to be their partner-coach, not because I'm attracted to someone who seems so much like an overgrown frat boy in a really nice suit. I get up and follow Alec out into the hall. Beth Anne lingers by the door, and once we are outside it, she shuts it behind us.

"Um, are you feeling ready?" I ask.

"Yeah," he says, "ready to get it over with." It occurs to me I'm not really sure what a partner-coach is supposed to do. I try to remember.

"Do you want to do One Nostril Breathing?" I ask.

"If you do it with me," he says, a little charmingly, and

I'm glad I suggested One Nostril and not Kalabati. One Nostril Breathing is slightly less embarrassing. He looks into my eyes. As he does, my stomach flips over even though I don't want it to. I can't like anyone right now, I remind myself. Not until I get through my speech, not until I get over Elliot, not until I've dealt with all the things I already need to deal with. I don't think my heart can handle much more safely.

"Dude," he says, once we've finished a few rounds of One Nostril Breathing. "I forgot to tell you last time. I was up in your neck of the woods a few weeks ago."

"Really?"

"Yeah, I went up to see that dude in the park with the orange flags."

Christo, I think, *The Gates.* And my stomach is still; my heart, for the moment, is safe.

"Uh, cool," I say. "Do you want to pick a Deity?"

"Trojan," he says and winks.

I don't think Trojan was actually a Deity. But then, I also don't think that was so much the point. *Yikes,* I think, as I look down quickly at the floor, and then lead the way back into the room.

I head quickly back to my chair-desk, hoping everyone doesn't notice how red my face now is. Alec walks suavely up to the front of the room.

He puts his hands on his hips. He looks around slowly, Taking the Room. Or at least he takes most of it, because when he gets to me I have to look away.

"Katie," he begins, "her name was Katie. I met her a long time ago in New York. Katie," he says again, "she was fantastic."

As he describes quite calmly, rather eloquently, how Katie was into politics, how she was out to save the world, he hardly stutters at all, hardly falters. He's so eloquent as he describes her.

"She was brash," he says, "loudmouthed, opinionated, but she had a terrific pair of legs." I think to myself what I'm sure everyone must be thinking: *Alec is very good at this.*

"We broke up for a while, and it was hard, but then she called me one night. She said she needed to talk to someone. She said when you're upset you talk to your best friend, and I was her best friend." He talks about how they got back together, how he *so very badly* wanted it to work.

God, I think, *he is so genuine, so real.*

Lawrence's hand shoots up in the air like a rocket. He starts waving it around. Beth Anne ignores him. Alec looks over at him quickly, but then keeps talking.

"Uh, Katie and I, we moved out to L.A." Lawrence is still waving his hand in the air, with even more zeal. His face is bright red and he has just started stamping his foot, quickly, rhythmically. I wish he would stop doing that, because Alec is such a good speaker, and his story of mismatched love is so heartfelt, *so true.* I'm feeling like all the "dudes" might not matter so much, I'm feeling like maybe I might be a little bit in love with Alec.

"Thing's got rough out in L.A. See, Katie didn't have a lot to do, and then, there was this girl, this girl I knew from Beekman Place, and—"

"No! No! No!" Lawrence is up and out of his chair, flailing his arms in the air above him, jerking his head from left to right. "Stop it! Stop it! STOP IT!" It's impossible not to notice the preponderance of spit that flies from Lawrence's mouth, after every "stop it!"

Alec stares at Lawrence, shocked. We *all* stare at Lawrence, shocked.

"You can NOT rip off *Barbra* for your One That Got Away!" he shouts and turns on his heel to face Beth Anne. "Beth Anne! Beth Anne! BETH ANNE!" He puts a hand on a hip, turns toward her, points a long arm in the direction of Alec. "*THIS* man is ripping off BARBRA! *THIS* man is just telling us the plot from *THE WAY WE WERE!*"

Oh, God, I think, *he's right,* and then I think *Oh, God, I'm such a gullible idiot.* Beth Anne stands up and actually starts laughing, and then, there just isn't anything else for me to do. I start laughing, too, because the truth that I am such a gullible idiot has gone quite beyond sad, all the way to funny. Sad things, I'm beginning to see, they have a way of doing that, of just eventually becoming funny.

"Dude, if it gets me out of the moment, if it's the way I interpreted the assignment, what's your damage?"

"How could you?" Lawrence hisses. He turns and storms back to his seat.

"Yes, Lawrence, class, I think Alec is right. I think if this is how he interpreted the assignment, then it's okay. What's important is that Alec is delivering a wonderful speech. Let's let him finish." She smiles at Alec and returns to her seat.

Lawrence lays his head down on his desk and covers his ears with his hands. The rest of us listen to Alec's speech, all the way to the end where he runs into Katie, years later in front of the Plaza Hotel, and she says to him, "Your girl is lovely, Alec."

"Great job, Alec," Beth Anne tells him. "What was your anxiety level?"

"About a four," he tells her. "I'd say, really not so bad."

"Marvelous, just marvelous! Now, Rachel, would you like to try again?"

"No! I cannot!" she blurts out, stealing a glimpse over her shoulder as she does.

"Okay, Amy," Beth Anne says instead. Amy stands up, smirks, and replies, "Hey, Hubble, want to be my partner?" and cracks herself up, all the way out the door.

* * *

Amy stands up very straight in front of the room. She takes a deep breath in and lets it out. It is the first time I have ever heard an exhale from her that is not solely for the purpose of hostile emphasis. She crosses her arms in front of her, which probably isn't the best thing in terms of proper public speaking posture.

She uncrosses her arms and begins speaking, "There was some guy. Some guy named Matt. We went on one date. We had some things in common." She pauses and looks down at the floor. I wonder if she is going to the bad place. She regroups, looks back up. I study her for further signs of failure. I'm awful like that, I know. She takes another breath.

"Among them: we both grew up in a suburb of Chicago, we both used Macs, we both liked the Book Review and the Travel section of the Sunday *New York Times* best. We met for a drink." She uncrosses her arms, she continues. "We sat at the bar, me with a bourbon, he with a Tom Collins. He quoted a line for me from the very book I was reading at the time. He thought it was the best book he'd read recently, too. I forgave him the Tom Collins. He thought I was pretty. He thought I was smart. Or at least he made the effort to say he did. He was polite; he was well read. He said during dinner how much he wanted to see me again. We made plans for that Friday, even before the first date was done. When I offered to split the check with him he told me he made egregious amounts of money." Amy pauses for a moment, looks over at Beth Anne, who smiles at her encouragingly, and continues.

"*Egregious.* He said it a second time just to make sure I had heard him. And he might as well have walked me out into the street right then and hailed a taxi. He might as well have just put me right in the back by myself and walked on over to the driver's side window. He might as well have leaned in, given the driver some of that *egregious* fortune and said to him, "'Take her, will you, to that place she has gone so many, many, *many* times before.'" But really he didn't have to bother, he had already taken me there himself. There I was with my *big*, big suitcase in hand at the Place Where I'm Sure There Won't Be Any More Dates."

Amy, I think, is *very good at this*. She is speaking so well, so smoothly, so confidently. She's very theatrical, very animated. So much more animated than I have ever seen her before, and though she seems a bit hostile to her subject matter she seems so much less hostile to all of us in the room. And more than that, as she stands up there straighter and straighter, intermittently, she takes deep breaths, and pauses to make eye contact around the room. I'm able to stop looking at her as just someone who's practicing a speech, I'm able to stop looking for where she's falling short. I'm able to stop looking for nervous tics to reveal themselves, stop waiting for telltale signs of a big breakdown: the gasping for air, the dry heaving, the running for the door. And her subject matter on top of everything else, it is so captivating to me. I sit back in my chair and give her my complete, undivided attention.

"I had something leaning toward a panic attack the next day," she says, "thinking about how he had quoted the rather high price tag of the apartment he was looking to buy; how he said that *his* Mac was the new titanium version; how he *always* bought dinner for his friends who didn't make the *insane* amounts of money that he did; how, that said, he bought dinner for his friends *a lot*. I got a little feverish thinking how he told me he would take me to Bond Street next, how he looked forward to showing me the wonders of fine dining.

"I called his home number during work hours and left a message and said I wasn't feeling well and got into bed with a book for the rest of the rainy weekend, thinking maybe being alone for the rest of my life might not be so bad. I'd get to see a lot of movies. I'd get a lot of reading done.

"What if he was The One?" She pauses, looks around the room, and *continues*.

"There was some guy named Kevin. When I met him at a bar on the Upper East Side, he was sipping club soda and told me he had just gone to his first AA meeting. Ten minutes later he said he was thinking that the better version of AA for him would be a 'modified version.' Ten minutes after that he ordered a Makers Mark and soda and in no time flat had drunk it and ordered two more. There was David, who picked me up at the end of our first date and twirled me. Jim sent me a stuffed bear holding a heart that said 'I Wuv You.' Justin wore a vest; Ron looked to me so much like Sam the Eagle. There was Gary, too emotional Gary, who cried more than I did, and I cry a lot. Josh, so promising, until he licked my armpit. Scott was unkind to waiters; Craig didn't know what amicable meant; Alan, old Alan, had his own house in the Hamptons but pronounced Nietzsche, *Nitzky*. Alex was a Republican."

I think how Evan was a Republican. Then I think of all my exes, and I think so many of them were.

"What if one of them was The One?" she asks us, looking around yet again. "What if they were all The One?" She looks down, looks back up again, and smiles.

Lawrence jumps to his feet and shouts, "Bravo, oh, bravo, Amy, bravo!" Amy thanks him, really rather graciously.

"Wonderful job, Amy!" Beth Anne exclaims. "Such an effective presentation!" And all I can think is, *effective indeed*.

"What was your anxiety level?" she asks, and all I want to do right now, all I want to do in the world, is raise my hand high, raise it high in the air, and say that my anxiety level is about a ten.

"Uh, you know, it wasn't so high," Amy answers, really pretty calmly. "It was, like, a three, at most a four."

"Well, claaaaaass, I hope you were all able to see this excellent, *just excellent,* example of how if you concentrate more on what you are saying than on the fact that you are saying it up in front of a room of people, that wonderful results can occur." She beams proudly at Amy.

But I'm not seeing that so much. Maybe I'm not seeing that at all! I look around at my classmates, all nodding sagely in agreement with Beth Anne. I wonder if they're seeing what Beth Anne is telling us we should see, or if they're seeing that maybe Amy could have found her happy ending, that things could have turned out so differently for her, if maybe she'd been just a bit more open-minded.

All I can wonder is, what would have happened if Amy had—instead of balking, instead of deeming each one of these men her own equivalent of a Sprocket—just looked at these men, one by one, and said, "Really, it's gauche to talk so much about money and it kind of turns me off." "Your name is Kevin and you are an alcoholic. Put the drink down, baby, one day at a time," or whatever it is that helps alcoholics. What if she'd just said, "I prefer, generally, not to be twirled." "I don't like stuffed bears." "Wear something other than a vest?" "Wear a baseball hat, maybe?" "I don't like my armpit being licked." "Be a man!" "Be nice?" "Would you like to see my dictionary?" "Would you like to see my phonetic pronunciation program?"

Or. What if she had said nothing? What if she had just accepted these men, instead, for who they were? What if she'd been more open-minded? What if she'd seen things differently, seen people for who they were rather than only for their mistakes?

* * *

As we all stand outside the elevator, as everyone agrees to go for a drink at Cedar Tavern, it isn't only Rachel who declines, it's me, too. As I turn in the opposite direction of everyone else, and walk north along Fifth Avenue, all I can think is, *What if I'd just laughed at Evan's jokes?*

chapter twenty-four

I Coulda Been a Contender

Okay. I'm over it. Well, I'm not entirely over it, but I feel I'm over the worst part of it. I'm over thinking that maybe Evan, after everything, was The One That Got Away. The fact that most of, well, to be honest, *all* of, his humor was entirely lost on me though, has been duly noted. The fact that Amy's speech resonated so completely has not been lost on me. The fact that Pamela has oft implied that I can be close-minded, as close-minded as I lamented Amy being, has not been lost on me. And another thing that hasn't been lost on me? When it comes to judging people, to forming opinions based perhaps on not a hell of a lot of pertinent information, I may very well need to lighten up. Just as soon as I figure out who was The One That Got Away, make a speech about it, graduate from Overcoming Presentation Anxiety class, make my speech at my parents' anniversary party, somehow get over my crush on Elliot, and rethink the amount of importance I tend to place on footwear.

I buy a second cup of coffee from the vendor right outside the museum; the past weekend was not one in which I got a tremendous amount of sleep. I drink half of it standing outside on the steps, before heading off to the Conservation Studio.

When I get there, the mood in the basement of unrequited love is, I have to say, quite tense. Elliot looks up as I walk in. "Hope," he says, and I almost drop what's left of my coffee right on the floor. Except for the very occasional telling me that I have a phone call, I don't think Elliot has ever just spoken to me, just like that, unprovoked. In fact, I'm sure that he hasn't.

"Hi, Elliot," I say, and damn it all to hell, my voice actually cracks.

"Uh, I just wanted to tell you. May just told Sergei and me that she's making an announcement after lunch."

"Oh, okay, thanks." I look over at Sergei: he looks surly, a little bit pissed. Elliot does not. I wonder if Elliot knows what the announcement will be.

I head to my desk where I sip my coffee and look suspiciously around at Elliot and Sergei. I'm pretty sure that when I am not looking, they are looking suspiciously at me. I long for the days before we all knew of this promotion, before we all entered silently into this world of competition. I've got this new feeling now, too, this premonition-type feeling, that as far as our competition is concerned, Elliot has pretty much got it in the bag. I mean, if I think about it, really think about it, in a way I have so far been loathe to do, Elliot, as you know, was a Head Restorer before he came here. And as you also know, to get the promotion, such would be the way of Elliot. But maybe, I think a bit positively, maybe that's just me. Maybe the rest of the world isn't in love with him from afar. Maybe the rest of the world doesn't jump to conclusions and think things like, "Such is the way of Elliot," as they sip their coffee.

I turn to the Rothko, and try to see if I can decipher any of the tiny, tiny dots I have painted on to it. When my eyes start to lose focus, I turn away and sift through my brushes to find the one I want again. Out of the corner of my eye, I can see Sergei. He's keeping to himself over there, by the hot vacuum table, wielding his canvas pliers in a way that now seems to me, and this actually might be just in my head, sinister. Sergei seems different as I watch him painting glue onto the back of some tortured canvas.

May returns to the Conservation Studio, talking quietly into her cell phone, and I can't help wondering how she could pick either of them over me. But then I remind myself that she hasn't picked anyone yet, and that she could still very well pick me. I pull my magnifier visor down over my eyes, but not before I dart accusing glances in the direction of Sergei, Elliot, and, maybe most of all, May.

An eternity later, I push my magnifying visor up, and look at my watch. It is ten-thirty. Ten-thirty in the morning, and already I am desperate for it to be after lunch. I'm not good with suspense. Not at all. Honestly, I'm almost wishing at this point that I could stop thinking that maybe Sergei and I have a chance. I'm almost wishing we could all just skip ahead to once we've already lost. Even if it means that once we've skipped ahead, Sergei and I might be looking back at it all with regret, shaking our fists at the tiny bit of light coming in through the basement windows, saying to each other, to Elliot, "I coulda been a contender!"

And though, clearly, this is not the best scenario that I could envision for myself, I'm pretty sure that it would be better than this, than all this tension. Because, really, there is so much tension.

* * *

I manage to work continuously through the rest of the morning, not thinking about any of it, thankful for the respite, until I hear everyone rustling around behind me, putting things aside, and getting ready to break for lunch. I've got that blurry feeling. Looking at what appears to be an endless field of red under a magnification lens for a few hours makes it so that your eyes don't just get blurry, your entire body does. I take the visor off completely and turn around to set it on my desk. I notice May heading out again, notice Sergei opening up a newspaper over at the lunch table, as far away from the paintings and canvases and chemicals as it is possible in the Conservation Studio to be. I glance over at Elliot, who's leaning back and squinting at what must surely be the twelve millionth Old Master landscape he's worked on today. I pull my visor off, and head over to join Sergei at the lunch table. As I do so, I look up at the April sun shining through the window. I am tempted to run away from this and head to Pug Hill, but I imagine it is not in my best interest to do that, regardless of what May's decision will be.

* * *

It all happens pretty quickly.

"Hey, gang," May says joining Sergei and me at the table. Elliot sidles up right behind her. "As you all know, in a month or so, I'll be heading off for a year." We all nod solemnly.

"Elliot's going to be in charge while I'm gone," she says and smiles shyly. There is no "I've given this a tremendous amount of thought," no "This was a very difficult decision for me to make because you are *all* so conscientious and studious and hardworking, just some in subtler ways than others, and I'd trust each of you to be in charge." Things like that would have been nice to hear, had they been said. The way she says it, so casually, like there was no contest, makes me wonder if she just thinks that will make it easiest, will make it so that Sergei and I feel okay. Because May is really nice like that, she wants us to all feel good. But also, I can't help wondering if it seems like there had never been any contest, because all along, there never really had.

"Thanks, May," Elliot says, and smiles. "Thanks a lot." He's not smug or triumphant about it all. Not that I really ever thought he would be, he's not that type of guy. Sergei gets up and claps him on the back. Elliot puts his hands in his pockets and looks down at the floor.

"Congratulations, Elliot," I say.

"Thanks, guys," he says to all of us, "thanks." And seeing him so humble, and so, well, *Elliot,* I get butterflies in my stomach. I forget all about everything I'd thought at first, how I'd thought that if Elliot got the promotion I'd be bitter, outraged, and how I'd maybe hate him for taking the promotion that was so rightly mine (well, not really but it's better to think of it that way in order to fuel said outrage). I forgot how all of that was supposed to set me free.

I spend the rest of the afternoon picking at my Rothko and occasionally sighing. Sergei scrapes glue off the back of a Rubens, and Elliot seems to be filling in the missing paint chips on an Old Master still life. And it seems like everything is, in a way that I think is probably okay, the same.

* * *

At the end of the day, after May has already gone, Sergei calls across the Conservation Studio. "Hey, we should go out and celebrate, all of us."

I am shocked. I do not know what to say. This has never been a normal work environment, has never been the type of place where office friendships are formed. It has never been the type of place where we all go out to grab a drink after work. I mean where would we even go in this neighborhood? The Carlyle Bar? I do not think, in fact I am quite sure, that in all my years as a paintings restorer I have ever actually seen another paintings restorer outside of the museum.

"Uh, yeah," Elliot says, leaning back, "that'd be cool."

"How about Saturday night? Make it really festive!" Sergei exclaims happily. I am now sure that in all of his disappointment over not getting promoted himself, Sergei has, quite clearly, gone insane.

"Hey, if you guys want to get out of Manhattan at all and want to come out to Brooklyn, I know this really cool new bar that just opened on Smith Street. We could go there?"

We, I think, *we. We,* as in *me and Elliot,* going to a bar together, on Smith Street.

"Sounds great," I say.

"The bar on Smith Street it is," Sergei says happily.

Right, Sergei, I think. *Me and Elliot and Sergei.*

"I'll look forward to it," Elliot says, and all I can think is, *I'll say.*

chapter twenty-five

I've Been Looking
So Long at These
Pictures of You

I've thought about it more, a lot more. And while I almost went the way of thinking that maybe I'd give a speech about The Promotion That Got Away, in the end, I remembered Benji Brown.

Benji Brown. It's that simple. The only answer—the only one—to the burning question of who is The One That Got Away is, of course, Benji Brown. Really, I can't believe it took me more than a second and a half to figure that out. I just hadn't been digging deep enough. All this time I'd been so busy sifting through exes that I'd had in my adult life. All this time I'd been reluctant to give the title to anyone, surely not to Evan, and definitely not to Rick, the one before him, the one who wore a Barbour jacket so well. And certainly not to Peter—the one before both of them—who must *never* be referred to. But if he absolutely must be referred to for some reason, he is only ever to be referred to as Cheater.

But then, when I went back a little further, back to eleventh grade—the year, coincidentally (or not so) right after Mr. Brogrann's English class and *The Grapes of Wrath*—I had my answer. The very second I thought his name, *Benji Brown,* James Taylor piped up in the background singing, "Only One." The more I think about it, the more I think James Taylor might have been trying to tell me that Benji Brown was The Only One, or at least he was trying to tell me how much nicer it would be to look back over my exes if he were. That James Taylor song has been playing in my head for a few days now, along with The Cure and The Smiths and INXS and all the other music Benji and I spent such a long time listening to together.

I walk into room 502, ready to give my speech.

"Okay, claaaass. Tonight we'll be hearing from Rachel—"

"I cannot go tonight," Rachel blurts out as her foot jerks out in front of her.

"But Rachel, tonight is the last night for presentations, next time we'll be watching the videos from our poems," Beth Anne explains to her soothingly.

"There are three others who have to go tonight. There is not time for me to go tonight. I cannot go tonight," Rachel counters robotically, pausing after each word. Beth Anne seems to consider the point.

"Well, yes, actually that's right, but I think if we work quickly, and maybe all agree to stay a few minutes late, we can get through all the speeches. Claaaass . . ." She looks around at us. "Can everyone agree to stay a few minutes late?" Everyone nods, murmurs in agreement.

"I CANNOT!" Rachel shouts and looks over her shoulder, says, more softly, "I *know*."

Beth Anne looks flustered, and smoothes down the front

of her skirt. Everyone else has started staring at the floor. "Okay, Rachel," she says, "I understand." Rachel says nothing and Beth Anne says to us, more brightly, "Okay. So we have Lawrence and Lindsay and Hope." Lawrence, and Lindsay, and *Hope. Oh my.*

Lawrence's hand is up in the air before Beth Anne can even ask who would like to go first. Lawrence, possibly worried that Beth Anne may ignore him, as she has taken recently to doing, jumps up out of his chair. He clasps his hands demurely in front of himself and announces, "I'm ready, Beth Anne!"

"Wonderful, Lawrence," she tells him.

He smiles, tilts his head, and says, "And I would like Alec to be my partner." Alec looks tremendously uncomfortable, a bit pained as he follows Lawrence, who has just skipped out the door.

*   *   *

Upon their return, Alec looks even more pained. Lawrence looks ecstatic as he takes his place proudly in front of the room. Then, suddenly, his expression changes, becomes quite serious, as he looks at the index card in his hand. He looks back up at us.

"I would like to tell you tonight about my wife," and I think what I imagine everyone must be thinking, well, what Amy and Alec and Lindsay must be thinking because really, I'd rather not think about what Rachel must be thinking. I think to myself, not for the first time, *wife*?

"I loved her. She was my life," Lawrence continues and though the rhyming is distracting, he is such a poised and proud public speaker, has been it seems from day one, that it's easy to sit back and listen. As I listen to his poem, part of me, for a moment, wants to cry. Though rhyming and rhythmic, it's also so sad. It's about how he loved his wife and wanted to make her happy but because he was gay, it could never work out. He talks about how she said she'd never forgive him and never wanted to see him again. As I listen, I look around: everyone, even disturbingly freaky Rachel, looks touched, sympathetic. I think about Lawrence, such a showman, so endlessly entertaining, the sparkly disco ball equivalent of a person, and I think about the sad things, and how enduring them can get you to a far happier place.

"And so, for her I will always wear this ring." He flips his wrist around, holds his hand up for us to see.

"I couldn't hold on to any part of her, but I hold on to this one thing."

He looks down at the floor, briefly traces a line on it with his Capezio and then looks back up. I remember how he stood and clapped for Amy, how he said, "Bravo!" to her, and how that seemed to make her happy. I stand up from my chair and start clapping. "Bravo," I say. "Bravo."

When Beth Anne asks Lawrence what his anxiety level is, he inspects his fingernails, and only says, "you know," before returning back to his chair, with a new spring in his step.

"Okay, wonderful job, Lawrence, and thank you for sharing that with us. Lindsay? Hope? Who would like to go next?" Neither of us makes a move. I don't really want to follow Lawrence, because he was so good, and I'm pretty close to sure that no matter how deeply I remember Benji Brown, I won't be that good. But at this point, I feel like I've been waiting so long. Longer, I imagine, than I even know.

"I'll go," I say, as I raise my hand high.

"Wonderful, Hope. Who would you like to be your partner?" I look around the room.

"Lawrence," I say, and we walk together out into the hall.

"Your poem was really good," I tell him once Beth Anne has shut the door behind us.

"Thanks, sweetie."

"I'm, um, I'm sorry it was so hard."

"Oh." He waves his hand in the air. "Don't be. It's *all* hard, sugar, and figuring out who you are might be the hardest part of all."

Wise words, I think, *wise words indeed.*

"Okay." He claps his hands together twice, right up by his ear. "Let's get you in fighting shape! Let's do The Lion!"

* * *

I stand up straight. I take a deep breath. I don't quite Take the Room; I take about half of it, but since the sweating has started, I figure the best thing to do right now is start. I steal a quick glance at my index card even though I'm pretty sure I know it all by heart.

"When I think about Benji Brown," I say as my voice falters a little, "a British Invasion band from the eighties is often playing—really loudly—in the background."

I pause, look up. Lawrence is smiling at me brightly, he pumps a fist in the air. *I can do this,* I think. I continue. "It's something about all the guys I went to high school with, something about the memory of hearing them blast their Smiths, their Cure, their Erasure, their Depeche Mode." I close my eyes for a minute, I can still see them all: the way they were back then. I can see all the Flock of Seagulls haircuts, all the bangs. I can see the baggy pants folded at the bottom and rolled up, the black penny loafers with nickels where the pennies should be, all the sockless ankles.

"The second I saw Benji Brown, I knew he was going to be important. I knew it the second I saw him," I say again, for emphasis, "I knew it right away. It was the summer before eleventh grade. There was Benji, at a party in someone's basement in Northport, and I couldn't take my eyes off him. I'd heard his name before; people had mentioned this guy who'd moved here from Boston and was coming to our high school in the fall. No one new ever came in eleventh grade, so by virtue of that alone he was special, and he was rumored to be this completely amazing soccer player, and then, of course, there was that name. His name, the first and the last name both starting with *B,* that he still went by Benji at sixteen years old, seemed so dorky, but at the same time so cool to me. *He* seemed so dorky and so cool to me." And he was. He had the combination down. Equal parts dorky and equal parts cool. It is a mixture I think I've been search-ing for for some time. Come to think of it, ever since high school.

I speak clearly and not too fast. I tell them how Benji had such thick, curly dark hair, how it was a little bit like an Afro. I tell them how he had eyes that always looked a bit sad. I tell them how Benji's family was Unitarian Universal-ist. I tell them how with Benji, I never felt weird for being Jewish and Catholic, something in high school I used to feel weird about a lot, and, as you know, sometimes still do. But Unitarian Universalist was like an entire religion that didn't care that I was Jewish and Catholic, it was like a giant reli-gious melting pot; the kind I'd always wanted to be able to see myself as. I tell them how Benji was a great athlete, but so sensitive, so completely void of any Captain of the Foot-ball Team behavior. Or rather, Captain of the Soccer Team behavior, because at my high school, all the cool boys played soccer.

"Also," I continue, "there was a little bit of cinematic romance in the fact that he transferred in eleventh grade. *Heathers* was playing in the theaters the summer that I met Benji, and I sometimes thought of us as Christian Slater and Winona Ryder. Before, of course, they killed all Winona's friends and blew up the school." Everyone laughs, and I think that's good, that I made people laugh. It's good and it buoys me, so I can continue, and tell them about the most important part, about the mix tapes.

"Benji made the best mix tapes of anyone I've ever met, and most of the time, I think, of anyone I ever will. A lot of the time we spent, we spent listening to his mix tapes. We used to drive around to nowhere in his car, listening to Erasure and New Order and Flock of Seagulls and R.E.M. and The Smiths and The Cure, *always* The Cure, for hours. And then we'd pull over, and listen to them for a few hours more. I can remember kissing him a thousand times in that car."

I leave out the part about how I can remember the exact feel of his body, the exact feel of my own, as he maneuvered himself over the stick shift, and reached over me to pull that lever on the side to get the seat to recline, while Robert Smith sang about looking so long at these pictures of you. It was the best kind of kissing back then, the kind that lasted all night, the kind that lasted forever because you didn't know what came after it.

"Sometimes," I continue, "Benji made mix tapes for me, and other times I'd just take tapes he'd made for himself, and pretend he'd made them for me. I'd take them home and sit on the floor by my stereo, hitting pause and play again and again, until I'd written down every last word to every last song in a notebook that I don't have anymore but wish I still did."

My speech is almost over. As I work my way through another few sentences about Benji, I remember kissing him. I remember kissing him in November when we were home from college. We'd gone outside at a party and were lying together by someone's swimming pool, on a lounge chair. Wherever we were, whoever's party we were at, I remember thinking how their family was much more relaxed than mine about when to pack up and put away the pool furniture. I remember telling him that, and I remember him saying that it was a good thing we weren't at my house. I remember thinking how it wouldn't have mattered, how I would have been with him in the wet November leaves. I would have been with him in the almost frozen pool.

I remember how we decided that November that we should see other people since my college was in New Hampshire and his was in Virginia, how college was important, and we didn't want to spend it on the phone. I remember how he went back to the University of Richmond where I'd wished I'd applied, and I met someone new at college, his last name was Glickman. I remember Nana called and said she heard that at last someone had the sense to date someone Jewish.

"Hope?" Oh, damn, I've stopped talking again. I have no idea how long I've been standing up here so very much like a deer in the headlights. I take a deep breath. I get ready for my big finish. I like my big finish. I begin speaking again:

"I've noticed in life that the older you get, the fewer men there are who will take the time to make you a mix tape. I'm not sure," I say slowly, taking care not to rush, "that there are any men left in the world who are going to make me a mix tape. I'm still optimistic, though. I like to think he's out there, and that I'll meet him, and on our third, fourth date, he'll say, 'Here, look,' as he pulls something out of his jacket pocket, 'I made this for you.'"

I look out at the room and then over to Lawrence. He is on his feet in a flash, clapping away quickly and saying, "Bravo!"

"Very good job, Hope," Beth Anne says, and I'm happy she doesn't want to talk about the part when I forgot that I was in the middle of giving a speech. But then I think, *Wow, I really did forget I was giving a speech.*

"Thanks," I tell her.

"What was your anxiety level?"

"You know, it really wasn't that bad. Like, at most a five."

"Excellent, Hope, good to hear."

Lindsay also selects Lawrence as her coach and they head off into the hall. When they return Lindsay delivers a slightly choppy, but actually very funny, speech titled, "The E-mail That Got Away." I don't pay as much attention as I really should, because my mind is still all tripped up, my mind is still a freshman in college, saying a long good-bye to Benji Brown, a good-bye that I didn't believe was ever going to be real.

I'm trying to remember the last time I kissed him, and I can't. I wish I had known when it was going to be the last time I was ever going to kiss him. Because I would have concentrated more, paid closer attention, tried to somehow record every last detail about it. If I had known it was the last time, I would have kissed him for longer than I ever had before. And then, just for old times' sake, I would have kissed him again.

*   *   *

As everyone except for Rachel sits around the big table up on the second floor of the Cedar Tavern, the air between us is softer, kinder than it's been. It's more familiar also, like we know each other more. I think how much more you know people when you know what they've lost.

I wonder where Benji Brown might be in the world at right this very second. I have no idea. The James Taylor album that's been playing in my mind skips over to a different song. I lean back a little in my chair, take a sip of my white wine spritzer, and listen as James Taylor sings so softly: *this is a song for you far away from me.*

chapter twenty-six

Standing on Smith Street in My Pumas, Waiting

"Listen, man, thanks for suggesting this, it was fun," Elliot says as he leans over and does some sort of guy handshake-snapping thing with Sergei.

"A lot of fun!" Sergei agrees. "See you all on Monday. Bye, Elliot. Bye, Hope."

"Bye, Sergei," I say and I wonder if that just came out slurry, or if I just think that it did. It is two-thirty in the morning. I can't remember when I was last out this late, and I think the possibility might be high that it was in a different decade. I also think the possibility might be high that I am wasted. Elliot asked Sergei and me at work on Friday if we minded if some of his artist friends came with us as they, too, wanted to celebrate Elliot's promotion. We both said that of course we didn't mind and then I couldn't sleep at all last night trying to think of what to wear that would make me seem cool to Elliot and all his artist friends, the type of people who surely sneered at people who lived on the Upper West Side, the type of people who only lived in artsy, exotic places like Brooklyn.

That I found myself at Foot Locker first thing this morning, buying a pair of Pumas (my thinking being that Pumas were indeed a hip footwear choice) actually did not do a whole hell of a lot to increase my confidence about my level of coolness.

Claire is not here. Maybe Claire is at fat camp. Or better yet, maybe Claire doesn't exist at all. The artist friends have come and gone. It's just Elliot and me. I have spent a tremendous amount of this evening thinking that Elliot is perfect. And dreamy. Though to my credit, when, over the course of the evening, Elliot has gotten up to get us yet another round, or to go to the bathroom, I have refrained from thinking things like, "God, look how fucking hot he is when he walks." Thinking such things, I know this, would generally not be a good idea. Thinking such things could be but a stop or two away from Penis-Lunging-Ville, a Ville to which I do not wish to go.

Elliot takes another sip of his beer, puts it down on the table. "So how's it going with the Rothko?" he asks. It is the first time tonight that I have remembered that Elliot is now my boss.

"Good, hard though," I say, and take another sip of my beer.

"Paintings Conservation," he says, draining his beer, "it's so hard. It's painful and you're always alone." I live for this shit, I really do. Elliot is so deep. And so blurry. I nod in agreement and take another sip of beer. Elliot reaches into his pocket and pulls out his cell phone. He glances at its screen, and as he goes to put it back away, I remember standing on the steps of my brownstone so long ago, imagining typing "Elli" into my phone. I know that I am drunk, yes, but I feel that the symbolism, whatever it might be, needs to be captured. I reach into my bag, grab my phone.

"What's your number?" I ask. "I should program you in."

"Uh, yeah," he says, "718-555-1212." I key in the number, type in E-L-L-I, smile to myself, and flip my phone shut. As I slip the phone back into my bag, I think that I'd like to have sex with my boss.

"Uh, what's yours?"

"Oh, um, 917-222-1515."

"Cool," he says and I watch him type in the number. A wave of dizziness sweeps over me. It occurs to me that I'm too drunk, that going drink for drink, for some inexplicable reason, with Sergei and Elliot wasn't a good idea at all. It occurs to me that possibly I'm *thisclose* to something I'll later regret. I watch as Elliot types the four letters of my name into his phone. H-O-P-E. It occurs to me that the only thing you can shorten Hope to is Ho.

"I think I'm just going to grab an ice water," I tell him.

"I'll get it for you," he says, and heads to the bar.

God, I think, *look how fucking hot he is when he walks.* He comes back and I thank him for the water. I'm careful not to drink it too quickly, lest there be unseemly vomiting. He's telling me something about some new black light he used recently, and I can't really listen. I'm looking at his eyes. They're usually green but in this light they look so much more like purple. And I don't think they're ever going to light up for me the way they do when you tell him that Claire's on the phone. I'm also thinking a little bit that it's happened, that even though I didn't want it to, that some-where along the way I might really have become a stalker.

When the bar closes at three, even though I've been on water for the past half hour, I am still much drunker than I'd like to be. I also have a very, very bad taste in my mouth from all the beer. But, also, I am blessed; I only have to dig in my bag for a second to find my gum.

"Can I have a piece?" he asks.

"Sure," I say, and hand him the pack. As he takes it from me, a thought pops into my head. I think maybe he doesn't just want the gum for the sake of the gum. He wants the gum so that he has fresh breath when he kisses me passionately, like he's been waiting his whole life for me. Like he's been waiting his whole life to kiss me. Really, it's not simply because the eleven beers he just drank left him feeling like a small burrowing animal crawled into his mouth, lied down, and quietly died. No, he wants the gum because he and I, Elliot Death and Hope McNeill, are destined, just destined, to be together.

We walk, each chewing silently on our gum, cosmic symbol of our togetherness that it is, into the quiet desolation of Smith Street.

"Okay," he says.

"Okay," I say and we look at each other and I move the cosmic gum around in my mouth a bit and then I bite down on it.

He stands in the street, just off the sidewalk, and he looks at me, really looks at me. And for as long as I've waited, for what seems like an eternity, for him to look at me, there is a part of me that doesn't need to wonder if this is wrong, because I know it is. Because of Claire. He hasn't leaned in to kiss me, hasn't done much else other than ask me for gum and stand with me in the street, but I wonder what will happen if he does. I think that all I've ever wanted in the world has been reduced to this very second, to how much I want Elliot to kiss me, if for no other reason than for all the hours I've logged.

But the universe, thinking about the universe, it keeps getting in my way. It's the way of the universe, I think, that you just don't kiss other people's boyfriends. I think of all the boyfriends I've ever had, all the way back to Benji Brown who might have been the only good one, and in a way, how sad is that, or is it okay? Right now, though, what I'm thinking about has less to do with Benji Brown, the best boyfriend even if he is, chronologically, the furthest away from me now. Right now, with the real possibility that Elliot Death might at any minute lean in to kiss me, I can't help thinking of the boyfriend who must only be referred to as Cheater. I can't help thinking that somewhere along the way, out there in the universe, there have been girls who kissed my boyfriend.

Standing on Smith Street, in my Pumas, waiting for Elliot to kiss me, I can't help thinking that maybe the universe owes me something.

"Okay, well, I am actually going that way," he says.

"Oh, right," I say, "I should get a cab." I wonder if cabs drive around this late at night in Brooklyn. I hope that they do, because right now, for so many reasons, I don't want to be on the train.

Something behind me catches Elliot's eye and he looks away from me, looks over my shoulder. His arm goes up.

"Here comes a cab," he says. He stares at it with determination as it approaches, like it is one of so many Old Master landscapes. The taxi pulls up, and the moment is gone. And then, as I bite down again on the gum, the gum that I thought was so significant only a moment ago, I wonder if there was ever any moment at all.

"Really fun night, Hope," he says as he leans over and opens up the door for me. "Thanks for coming out."

"I had fun, too," I say. "Bye, Elliot."

"Good night, Hope. See you Monday," he says and the door slams shut and even though we're already driving away and if I turned around, which I won't, I'd see Elliot getting smaller and smaller on Smith Street, I say, "Yeah, see you Monday." Only the cab driver is here to hear me say it, and I don't think he's listening either.

As we speed over the Brooklyn Bridge, as I look at the lights of the city in front of me, I think that if there is any part of being single that I actually really want to run away from, it is the hopefulness, the feeling that at any moment, everything might be about to change. It's the hopefulness that's got to go.

I wonder if maybe instead of getting kissed by Elliot, if what the universe owes me now, after everything, is a really good cry. I wonder if what the universe owes me is a hall pass to just sit in the back of a taxi and sob.

And then it hits me. I don't want to be this type of person. I don't want to be the type of person who will spend as long as I've spent thinking so much about someone else's boyfriend. I don't want to spend any more time staring across a room, wondering what's going to happen next. I don't want to wait so much for things to change, for things to get better, for things to pass. I don't want to be a spectator, staring across the giant Conservation Studio of my life, waiting for something to happen.

Starting right now, I think, *I don't want to wait anymore.* I don't want to be standing on Smith Street wishing someone else's boyfriend, no matter that he is Elliot, would kiss me. I think that the first thing I'm not going to wait for anymore will be this: I'm not going to wait anymore to not have a crush on Elliot.

And I know, as much as I feel I've known anything, that with Elliot, at last, it's over.

I wish I'd known all along that turning the corner, and leaving Elliot, someone else's boyfriend, someone not at all interested in me, behind, would be so easy. But the thing is, and I know this, it wouldn't have always been so easy.

chapter twenty-seven

I Want to Tell You
a Story

"Claaass," Beth Anne says, looking around, full of assurance and nurturing, at the six of us assembled. "Today, we'll be watching our videos," and with the word *video,* I feel myself tense up. I feel everyone around me stiffen, so automatically and so uniformly that it's as if I can actually feel the air, the energy, changing completely.

We watch our poems in the order they took place. A month earlier version of Lawrence looks out at us from the television screen. He's just finished saying the first of many lines that end in the *ee* sound. I think of the first time I heard Lawrence's birdie poem, how it seems, so concretely, like years and years ago.

Throughout the video playback of Lawrence's poem, he's saying, really loudly, "I'm never wearing white again," and "I'm *definitely* never wearing that sweater again," and then,

"Maybe I need to overcome my weight problem before I overcome my presentation anxiety! I'm sooo fat! Beth Anne, really, do I look that fat?"

As soon as the videotaped version of himself finishes his birdie poem, Lawrence stands up and wails, "The camera adds ten pounds!" and I look at the television screen and look back at Lawrence, and I have to agree with him, it really does.

When we get to the end, to my poem, I feel like I must speak, like I have to jump to my defense, and I have to do that not in a little while, not after I mull it over for minutes and minutes and hours and hours and days and days, but right this very second, right now before everyone, my poor introverted self included, has to watch the hideousness of those first few moments of my poem.

"I really think we should start my tape after I left the class," I say. Beth Anne looks over at me.

"Um, I just think it'd be better to start it from after we talked," I explain and Beth Anne, bless her, says that she agrees.

Unfortunately, she also seems to lose her prior mastery over the fast forward and rewind buttons and keeps going forward too far, and then back too far, and then eventually just rewinds it to the beginning of my poem, and we start watching from there. I focus all of my attention on the surface of my chair-desk; I don't look up at all, but I still hear that croak that came out instead of "corner." I don't look up until the part after Beth Anne and I left, until the part that I remember as not being so bad. And really, it's actually not so bad, except that those light blue corduroys I love so much and wear all the time, actually make my thighs look gargantuan. It is only in hindsight that I am able to see that pairing those light blue corduroys with a light purple sweater, something that at the time I remember thinking was an excellent idea, was clearly a mistake.

* * *

"Class," Beth Anne says, right at the end, "it has been my pleasure working with each of you. I hope this class has helped each of you."

One by one, everyone thanks her warmly and though I want to jump up from my chair-desk and envelop her tiny caftan-covered body in a bear hug, I satisfy myself with just saying, "Thank you," again, so that I've thanked her twice. I hope she knows that's just another way of saying, "I really can't thank you enough."

"One last drink?" Alec says as we all stand at the elevator, and I'm struck that it's sad, that this is the last time we'll all be together. Everyone agrees, even Rachel, who looks over her shoulder and then looks up at Alec and says, "I would like that. Thank you." The six of us pile into the elevator, head over to Cedar Tavern and then up to our big table in the back.

We sit with our drinks and everyone even stays for a second round. We reflect back on the class, and it's surprisingly unanimous, even Amy has some positive things to say. Everyone agrees that they have learned something.

I look around the circular table: Amy scowls across the table at Alec, and Alec winks at the waitress; Lawrence primps a little bit, his eyes dart everywhere; Rachel stares freakishly into space and doesn't say very much; Lindsay sits up straighter than she used to, I think how we all do.

I remember that when the class first started I was wondering if in it I'd find out the secret of how to be normal, if some secret answer would at last be revealed to me. I think how long it's been that I've been wondering where my normal is.

"Oh, before we go I want to tell you a really funny story," Lawrence says. And I think that, in a way, that's all that public speaking is: it's just standing up and telling people your stories. And maybe the trick in life is just finding the people you want to tell your stories to? And finding people who want to listen to your stories, and tell you theirs, too?

"Ha!" I hear around the table, and "Ha," again. As Lawrence finishes his story, Amy spits bourbon out across the table because she's laughing so hard. "Sorry about that," she says, and everyone's laughing, even Rachel. No one can stop laughing, and then neither can I. I think, through all the laughter, that in addition to finding people who will listen to your stories, and who will tell you theirs, the gravy in all of that, the cherry on the ice cream, is that some of those people will make you laugh, too.

I take a sip of my white wine spritzer, look around one last time at our peculiar little group. A frustrated novelist, a rather poetic real estate broker, an accountant who lost mastery of her e-mail program at a most crucial time, a well-dressed attorney, a paintings restorer, and Rachel (to tell you the truth I've forgotten what her job is). I wonder if maybe this is my normal, and if it is, I don't think that's such a bad thing at all.

*   *   *

Out on the corner of University Place and Tenth Street, we all say good-bye to each other, and taxis pull up and take people away, one by one. The good-byes are quick, as if we'll all meet again next week. Mentions of getting together soon are thrown around, but I don't think we ever really will.

"Bye, Lindsay! Bye, Lawrence! Bye, Amy! Bye, Rachel!" I say cheerfully, one by one. But as I watch my classmates drive away in the back of taxis, I can't help thinking that this is a sadder good-bye than we're all giving it credit for. I can't help thinking that this is one of those good-byes, the kind that is the hardest, the kind where you know, if you stop to think about it for a second, that you won't ever see these people, this group, that was important, that meant something, ever again.

I want us to hug each other and say that we're glad to have known each other, and that even though we only knew each other for six weeks, it was an important six weeks, and we'll remember each other because this meant something, it did. I want our good-byes to be heartfelt. Or maybe I just want someone to tell me that when I make my speech next week, it will, in fact, be okay.

And then it's just Alec and me standing alone on the corner.

"Do you need a taxi?" he asks.

"Uh, yeah," I say, "I do." He reaches his arm up.

For a moment I can see my thirties, stretching out in front of me: years and years of saying good-bye to men outside of taxis. I hear Ben Harper playing in the background. It's a song called "She's Only Happy in the Sun." I listen for a moment, up until Ben Harper gets to that line that says, *The story of your life is hello, good-bye.* I walk over to Alec and stand right next to him. He looks down at me. I reach up to his arm and pull it down. He smiles at me and I smile back. I notice a few taxis driving by, their numbers all lit up, as Alec leans in to kiss me.

chapter twenty-eight

Breakfast at Pug Hill

Okay, in case you were thinking, well it's *about time* the poor girl got some action, in case you were thinking that you were about to turn the page, and at last, find yourself at the big juicy sex scene chapter, you can stop thinking that. Nothing happened, it was just a kiss. But it was a really good kiss, a really cinematic kiss right there on Tenth Street with all the empty taxis whizzing by. It was a Woody Allen kiss if ever there was one. And I think it helped me out with my need for a heartfelt good-bye. But that's all it was.

I'm leaving in a few hours to go to Long Island for the week, a week at the end of which I'll be giving my speech. Before I go, I'm meeting Kara and Chloe for an outdoor breakfast. And of course, no question, we're meeting at Pug Hill.

I head to the park and walk across it, drinking an iced coffee from Columbus Bakery. When Holly Golightly went to Tiffany's, generally she got out of a limo, generally she was wearing an evening gown and, of course, she looked just like Audrey Hepburn. My eyes are nowhere near as big as Audrey Hepburn's and my neck is nowhere near as long. I'm wearing yoga pants and I'm holding an iced coffee and a brown paper bag with three muffins in it, as opposed to, say, an antique cigarette holder, and a really fetching clutch. I'm wearing a ponytail, not a French twist. I don't have the long gloves. Holly Golightly was going to look at the most elegant of accoutrements, at so many diamonds, and I am going to look at a bunch of pugs. But surely you see the poetic connection, the pure beauty in actually eating breakfast at Pug Hill, and on a Saturday morning no less, when the pugs are actually there.

There are so many pugs. There's one of the extremely girthy ones: his name is Buster; and there's Roxy, resplendent in a new faux-leopard harness. I sit on the bench so as not to torture the pugs with the muffins. It's not that I don't like to share with the pugs, of course I do, it's just that I've learned that pugs, more often than not, are on a diet; it's just that I've also learned that if you feed the pugs, more often than not, their owners will look at you disapprovingly, and ask if you could please not feed their dog.

"Hope!"

"Hey, Kara," I say, motioning her over. "And hello, Chloe."

"Ho!" she says.

"Sorry," Kara says, smiling sheepishly.

"It's okay," I say, "it's nice she knows my name."

"Right?" Kara agrees enthusiastically, beaming at Chloe. "And she's getting the *H* sound down, which is great." I see that Chloe is carrying the Groovy Girls doll I gave her, minus all of its clothes.

"Who's this?" I ask her.

Chloe throws the doll in the dirt and says proudly, "Ho!"

"Hi, Ho!" I say, and turn to my bag and hand out our muffins.

As soon as we're done with our muffins, or rather, as soon as Kara and I are done with our muffins and Chloe has thrown her muffin in the dirt, gotten end-of-the-world hysterical about it, and miraculously regrouped at the appearance of an Elmo sippy cup, we all get up and walk over to the scraggly pine tree and sit right in front of it. Right away, Roxy runs over to us, snorting: a first for Roxy. Roxy, so fiercely independent, rarely displays any of the emotional sluttiness found in other pugs. Thinking of emotional sluttiness, I recall, of course, Annabelle, my parents' French bulldog, who is as good an example as any of an emotionally slutty dog. Annabelle, I think, is as about as close as you can get to being a pug, without actually being one; I'm happy for that, that all next week on Long Island, Annabelle will be there.

Roxy jumps up and puts her front paws on my shoulders and begins slobbering wet kisses all over my face. I lift my chin up to take my face out of the line of slobber, and as I wipe my face with my sweatshirt, I tell her what I always tell Annabelle, "We don't have to make out. We can take it slow."

And Roxy, like Annabelle, is nothing if not respectful of my desire to take things slow. Within moments, Roxy trots off. I try not to think that she trots off in search of better action. Chloe squeals and claps her hands, and screams, "Lalo," which I think means "Elmo."

And then, just like that, like a good omen that's always been there and has simply been waiting for the right time to happen, Kermit, the little black pug, comes bounding up the hill.

"Oh, Kermit!" I say, and Kara smiles, because I've mentioned Kermit to her before, and I think she understands. Chloe squeals as Kermit sits down right in front of us, positioning himself so as to best display his rounded belly, and opens his mouth wide for us, and sticks out his tongue. As if all that wasn't a good enough display of all the wonderful pug behavior, he cocks his head to the right quizzically and then to the left.

"Chloe," I say, "this is Kermit."

Chloe squeals and claps, and Kermit, as if on cue, jumps up and spins around.

"Chloe," Kara says, "do you remember the song we sang that Kermit sings?"

"Ah," says Chloe and I think she really is trying to remember. Kara helps her and sings the first line,

"Why are there so many songs about rainbows?" she sings. And I know this song, *I love this song,* and so I join in, too.

"And what's on the other side?" I sing.

As Kara and I sing together to Chloe about rainbows being visions and only illusions she is rapt with attention, as is Kermit. I have to say I think Kermit is quite enjoying the song. When we get to the part, *Someday we'll find it,* Chloe lets out one of her higher-pitched squeals, and Kermit trots off. Before he does so, though, he throws me a quick look, and I smile right at him.

Right as we get to the last line, *the lovers, the dreamers, and me,* I think how such a long time ago someone had said to me, "A girl can dream." I hadn't listened because I believed at the time that the person saying it to me was being annoying. I wonder, though, if maybe I didn't listen, because I didn't think it was true. It occurs to me right now, as I sit on a beautiful spring day, surrounded by so many pugs, that a girl *can* dream, and more importantly, that *I* can.

Chloe continues squealing and clapping, so for the next half hour, none of the other pugs run over to visit us. But even so, it's so nice to sit in the sun with an iced coffee and admire them. I can't help thinking that as long as you have a place like this to come to, the bad things, really, truly, aren't as bad.

I think of Holly Golightly and her "mean reds," the feeling she used to get that was worse than the blues, and always sent her off to Tiffany's. And the thing is, and I know this now, if Holly Golightly had been a paintings restorer instead of a party girl the "mean reds" wouldn't have seemed so bad at all. Because everyone who's ever had to restore a painting with red in it knows that red is so hard to restore because red is what we call a fugitive color: the kind that just flies away.

chapter twenty-nine

How Do You Know?

As the train pulls out of Penn Station, I try not to listen to the little voice inside my head, the one that lives in the bad place, the one that tells me there's something slightly uncool and maybe a little bit stunted about spending your vacation time with your dad. I try not to listen, but of course I do, and am compelled to answer back (inside my head, of course) that I'm really lucky to have an entire week to hang out just with my dad; that, really, how many people get to do that?

I'm taking the train out to Huntington, but actually I'll get off at Cold Spring Harbor because Dad decided at some point in my train traveling career that he preferred the drive, so much more scenic, to and from the Cold Spring Harbor station, even though the Huntington station is so much closer to the house. And I believe the part about the scenic, I do; my dad is very into scenery, is very much a proponent of

stopping and smelling the roses, and will often go ten, fifteen, twenty minutes or more out of his way to do so. But I
also think he picks me up at the Cold Spring Harbor station
because it's about ten minutes before the Huntington station,
and he knows that I'm not the biggest fan of train travel. My
dad is one of those dads, and I've always felt so lucky for it,
whose greatest joy in life has been being a dad.

But as much as I'm looking forward to a relaxing week
with Dad, it's not like I can't say I wouldn't like a spa week
for myself, but I understand the logic that it's much nicer for
Dad to have someone helping him with the dogs for the
week. Not that that is *entirely* the logic, but still. And it *is* a
lot of work these days, especially with Captain and all, and
I know Mom felt she *had* to take Darcy to the spa with her,
because of the commune of course.

The train is just pulling up to Mineola. I've always thought
of Mineola as the halfway point to home, even though I have
no idea if it really is anywhere to the halfway point at all. I
pay very little attention on the train. After a train ride I've
been taking for most of my adult life, you'd think I'd know
exactly the midway point, like I'd be able to say, "Oh, I know.
Mineola is thirty-four minutes into the sixty-eight minute
trip," but really, I have no idea. There are mysteries to the
train that I feel, for me at least, will never be solved.

Like when they announce right before my stop sometimes
that the last three cars will not platform. How do you know
if you're in the third-to-last car? I mean the last car, fine, you
know, because you can look out the back window and see
nothing else, but if you look out the back window in the
third-to-last car, all you know is that there are cars behind
the car you're in. It's too hard to tell, looking through windows reflected in windows if you're in the third- or, let's say,
fourth-to-last. I never know what to do; I always wonder,
should I move forward just in case? But I hate walking

between the cars, along of course with public speaking, walking between train cars really freaks me out.

I always remind myself to pay more attention when I'm getting on the train, to take note of where the last car actually is, in relation to the car I'm getting on, rather than simply getting off the stairs, and with tunnel vision, right onto the car that's right there. But I never leave enough time to get to Penn Station, and I'm always frazzled and hectic once I get there, running for my train. I so often forget all about the possibility that I might be in the third-to-last car.

And I have forgotten to figure this out today, and so of course, the announcement comes, "Next stop, Cold Spring Harbor. The rear three cars will not platform in Cold Spring Harbor. If you're in one of the rear three cars, please walk up."

But how do you know?!

I see two people gathering up their things and walking between the cars toward the front of the train. I have to believe that could be as good a sign as any. I get up quickly and gather my things. I begin wheeling my suitcase to the connecting doors, certain that the wheely suitcase will surely make the death-defying leap between train cars that much harder. I slide open the door and step out into all that open air and fear, and somehow I make it through to the next car. I see that the two people from my car, along with two other people, are standing in the middle of the car, waiting there, as we approach the station. The tight feeling in my stomach loosens up again, and I know I'm in the right place, and that, for now at least, I don't have to face the fear again.

"Cold Spring Harbor," the announcement says. I step through the doors, onto the platform, wheeling my suitcase behind me, and scan the parking lot. I see Dad at the wheel of his car, and he sees me, and he smiles. He gives a little wave and drives up to meet me.

"Hi, Dad," I say as he helps me put my suitcase in the back.

"Hello, sweetness," he says, and after we get back into the car, after we've said our "how are you's?" and answered them with "Great's," Dad turns to me, as he always does, and says, "Isn't it a beautiful day?" I agree, and as we pull out of the station and head toward Shore Road, he points out to me how many of the sailboats are back in the water.

For everyone who hates Long Island, who makes a face like they've just eaten soap when you say you are from there, or going there, for everyone who wonders if Amy Fisher is your neighbor or if it's true that everyone there really has a horrid accent, there are people who love Long Island and see everything that is good about it. My dad is one of those people. He's been out here, in Huntington and Cold Spring Harbor, for well over thirty years, and he still loves to drive a little farther, if it's along a scenic road. He loves it even more so if the train comes in at sunset, so that we can drive home along Route 25A, right along the water all the way to our house. He still tells me, no matter how many times we've driven together along this road, to look at the sailboats, to see how pretty they are.

chapter thirty

You Are My Best Friend

Dad and I walk together into the entrance hall of the house. Dad's taken my bag from the car, and tells me he's just going to put it up in my room for me, to give me some time to properly say hello to the dogs.

Mom calls out, "Hi, Hope!" from the kitchen and I call back. She stays in the kitchen, and Dad slips upstairs, because it's easier for everyone this way. It's easier for everyone because it's easier for Betsy if she's given the opportunity to greet people coming into the house without my parents being right there. For some reason, should Betsy be faced with the task of greeting people at the front door in the presence of my parents, she freaks out a little bit, gets a little too hysterical, and being as "conversational" as she is, Betsy's freaking out can get very high-pitched, very noisy, very, at times, headache-inducing. Betsy, as you know, is a Jack Russell terrier; Mom says such hyperactivity comes with the territory. I'm not so sure.

The dogs clamor around me in the entrance hall. Along with Betsy, there is Annabelle, the French bulldog of whom we have spoken, and though he's not here yet, because it takes him a little longer to get around these days, there's also Captain, the corgi.

"You are my best friend," I say to Betsy, because she's started gurgling. Betsy barks, indeed she does, but she also does this thing where she starts out gurgling and it's actually quite charming, some would say adorable. It's, as my mother would say, seemingly very conversational. The thing is though, right after the gurgling, if you're not vigilant in the attention that you give to Betsy once she's started gurgling, she moves pretty quickly to screeching, and the screeching is horrible. No matter how you slice it, it is not charming at all.

"You are my best friend," I say again, with a little more feeling and not because she necessarily is, but because the thing with the screeching is that Betsy has extreme issues with jealousy. Everyone has consulted and everyone has agreed on the protocol: it's important, for Betsy's ego and also for everyone else's peace of mind and sanity, that Betsy is to be told, especially loudly, and especially in large groups, that she is the "best friend" of whoever has just walked into the house.

"You are my best friend!" I say even again, switching over to a high-pitched, breathless voice, the tone and pitch of which has been determined as the most soothing to Betsy. Thankfully, it takes. She flips over on her back to display her belly that of course I am inclined, as anyone would be inclined, to squat down and rub.

With Betsy so briefly occupied, I have a moment to say hello to Annabelle. Annabelle is much smaller in stature than standard French bulldogs, and like so many of the pugs I adore, very girthy. She's a free spirit, a rough-and-tumble-type of girl, looking for love and adventure everywhere. I know you're not supposed to pick favorites, but since they're not really my dogs anymore, they are my parents' dogs, Annabelle is my favorite. This information should stay between us, however; I would hate for Betsy to find out about it. Annabelle runs around us in circles and does this thing she does, just like the pugs, where she stands in one spot and leads herself, with a throw of her head. She jumps up, and spins a tight, tight, standing-in-one-place circle. Then she does this other thing that just kills me: she gets on the entrance hall rug, lies down, front legs stretched out in front of her, back legs stretched out behind her, and proceeds to drag herself around by her front legs, in an almost perfect figure eight. Really, it just kills me.

I can hear Captain lumbering in, coming slowly down the hallway. I can hear the quickening of his toenails against the hardwood floors. I can tell that he's trying to walk as fast as he can, even with his diabetes, even with his cataract, and his malignant sarcoma that has left him with a large goiter-like thing on his back. The doctors said that surely, the goiter-like thing didn't cause him any pain, but that it also meant he wouldn't make it past Christmas. But here he is in May. Captain reaches the group and I try to settle down Annabelle and make sure that Betsy stays flipped over on her back. I look right at Captain, and as I do so, his eyes remind me so much of Spanky, and the thought of Spanky can still almost bring tears to my own eyes. In case Captain's eyes remind me of Spanky because Spanky (as I think he has a way of doing) has come to visit and is taking residence temporarily in Captain's eyes, and because it will still be nice for Captain to hear it a few more times, I look at him and say very softly, "You are my best friend."

Coming home—or is the right term going home?—it can bring up a lot of things, it can make you feel a lot of things, is what they say. And it does for me, of course it does, but at times like this, kneeling on the floor with all the dogs gathered around me, I feel like all I need is for Betsy to stay quiet, and for a little blue cartoon bird to fly down and land on my shoulder where it will sing a peaceful melody and I'll turn my head and bat my eyelashes and then, pretty much, I'll be Snow White. You know when she sits in a meadow with all the baby animals flocking to her because she is so lovely? Right now, that's exactly how I feel.

After a few more minutes of being a modern-day Snow White, I get up and head to the kitchen. I walk in and see Mom, where I expected to see her, standing at the counter, chopping something. Mom, nine days out of ten, likes to spend a large portion of the day involved in food preparation. Should you question this, she will tell you it makes her very happy, and she will tell this to you in a way that says, really, don't question this again.

"Hi, Mom," I say, and she puts down her knife and we hug and we kiss and she pulls away and studies me for just a second and says, "You're looking well, Hope."

What I actually hear is, "Your hair looks frizzy and with everything colorists can do these days I don't know why you insist on walking around with it red; have you switched foundations because I'm not sure the one you have on properly matches your skin tone; have you done something new with your eyebrows, dear? and, I don't see why you insist on wearing these camisole-type shirts out in public when a) they are not appropriate and b) no one ever said your arms were your best feature."

I try to go back, to hear only, "You're looking well, Hope," but it's impossible. When you live so much of your life really close to the bad place, it's hard not to occasionally take quick trips back there.

"How's everything?"

"Everything's great," I tell her, and ask, "Are you excited for your trip, for your party?"

"Oh, I am, it's all very nice. And I appreciate it, that you're here," she tells me.

"My pleasure," I say, and without even realizing that I'm doing it, I tuck my hair behind my ears.

"Don't screw your hair behind your ears, Hope. It looks so unattractive that way," she says, reaching forward and pulling my hair out from behind my ears for me. "Here, let me show you," she continues, but rather than actually tucking her own hair behind her ears to show me how much less attractive she feels one looks with their hair "screwed" behind their ears as opposed to not (which she has been known to do on numerous occasions), she turns instead to the kitchen counter, to show me something there.

"I've made lists, and I've separated Captain's medicine into packets. One for each morning I'll be gone, and one for each night. It'll be easier for you and Dad this way. Dad will do the insulin shots, you don't have to worry about that."

Mom shows me her lists, her packets of medicine for Captain, shows me a chart she's made where we can check off what medicine has been administered and when.

"Do you want me to show you how to put the pills in the cream cheese?" she asks.

"No, thanks," I say, "I'm okay."

We talk a little about how things are at the museum and how I'm fine with not getting the promotion, and how it hasn't clouded everything else. We talk about her book club and what they're reading, and the incident with the hair tucking is forgiven.

"Hope," she says very seriously, "while I'm gone, please do not bring up the tent again to your father. Your father is very upset about the tent."

"No, I won't," I say, and while part of me still wants to

explain that I didn't technically bring up the tent, right now, really, it's better just to leave it. But for some reason, I feel compelled to ask instead, "Is Darcy sleeping in the tent, too?"

"Yes, I imagine she is."

Clearly, this whole thing is terrible, because the tent will, of course, serve all next weekend as a blatant reminder of the commune that may very well be kicking up dust in the future.

"This REI, this was your idea, I understand?" she says.

"Uh, yes."

"Well, your father is very upset. He went online and ordered up a tent from REI, and it's in the garage in this very large box, you can go see it."

"No," I say, "that's okay, I don't want to see it."

"Well, apparently C.P. won't sleep in an REI tent either. C.P. himself actually called up your father, he said, to *explain*. He said he is trying to shun materialism and that sleeping in an L.L. Bean tent *or* an REI tent doesn't *jive* with his beliefs."

I am afraid, very afraid, that I'm going to start laughing. I focus all my attention on trying not to; I focus all my attention on trying my best just to listen.

"I swear to God your father had to just give me the phone. I just said, 'Henry, just hand me the phone,' because I think your father is about ready to kill C.P. and that won't help anything,"

"No," I say.

"I think the spa will help, do you think the spa will help?"

"I think the spa will help," I say, even though, at this point, I'm not so sure.

My mother sighs. She walks over to the coffeepot, empties it and rinses it. I grab a dish towel and go stand next to her. She gives me the coffeepot to dry, and I return it to its place in the coffeemaker and go back to sit down on the stool. Mom heads immediately to the coffeemaker and lifts up the back of it, the part where you put the water in.

"It's important to leave the back open for a while so the water can dry out properly," she explains. "You don't ever want to get mildew in your coffeemaker."

"No," I say, but in agreement, nodding my head as if no is yes and there's really no difference between the two. As I do so, I realize that she'll tell me things like this all the time, like how often one needs to bring their knives in for sharpening, or how to care for your coffeemaker, and it doesn't matter in the least that I never cook in my apartment and that I rarely make coffee in it either. What matters the most I think is that she still wants to teach me things, even if sometimes those things might be that I'm not good at matching my foundation to my skin tone. *All these little lessons,* I think, as she spins the part of the coffeemaker that holds the filter out to dry, too. There's something about these little lessons she's always given. It's these little pointers, I sometimes suspect, that keep everything in place.

I look at the coffeemaker and I think about this thing with Darcy, this worrying over her that my parents do. It has something to do, in a way, with leaving open a coffeemaker, and I understand the trip to Canyon Ranch a little more. I don't know very much about being a parent, but from what I've learned from coffeemaker maintenance and from sisters who, after everything, might go live in communes, I'm pretty sure a parent's work might never have an end point.

"Caroline, Hope," Dad says, walking into the kitchen with Captain at his heels, "we'd better get going."

"Where are we going?" I ask.

"We're going for a boat ride!" Dad says enthusiastically. "Didn't I tell you last week we planned a boat ride?"

"No, I don't think so."

"No, I'm sure I did," he says, and I still don't think so, but really, why not just drop it?

"You'll join us we hope?" Mom chimes in.

"Of course," I say. Then she adds in, "The Gerards are coming, too."

"Oh, no, why?" I ask. "I don't like the Gerards."

"Hope, don't be intolerant," my father says, because even though it's completely unfounded, and in my opinion completely unjust, somehow in my family I have gotten the reputation of being intolerant. "I'll go get Betsy's life preserver," Dad says, and then, "five minutes?"

"Why are we going on a boat ride with the Gerards?" I ask as soon as Dad is out of earshot.

"I don't know. Your father had to buy that Boston Whaler when no one wanted it and now it seems to make him happy to go on it, so we're going." It occurs to me that my question about the Gerards is not going to be answered.

"And anyway," Mom adds on, "Betsy so enjoys it." Betsy barks from the corner of the kitchen at the sound of my mother mentioning her name. Mom's right, I mean she often is of course, but she's right about Betsy. Betsy loves few things in this world as much as attention; a close second, however, is the wind.

I sigh and head upstairs to change.

chapter thirty-one

You're Not Ready
and You Don't Know
What You Want

I'm standing at the far end of the dock, watching as my mother approaches, carrying Betsy. Mom thinks Betsy doesn't like to walk on the dock.

It's windy out today, even windier down at the end of the dock. Betsy looks quite serious as she approaches. She's often very serious about being carried, and also about being walked on a leash, two things you'd think, given her hyper-activity and propensity to screeching, would be put into use a bit more often than they actually are. Mom arrives at my side and puts Betsy down at our feet. We both shield our eyes at exactly the same time to look out at the harbor where Dad is rowing the dingy out to the moored Boston Whaler with Mr. Gerard, who now after thirty years I am supposed to call Walter. I almost always forget, something that doesn't annoy Mr. Gerard nearly as much as it annoys Mrs. Gerard, and also makes me feel like I'm still fifteen.

We watch as they tie the dingy to the mooring and get up onto the Whaler, and then, at the same time, we both look down to check on Betsy.

"Hi, Bets," I say.

The wind is making ripples in her fur and you can see this pleases her to no end by the way she throws her head back with abandon. She throws it back that same way when Mom gives her Lil' Cesar's dog food. Actually though, when I'd seen her do this once while eating Lil' Cesar's, I'd commented on it, how she throws her head back with abandon when she chews, and Mom had explained to me, very seriously, that she thought it wasn't so much with abandon, as it was with joy. And actually, looking right now at Betsy, I think she's right; I think it is much more with joy.

"When I give her Lil' Cesar's, she does that with her head, throws it back with joy that way," Mom says, and sometimes it's so scary, how much it seems at certain times like she can just read minds.

"I worry though," she continues, "as much as she enjoys it, the Lil' Cesar's has so many chemicals in it. I don't know why I ever started with it."

And I say, "Uh-huh," and then from the end of the dock I hear, "Yoo-Hoo!"—yes, really, *Yoo-Hoo*—as Mrs. Gerard, so tall and dark, approaches.

"Hi, Mrs. Gerard," I say when she reaches us.

"Nancy!" she corrects me gruffly, and then tries to make it un-gruff by smiling a big smile at me.

"Nancy," I repeat as she leans over and kisses me on one cheek, and then the other, and then tells me, "I'm very European!" I assume she means the kissing and I agree, and then she turns away from me and swoops in on my mother. I'm happy for that, I'm happy not to be the focus of Mrs. Gerard's attention. I wonder though, somewhat nervously, how long can it possibly last?

Betsy starts barking again, until Mrs. Gerard looks down and tells her, "Yes, hello, Betsy. You are my best friend."

I turn back to the water, shielding my eyes to see the Boston Whaler as it glides toward us. As we all get onto the boat and pass out life preservers and take our seats, I try, tremendously unsuccessfully, not to sit anywhere near Mrs. Gerard. Sadly, tragically really, if you ask me, as we take off into the harbor, I realize I have not been as vigilant as this day has been demanding that I be. I don't quite know how it happened, but somehow I'm sitting right across from Mrs. Gerard. Mom is in the front V section of the boat with Betsy, who is ecstatic now, intermittently barking and gurgling and screeching, while still managing at the same time to bite at the wind.

"Now, now, Betsy," I hear Mom saying to her, accomplishing, it seems, nothing at all. Dad's at the steering wheel, and Mr. Gerard is in the chair next to him, so not only am I right across from Mrs. Gerard, right there squarely in her conversational line of fire, there isn't anyone else around to distract her. You might have noticed my dad telling me earlier in the kitchen not to be so intolerant, and you might be thinking right now that I'm being intolerant of Mrs. Gerard just because she says things like *Yoo-Hoo* and *Yodel-eh-hee-hoo* (she says that, too) and announces that she's European when she double-cheek kisses you and worse than that, sometimes speaks in really poorly accented French. But it's not just that. No, Mrs. Gerard is, far and away, not exactly one of my favorites, but not because of any of the previous (and in my mind perfectly legitimate) reasons.

See, Mrs. Gerard is obsessed, *obsessed,* with the fact that I am not yet married, with unearthing the mysteries of it, with trying tirelessly, endlessly, to figure out *why*. And I can't handle it, not from her; I mean, I do enough of it myself.

And just like that, as we begin to motor slowly out of the harbor, before the engines have gotten too loud to talk over, Mrs. Gerard turns to me, eager, and asks, "How's Evan? Is Evan coming out next week for the party?" There is no escape, I take a deep breath, look back at her and start to say, "Oh, we br—"

"Now, which one is Evan?" Mr. Gerard pipes in before I can answer all the way, before I can explain that it's really for the best. "It gets so hard to keep track, heh, heh."

Heh, heh, I think, and really, I'm about to jump in and explain that there is no longer any Evan, that really there never should have been any Evan, but then I hear the as-far-away-as-you-can-get-from-dulcet tones of Mrs. Gerard's voice. "You know, Walter, you met him last Christmas at the McNeills' You remember."

Mr. Gerard looks at her blankly.

"The one who looked like Jean-Paul Belmondo," Mom shouts back from her perch at the front of the boat.

Why she feels that this is what she must add to the conversation is beyond me. *Thanks, Mom,* I think to myself, narrowing my eyes ever so slightly as I turn in her direction, wondering when it happened, when Evan managed to revert from schmuck, back to his previously revoked status as Jean-Paul Belmondo look-alike.

"Right, right," says Mr. Gerard, nodding his head in thoughtful remembrance, "nice fellow, banker, right?"

"Well, he worked at a hedge fund, so it's a little different," I explain. I feel that speaking of him in the past tense is as good a place as any to start, and now, here's my moment, I jump in before any more praises of Evan can be sung. "But we're not dating anymore."

"Oh, that's too bad," Mrs. Gerard says to me right before she yells up to my mother, "Caroline! Why didn't you tell us that Hope was single again?" My mother, now occupied with pointing out every sailboat we pass to Betsy, either doesn't hear her or pretends not to. With a concerned tilt of her head, Mrs. Gerard turns back to me. I'm sure that if I listened closely enough to her, something which in actuality I will go to great lengths to avoid, I would be able to hear her making a little *cluck-cluck* sound. "What happened?"

"Uh," I say, and as I say it, I know it's long past the time to say that it was all Evan's fault. I know it's long past the time to explain that Evan was too critical and too in love with squash, and The Club, and the cold. In the end it doesn't even really seem to matter that Evan loved all those things, along with Republicans, because when it came right down to it, he didn't love me, and I didn't love him.

"It just didn't work out," I say. I think how that's really, given all the things I could say, the nicest thing to say. Maybe when I was with him, I wasn't all that nice to him, like he said. So I say only that, and think that being nice to Evan in memoriam, being nice to him now, is better than nothing.

"Oh, I see," says Mrs. Gerard, sagely nodding her head.

"What?" I ask, even though I know better.

"You're just not ready."

* * *

As we leave the protected cove, and begin cruising around faster through the open water of Lloyd Harbor, I am thankful for the noise of the engine. We pass all the beautiful houses right on the water, and even though we've all seen them so many times before, Dad points them all out, yelling loudly over the engine, "Look at that one, Caroline." "Hope, look to your left." "To your right!" Betsy's barking is muffled, too, and I can see that Mom has one arm around her and is pointing out houses with the other. I think I can hear her saying, "Yes, Betsy, feel the wind," but it's entirely possible that's all in my head.

I can feel Mrs. Gerard staring at me and I know that as soon as we stop she'll be all over me and I look around, feeling very much like a trapped rat, and I try to plan my escape. As soon as we stop, I think strategically, I will head straight past my dad and Mr. Gerard and up to the front part of the Whaler and sit with Betsy and Mom. And that will be so much better. Even though Mom will slowly drive me to despair in her own way because she will be cooing to Betsy and pointing things out to her like the water, and other boats, and seagulls, and truth be told, no matter how old I am, when she does things like that it makes me feel very second-rate, and truth be told, I've never really gotten over always feeling like that because of Darcy.

"Look, Betsy, look at the seagull!" my mother shouts out, as if this has all been scripted long before I even got here, and I've always been destined to play some supporting character, the token surly, belligerent teenager. I am about to reconsider my plan. But one look at Mrs. Gerard, perching forward now on her seat, ready to pounce, makes me certain she is by far the worse of two evils. I feel the boat slowing down as we motor slowly into a cove. I brace myself. I get ready to make my move.

"Are you dating anyone new?"

I kid you not, the entire sentence is out, thrown at me like a lightning bolt, the second the engine is cut.

"Oh, you know, not really," I say, "but I'm sure something will pop up soon." I try to say this breezily, in what I hope is a nonchalant tone, in what I hope is a tone that says, "This is *so* not an important topic, and really, it's rather boring, so let's move on to something else, or better yet, let's not talk at all, let's just be quiet and listen to the water splashing against the side of the boat because that's such a nice sound."

"You girls today, you think it's all a race," she says to me. Mrs. Gerard, she does this, she sets you up so that she can say these things, these things she must think are wise and sage, along the lines of *my not being ready*. I would very much like to explain to Mrs. Gerard that I don't think it is a race, and that if, indeed, I did think of it as a race, it's a race I lost, a really long time ago. But what I want, so much more than to point out to Mrs. Gerard that her wise and sage advice is as unwise and un-sage as it is unwelcome, is to not have a conversation about dating. So I smile, and stand up, believing foolishly in my mind that there is actually an escape.

"Maybe," she says next, "you just don't know what you want?" and I am torn. I am torn between explaining something that I don't know if I even have the language for, and just walking away, figuratively and literally, heading to the front of the boat and away from her. I opt for the front of the boat. I look in that direction, and realize sadly that the path is blocked. Literally, it's blocked; Mr. Gerard and Dad have inexplicably gotten out some giant pile of rope and set it between them. It seems they are now engrossed in discussing it, as engrossed as Mom seems to be up there. "Betsy, yes, yes, that's another motorboat."

"No, I know what I want," I say. I sit back down, because the boat is rocking now and the rocking is making me dizzy.

"What do you want?"

Oh, for crying out loud!

"What?" I say for no other reason than to stall for time. I look over in the direction of Mom, of Betsy, to see if maybe they're going to step up, at any moment, and save the day. Mom is now just gazing adoringly at Betsy; Betsy is sitting with her tongue out, blissfully tired from all the wind.

"That's quite a big pile of rope," I hear Mr. Gerard say, and I think, *Yeah, it is.* I watch a seagull that is diving head-first into the water, and the way he does it, I wonder if there might be something wrong with him.

"What do you want?" Mrs. Gerard says again, even though we both know I heard her the first time. Part of me wants to tell her that I've stopped believing in my ability to answer questions as big as that. She smiles at me again and I'm not sure it's a smile anymore, I'm really starting to think it's a sneer. And I know what she thinks my answer will be. I know she thinks it will be a way-too-long list, far too specific to ever be met. I know she's expecting me to get all worked up in a dither, and say something really fast, something along the lines of:

"I want someone who would pick me up at the airport when I haven't asked and I'm not expecting it, someone who would just surprise me, waiting right there at the gate, if he could get to it what with all the extra security these days, and I'd like it even more if he had to take a taxi to La Guardia or Kennedy or Newark to pick me up because he lives in Manhattan and might not have a car. Though, I think it would be nice if he had a car, though not for materialistic reasons but just much more so because one of my favorite things is being taken for long drives, and because I'm afraid of trains. I want what I've had, when it made me happy before, even though for whatever reasons it didn't last. I want someone who likes art and who would never dream of referring to Christo as 'that dude in the park with those flags.' I want someone who likes books more than he likes football. I want someone who will make me mix tapes. I want someone who doesn't think it's weird and/or wrong that I'm a Catholic Jew or a Jewish Catholic and that really, I'm no religion at all so much more than I am both. I want a Unitarian Universalist. I want someone who cares about me and about something else, who cares about the environment and people and while he's at it, social security. I want someone who is good at percentages, and someone who is good at tossing things coolly from one hand to another. I want a non-hairy chest. I want lanky. I want someone who will go to Woody Allen movies with me, and who, afterward won't feel the need to talk my ear off about how Woody Allen was a better filmmaker years ago, but is rather just happy Woody Allen is still making films at all, and who will maybe say something positive about how nice the apartments were. I want Patrick Dempsey. I want Zach Braff. I want Joaquin Phoenix. I want Adrien Grenier. I want Jon Stewart. I want Ed Helms and I want Stephen Colbert. I want David Duchovny. I want Jason Bateman!"

But I wouldn't say that. Besides for maybe the thing about the airport, I know enough now to know you can't get that specific. Really, I think I want just what everyone else wants. I want love. And I want finding it not to be so hard.

I look out at all the sailboats, and I've always loved the sailboats, and I think that I want someone who would maybe take me sailing. I think I'd want that, too.

"Hope?"

"Uh," I say, and I don't want to tell her anything. But I feel, right now, like it's so important that I tell her something, if for no other reason than to make her be quiet. I want to tell her something so that we can have silence, so that we can just listen to the sound of the water splashing against the side of the boat. Even if it is intermittently interrupted by my mother saying, "Betsy, look, look at the seagull," at least it'll be mostly silence, at least it'll be mostly just the sound of water splashing against the side of the boat.

My eyes fall on Mrs. Gerard's tote bag. There's an elephant on it. I look closer at the elephant: it's red, white, and blue. I look up and say, "I want a Democrat."

Mrs. Gerard takes in a little breath, and then she doesn't say anything else, and for just one moment I can hear the sound of the water splashing against the side of the boat.

Betsy starts barking and I try, for what seems like forever, to catch Mom's eye. Mom looks over at me, and then looks over at Mrs. Gerard, and before she says anything, for this one really tiny, but really important moment, I feel understood. She turns to my father, and says, "Henry, it's enough already. Let's keep moving."

I close my eyes and turn my face to the sun. I listen to the engine sputtering as it turns over and at last, starts back up.

chapter thirty-two

Ready?

"Ready?"

It's six in the morning and Dad is standing in the doorway of my room. Right, I remember, we planned this yesterday. Yesterday, after Darcy had arrived and everything had turned awkward, after we'd all spent the afternoon skating around the subject it seems we all spend a tremendous amount of time thinking of. But no one brought the commune up to Darcy, and she didn't mention it either, which I have to say is something. But still, all the skating we were doing, it felt very much like it was on the thinnest kind of ice.

Of course a few times during the afternoon, I felt ever so compelled to point out that I just didn't think that a person who arrived with a manicure and pedicure, a fresh set of highlights, and what looked suspiciously to me like quite a bit of collagen, was the same person who was going to pack up and join a commune. But I did not actually go so far as to point this out, ironically of course because Darcy *might* join a commune and because, as I may have mentioned, I have been labeled in my family as the judgmental one. And as Dad explained right before he went to the airport to pick her up, Darcy doesn't need judgment right now; she needs support and love from her family.

And really, you might wonder, what does something like that leave you with? It leaves you with the fact that unless you want someone who's never going to move to a commune to actually move to a commune, unless when that happens you want it to be on your head, unless you want to be the judgmental one who sent her to the commune, you better not be anything but nice. Regardless of whether or not the person to whom you must be nice spent the first three years of your life making you eat sand.

Darcy and Mom left to drive up to the Berkshires, up to Canyon Ranch, right after lunch. Later, at dinner, Dad asked me if I wanted to get up early tomorrow morning and help him with the new routine.

"New routine?" I'd asked.

"Yes," he told me rather enthusiastically, "we've got a new routine now!"

"What time does it start?"

"Six," he said, and I said that sounded great to me even though in truth, six pretty much sounds a touch on the early side.

"Great," he said, happily. And here we are.

"Five minutes?" I ask without opening an eye. I hear Betsy gurgling, and I hear Annabelle snorting in the hallway and I think, from right at my father's heels where he always likes to be, I might hear Captain panting.

"Five more minutes in bed, or five more minutes until you're ready to go?"

I hear a soft thumping and I think it might be Annabelle dragging herself around the hallway on her stomach. I open my eyes and see that Dad's in his sweatpants and his sneakers are already on.

"Five more minutes until I'm ready to go," I say and I hear Dad leave the room. I marvel at how much harder everything feels at six in the morning, and I get out of bed.

*   *   *

"First," my dad explains, handing me Betsy's harness, "we take a walk twice around the block with Betsy and Annabelle."

"What about Captain?" I ask over what has so quickly escalated on Betsy's part to screeching, over the sounds of Annabelle's barking which is much softer, much easier to talk over, and sounds very much like a muffled, "Whoa, whoa, whoa."

"Ah, Captain." Dad looks over at Captain, who seems to know he's not coming, seems quite resigned to that fact, and is resting peacefully in his dog bed. "No, Captain can't make the walk; Captain just comes for the beach part," he explains, and I wonder how many parts actually constitute the routine, and then we both focus completely on harnessing Betsy and Annabelle, not an easy task when Betsy is well, Betsy, and Annabelle, this morning at least, seems to find the hysteria contagious.

"Annabelle," Dad begins, as we turn right out of the driveway, walking out onto the quiet street, "she just sits down on the grass as soon as we get to the beach. She doesn't get any exercise, so we do this for her, we take a walk twice around the block each morning."

"I see," I say, as Betsy marches very seriously right next to my feet, very much like the trained dog she is not, and Annabelle sits down.

"Or we drag," Dad explains, pulling gently on Annabelle's leash. Annabelle, indeed, does not seem to be such a fan of exercise, and any chance she can get, she sits down, digs right into the cement of the road. She seems to be just slightly more inclined once we coax her.

"Ann-a-belle! Ann-a-belle!" Dad says enthusiastically.

"Ann-a-belle! Ann-a-belle!" I say, too. Betsy starts barking.

"You are my best friend," we both say to her, at exactly the same time.

"Does Betsy still walk at the beach?" I ask, once Betsy has settled down, and Annabelle has reluctantly gotten up again and we are walking again, in something that marginally represents a forward motion.

"Oh, Betsy *loves* the beach. She just loves it. I let her off her leash down there and she runs and runs. She just comes on the walk with Annabelle, because, well, it's a little easier than leaving her at home." He laughs then, and tugs gently once more on Annabelle's leash. We walk on, stopping occasionally for Betsy or Annabelle to sniff something, and I think how my dad does this every morning, and how probably not that many people would.

After two laps, I stand waiting in the driveway with Betsy and Annabelle. Betsy is barking and running back and forth across the entrance to the driveway, and Annabelle is panting, lying on the cement. Dad emerges from the house a few minutes later, with Captain, also in his harness, walking lopsidedly alongside him. At the sight of him, Betsy starts to screech, and Annabelle sits up slightly and utters one soft, "Whoa." We pick up each of the dogs, and put them down in the back of the Jeep, onto the green plaid blankets that are always there, always laid out across the seats. The Jeep, my dad will tell you, it's really the dogs' car, they just let him drive it.

The dogs all sit remarkably quietly, all three in a row, all seemingly very patient and not grousing at all with each other. I look at them back there and really, they do look happy, at least to me they do. We head out of the driveway, and drive the half-mile down the hill, to the beach, because even though it's so close, Captain can no longer walk it.

There's a big grass field to the side of the beach, and this is where we pull up with the car.

"Alright, guys," Dad says to them after we've lifted them all down from the car and off Betsy goes, running across the field like a whippet, just as graceful, just as free. Captain galumphs after her, and I watch him as he goes. I try not to think how he used to run across this field, just like a slightly stockier version of a whippet himself, when we were all younger. Annabelle sits down and leans herself, lumpen, against the front tire of the Jeep. Dad picks her up and she reaches up to his face, all long slimy pink tongue, and licks him. "No, no, Annabelle, you don't have to kiss," he tells her, and we all walk together, Dad carrying Annabelle like a football, out to the center of the field.

I keep my eyes on Captain, gimping across the field, off-balance because of his goiter. And I know it's not really a goiter, I know it's something so much worse than that; I know that it is really a malignant sarcoma. But I prefer to call it the goiter because even though I imagine there is nothing funny about goiters per se, especially, I'm sure, if let's say, you happen to have a goiter, I think it doesn't sound as bad. It's easier this way; easier when you think of the malignant sarcoma as a goiter, to believe what the vet says when he says Captain is not in any pain.

"Do you think we're a dysfunctional family?" My dad asks me, breaking the silence.

"I'm sorry?" I say, startled not so much by the breaking of the silence, as by the peculiarity of the question. Dad's never struck me before as being the type of person to bandy about psychological words like *dysfunctional*. But then I remember that Dad now knows how to Google.

"Dysfunctional. Do you think we're a dysfunctional family? I read that people who join communes tend to come from dysfunctional families."

"Um, I've never really thought about it before," I say and look out, across the field, at the water. To tell you the truth, I never really have. And I know that might sound absolutely insane, that someone who spends as much time thinking about *so many things* as I tend to do, that someone who's part of a family that spends as much time as we all do talking about a commune, has never once thought of her family and felt the desire to use the word *dysfunctional*.

Though, I must admit, I have had my moments in which I might have come close. I have sometimes asked myself why it seems that *everyone* has a sister who is just their very best friend, that *everyone* has a mother who tells them how beautiful they are four hundred times a day, but I don't. I wonder if that's sort of the McNeill family way of thinking we are dysfunctional.

"Look over there, Hope, look at the rabbit running across the field," Dad says. I watch as a rabbit disappears from view, and Betsy charges after it. I wonder if the things I think sometimes when I think about my family are simply the "look over there, Hope, look at the rabbit running across the field" way of thinking we are dysfunctional.

"Betsy! Come back here!" Dad calls out to her. She doesn't listen. I look over at my dad; he's such a great dad. I think of what a good father he's been, what a nice childhood he gave us. I don't think he could have done anything better, I really don't.

"No, Dad," I say, "I don't think we're a dysfunctional

family," and we both watch as Betsy comes back up over the dune.

"And Dad?"

"Yes, sweetheart?"

"I don't think Darcy's going to join a commune. I really don't."

He looks over and smiles at me. "That's good to know, sweetheart."

Captain is walking up closer to us now. I can see his eyes better now, and his expression, the jauntiness to his step, which seems in this moment to be only slightly lopsided. As I watch him approach in a way that is so clearly as joyful as it is labored, I feel like I don't need language for it anymore. I don't need to switch up words and change them around, substituting ones that are funnier, less scary, in order to be able to believe he's not in any pain, or at least not too much. All I have to do to be able to believe that is all I've ever had to do to believe in things or make sense of a lot of things. All I have to do is just look into a dog's eyes. The eyes of a Saint Bernard, an English mastiff, a shar-pei, a Jack Russell terrier, a French bulldog, a corgi, a pug. A lot of the time I think all you have to do is look into any dog's eyes, and there'll you'll find honesty; there, I think so much of the time, you'll find the truth.

Captain's journey across the field has, at last, come to an end. He sits at my father's feet and looks up at him with so much happiness, his eyes so filled with love. And I know there are those people, those people who will tell you that dogs don't have our kind of emotions, don't share what we call feelings, and all I can say about those people, even if you happen to be one of them, is that really, they are insane.

Dad gives Captain one of his special sugar-free bones and Captain plods a few feet away from us to enjoy his bone in what I can only guess he has decided is a bit more privacy.

Captain looks back over at us as he chews his bone, throwing his head back in the air.

Half an hour later, we load all the dogs back into the car, and head back up the hill, where we'll finish the routine, the part of the routine I'm familiar with because Mom wrote it all down, and made charts and lists to follow. She did everything except make a PowerPoint presentation entitled "How to Feed the Dogs and Give Captain His Medicine."

Once we're home again, we'll get out the three different kibbles, the special diabetic kibble for Captain, the regular kind for Betsy, and the RD (restricted diet) for Annabelle. We'll give Betsy some of the Lil' Cesar's that she loves so much, and we'll give a half of a slice of fat-free American cheese to Annabelle. Captain will get a fried egg, and his cream cheese packets with his different medicines, and his eye drops, and once he's done eating, his insulin shot.

They say that girls grow up and they marry men who are just like their fathers. And my question to "them" is this: how do you find someone who does things like this? How do you find someone who gets up early in the morning to drag his obese, sedentary dog twice around the block? How do you find someone who lets his neurotic, jealousy-ridden dog come, too, so that she doesn't get yet another complex from being left at home? How do you find someone who will then load three dogs into the car so that the oldest dog, the one so literally on his last legs, can enjoy just a few more hours spent on the field he loves, right next to the beach? Really, *how*?

I turn around in my seat for a moment and I look at the dogs. Captain is rocking back and forth in his seat, happily tossing his head.

chapter thirty-three

She Really Was Magnificent

"Henry, Henry, man, you gotta listen to me," C.P. says urgently, leaning across the breakfast table. I wonder why it does not occur to C.P. that the chances of Dad listening to him would increase tenfold if he could refrain from calling Dad "man."

Mom and Darcy returned last night from Canyon Ranch, both looking more rested and svelte and golden than they generally already do. Mom arranged it so that they were able to pick up C.P. at the airport on their way home. She believed that if C.P. arrived here first, and was here with just me and Dad, without Darcy as a buffer, that, as she explained to me before she left, "Your father may very well kill C.P." The way Dad is looking at C.P. right about now, I have to concede that Mom, as she so often does, may have a point.

Dad doesn't say anything. He angles his chin in toward

his neck and looks up over his glasses. The carton of milk that is the focus of C.P.'s attention and near-revolutionary zeal is still in Dad's hand, poised over his bowl of cereal.

"Do you have any idea what they do to dairy cows? Do you? It's horrible, man, it's so inhumane." I watch Dad's face get redder, see the cardboard on the milk carton compress slightly under the weight of his grip. "For one thing—"

"C.P., honey sweetie," Darcy cuts in, leaning over in her chair to rub C.P.'s newly shaved head. "Let's let Daddy enjoy his cereal. We don't need to talk about dairy cows right now." C.P. looks over at Darcy, as if it were really she who got up there and hung the moon. "You know what?" she coos to him. "Why don't we go for a walk? I want to show you the beach."

"Okay, honey sweetie," he says, forgetting for now about the plight of the dairy cow. Darcy jumps up from her chair and reaches for C.P.'s hand. As C.P. pushes his chair away from the table, Darcy bounces back and forth happily from one foot to the other. She is the bounciest, bubbliest thirty-four-year-old to ever walk the face of the earth, I'm sure of it.

As C.P. stands, all eyes are on him. He puts his hands in prayer position right in front of his chest, his elbows sticking straight out at ninety-degree angles. He closes his eyes, bows his head for a moment.

"Please, enjoy your meal," he says and turns and walks out of the kitchen. Darcy hops along behind him.

You can see and hear and feel my mom and me exhale. Dad pours the offending milk onto his cereal, puts the carton down with just slightly more force than usual and turns to his paper. Mom shakes her head back and forth a few times, pushes her own chair back and leaves the room.

I sit for a few minutes with Dad, but it's pretty clear that right now he probably doesn't want to talk. I think of Mom, how she looked upset right before she left the kitchen. I don't want her to be upset on the day of her party, this party that she and Dad, and just about the whole world, have been looking forward to for so long. I put my coffee cup in the dishwasher silently and head off to find her.

I find Mom upstairs, in my parents' room. She's standing by the window, looking down at the large, round, skirted table in front of it. I've always liked this table: the dog table. On this table, Mom has only pictures of the dogs. Silver picture frames, in all shapes and sizes, display so many photographs of all the dogs, individually, in various group-ings and pairings, engaged in different activities, over the courses of each of their lives.

I walk over to Mom and look down at the dog table, too. There they all are. There's Morgan outside by a pond; Brent-wood in a snow-covered field; Spanky, my Spanky, next to a peony bush; Boswell next to a Christmas tree; Captain and Annabelle at the beach; Betsy at a café in the south of France. So many moments of their lives displayed here are the most joyous ones.

I notice that Mom has another picture of Boswell in her hand. This one is in a round frame; it shows Boswell in profile, from the shoulders up. Mom looks up at me then, and her eyes are filled with something. I am so sure it is regret. Cra-zily, I am so sure that what she is going to say next is that she regrets that sometimes, a lot of the time, I never got any atten-tion because it was always Darcy, always, *always* Darcy, who needed so much more. I am so certain that is what she is going to say next, that I wonder if I am actually psychic.

"Bos was really magnificent, wasn't she?" My mother asks me, looking back down at the picture frame in her hand. Perhaps I am not quite as psychic as I so briefly believed myself to be.

"Yes," I agree, "she was magnificent."

"She was. She really was. But, see, look here," she says holding the picture out toward me. I lean in to get a closer look. My mother whispers loudly, it is too terrible to say at a normal volume, "I had a chain collar on her!"

"Yes," I say and I'm not sure; I'm not sure where this is going so I wait, to let it go there.

"I just don't know what I was thinking," Mom laments. "*How* could I have had a chain on her? It's so undignified! So cruel! She was never even on her leash, why would I have her in a chain collar?"

"Well, she was very big, she probably needed it," I offer.

"But she was so gentle!"

"Yes, she was, Mom," I say, because I really don't know what else to say. "She really was."

"It's just one of those things, one of those things that you'd never do if you'd known everything that was wrong about it when you were doing it," my mother explains, as much to me, I realize, as to Boswell. I nod my head in agreement.

Rod Stewart is playing in the background. *I wish that I knew what I know now when I was younger.* But he's not just playing in the background of my mind. I glance over at the stereo, and see the *Rod Stewart Greatest Hits* CD lying in front of it, the CD player turned on. Mom's really going with this; she has gotten out Rod Stewart to accompany the moment lyrically. I look at the CD there, and think, *This is where I get it from.* I look over at the dog table, and think exactly the same thing.

"I'm sure she didn't mind, Mom," I say. "She had such a lovely, lovely life."

"You think?" she asks me. I have never known Mom to need reassuring before this instant. I have always been the one so badly in need of reassuring, the sometimes close-to-the-edge-and-not-wanting-to-turn-around wreck, with all my insecurities and fears and issues and flaws. I want right now, more than anything, to be sure Mom knows that Boswell never minded for a second about the chain.

"Oh, I'm absolutely positive. I'm sure of it," is all I come up with at first; I don't want to hesitate for too long because hesitation can sometimes seem like doubt; it could seem like maybe I did think that Boswell was oppressed.

"And she really was magnificent," I add on in a flash.

"Yes," says my never-wistful mother wistfully, "she really was."

We stand side by side for a while, listening to Rod Stewart and looking at all the photographs. At one point my mother sighs. And I sigh, too, because it'll be afternoon soon enough, and then evening, and then it'll be tonight, and I'll be making a speech.

chapter thirty-four

Do You Want to Dance Under the Moonlight?

Clapping.

Clapping.

There is clapping, and the clapping is for me. I am standing on a stage, just to the left of the band, next to a microphone, and I've just finished my speech.

People aren't gasping in horror at how bad I was. People aren't stifling embarrassed smiles because they feel so bad for me. There isn't even anyone running up to the stage with a towel to clean up the throw-up at my feet. All there is, all there is right now in the world, is *clapping*.

This afternoon, Darcy and C.P. disassembled the non–L.L. Bean, non-REI, non-objectionable tent they'd put up last night in the backyard. Once their tent was taken down, people came and set up a much bigger tent, a much more festive tent, a tent that didn't drive my parents slowly insane but rather made them quite happy as they looked outside, watching as it went up.

Up in my room, as I got ready for the party, I looked out my window and saw the band arriving. I noticed that someone in the band actually did have a mullet as I imagined he might, such a long time ago. I thought how weird that was and how maybe that wasn't such a good sign. Then I had to practice The Lion and my One Nostril Breathing for about twenty minutes before I was able to leave my room.

I walked downstairs in my lavender dress and my high heels and my makeup. I walked over to my parents, and my mother stepped back for a minute to look at me. She smiled at me, no, she beamed at me, and then she said, "Hope, you look just beautiful tonight."

And I thought how I agreed with her, how it must be true since she was, after all, so often right. I felt something start to sting in the back of my eyes and I thought how completely simple it was, and how endlessly complicated, that maybe this, all along, had been all that I'd needed.

"Don't cry, Hope," my mother said, "your mascara will run."

And so I went to the bathroom and I cried. But only a little bit, and then I fixed my mascara and practiced The Lion one more time. I walked around and said hello to all my parents' friends. I assured Darcy that the hot pink boa she had opted for was nothing if not appropriate and tasteful. I tried not to drink too much champagne for what seemed like an eternity, but I think was only for an hour. And then, the mullet-headed band singer tapped on his mike, and announced to everyone, "Hope would like to make a speech."

Hope, I repeated to myself. *Hope would like to make a speech.*

I don't think I can really say that I stood up there brilliantly. I don't think I can really say that I *Took the Room* and made eye contact with all the different people in the room. But I can say that honestly, truly, I did okay. And I can tell you with complete accuracy that at the end, there was clapping.

* * *

Dad leads Mom out onto the dance floor, and I listen to the clapping and step back from the microphone, officially ending my speech, officially ending my Overcoming Presentation Anxiety, and maybe a few other things, too.

The band guy, the one with the mullet, looks over at me and winks and I think, *Really?* And then I think, *I wonder if a band guy with a mullet is the way it all turns out for me,* and then I hope not. I don't have to worry for long though. I realize that the band guy is winking at me because I'm still standing in the middle of the stage, grinning. The band guy's winking is not so much, "You and me, babe, how about it?" as it is, "Honey, it's over, you need to get off the stage."

"Okay, everybody!" he shouts into his own microphone. "Let's bring it on back to the sixties!" A few woops rise out from the crowd. "Let's put our hands together for The Beach Boys!" The band starts playing "Do You Wanna Dance," as a horde of sixty-to-seventy-year-olds pile enthusiastically onto the dance floor. Many of them, I notice, are doing creative renditions of the twist.

I make my way down the steps, to the edge of the dance floor, just as Darcy and C.P. sashay on by. And they really are sashaying: they're facing each other holding hands, letting go on one side and fanning out their arms and then holding both hands together again. They're passing right by me and I smile. They both smile back at me and then, something bad is happening.

Both C.P. and Darcy have stopped anything that resembles forward motion. They are both facing me and dancing in place in front of me. They've let go of each other's hands. They hold their hands out to me to join them. C.P. even gives a little flick of his wrist to be sure I'm quite clear that he wants me to join them. I start to shake my head "No," because sometimes, as much as I endeavor not to be, I am nothing if not a creature mired in habit. But I don't quite get the shake out, and I change the "No" at the last minute to "Yes."

Darcy is bouncing up and down like the Energizer bunny, and singing along to the Beach Boys, "Do you wanna dance and hold my hand?"

I step forward a little bit and take Darcy's hand with one hand, and I take C.P.'s hand with my other. And the three of us together, we sashay. We sashay around the perimeter of the dance floor and for the time that it takes us to get all the way around, I manage to forget that Darcy and I were always so much more enemies than we were ever sisters, and that after that, we were so much more strangers. Because right now, as we're sashaying, as I'm holding hands with Darcy and her Spiritual and Life Partner (as he likes to be called) none of that really matters. I realize that while you can forget about being enemies, or try to stop being strangers, we'll always be sisters.

The three of us, me and Darcy and C.P., we sashay right up to where my parents are dancing. Darcy and I stop holding hands and we reach out to our parents. They join us and the five of us dance together in a circle in the center of the dance floor. Everyone smiles, everyone laughs.

Part of me knows that moments like these will always be few and far between, and so I try my best to stop being so damn philosophical about everything. I try to just be fully and completely in this moment. I sashay and swing and laugh and dance and I try to enjoy it, to feel only love, as much as I can.

chapter thirty-five

The Beginning

Mom and Dad are sitting at the kitchen table, happily recounting the party and yes, saying how much they enjoyed my speech.

"Hope," Mom says as I'm filling my coffee cup, "you were magnificent."

"You really were," Dad says, too.

"Thanks," I say and smile.

The bay window is open and a light spring air fills the kitchen. Betsy is running a quick circle around the table; Captain is asleep at Dad's feet. Annabelle looks up from her dog bed by the window, cocks her head at me slightly, just the way pugs always do. Just outside, I can see Darcy and C.P. practicing yoga on the wood floor of the tent.

I want it to stay this way. And, more than that, I want it to stay the way it was last night when we were all sashaying.

I look out the window at the wood floor that was, just for last night, a dance floor and a stage. I think of someone telling me once how everything is replaceable and I see now that that's just another way of thinking that everything is temporary. I don't want everything to be temporary, even though so many things are. I think of my parents, of forty years, and know that there are also things that endure.

"I'm going to take a walk down by the beach," I say, and my parents both look up at me. Mom says, "That's nice, dear," and Dad says, "Would you like some company?" And as nice as a walk on the beach with my dad is, I know he's probably just gotten back, and that Mom likes to have breakfast with him.

"No, but thanks," I say. "You enjoy your breakfast. I think maybe I'll take Betsy with me." Betsy halts midcircle and barks.

"Okay, have a nice time," they both say in unison. Betsy barks again and as I head into the laundry room to grab her leash, through the window I hear Darcy and C.P. saying, "Ohm."

I walk down the road to the beach, working out in advance what our route will be once we get there. I think I'll stick with the most frequent route, all the way across the field, then down to the water there, to the jetty, and then back across.

As we approach the field though, Betsy keeps pulling away from me, in the direction of the beach. At first I hold on to the leash and try and bring her back to the route I'd already planned on. Betsy strains harder on her leash and then turns back toward me. She sits down, digs her feet into the grass right where she is and looks at me as if to say, with every core of her being, *No way*. Betsy is pointing something out to me. The fact then that I am holding on to her leash doesn't seem to make any sense and, after all, there's no rule saying that we have to go the way I'd planned. I loosen my hold on her leash and Betsy gets up and walks over the little hill and onto the beach. I follow her lead and quicken my step in order to catch up, so as not to pull so tightly and impolitely on her harness again.

As soon as we get over the hill, as soon as my feet are on the sand, I notice that we're not alone at the beach this morning. I look down at Betsy and I think she knew that, the way dogs sense things a long time before people do. I look toward the water at this guy, this lanky guy, by the way, who's standing at the edge of the water, looking out. He's wearing khaki shorts and a rust-colored windbreaker. He has really close-cropped black hair. Something about him, the back of him, gives me this feeling I've seen him before. His legs and the back of his neck are tan, quite tan I think for this time of year. I feel weird actually, standing on the beach unannounced right behind a stranger, like I'm spying, but I don't want to announce myself. I'd rather walk back over the hill, but Betsy seems so intent on staying here. Even though, for the time being, I am letting her stay I can still hear that very distinct gurgling of protest rising in her throat.

Honestly, Betsy, I think, *could you maybe just this once, with the stranger right there, give it a rest?* I tighten my grip on the leash and I'm about to roll the dice, I'm about to see if maybe, just maybe, I can get her back over to the field to take the walk I'd planned. The guy bends down and picks up a rock and throws it out into the water.

Betsy barks, right at him, and he turns around. And then he smiles, a really big white toothy smile, and Betsy barks again and he walks toward us.

And all I can think for a second is, *No way.*

He looks exactly the same as I remember him but I can't, looking at him, make out whether he looks really young now or if he must have looked older than the rest of us back then.

I'm sure though that he looks no different; his eyes are the same, the way they were always a little bit sad, only now they don't seem sad as much as they seem wise. Maybe that's what they always were, wise, and I was just way too young to know what wise was.

"Hope McNeill?" he says, grinning as he walks over.

"Benji Brown," I say as he stops, right in front of me. Betsy barks again and Benji Brown bends down to pat her. She flips over to display her belly. As he rubs it, he looks up at me and smiles again and I notice that the sad/wise eyes are actually different from how they used to be, because now they're a little bit sparkly, too. *Benji Brown,* I think, *the only man to ever make me mix tapes. Benji Brown, The Only One That Got Away.*

"Wow, Hope McNeill," he says again, and then hesitates. "Is it still McNeill?"

"It is," I say, and I'm really happy to be able to say that.

"You still have that pretty red hair," he says, and smiles, and then he laughs.

"Yeah," I say, "I do," and then, as I say that, the church bells start to ring. No, really, it's nine A.M. on a Sunday morning; they're actual church bells ringing.

"Wow," he says, "it's great to see you."

"Wow," I say back to him, because, really, *Wow!* "Benji, it's so great to see you, too."

"Um, actually, it's just Ben, now," he says and smiles back, a little embarrassed, and I don't think he should be embarrassed. Benji, in its day, was a very cool name. In spite of myself, in spite of everything I've learned in these past few months about the complete unimportance of footwear, I steal a glance at his feet. He's barefoot.

"Ben," I say. "How have you been?"

"I've been great, really good, how have you been?"

"Great, great," I say and right at this moment, I feel like all along, it's been the truth.

"Do your parents still live here?" he asks.

"Yeah, they do. Yours?" I ask, and for the life of me, I cannot stop smiling.

"Yeah," he says, "just came out for the weekend." He's smiling a lot, too. "You work at the Met, right?" he asks, and I think it's nice that he knows, and it's nice, too, that after all these years I still really like the way it sounds when someone says, "you work at the Met," even with all the things lately that have been distracting me.

"Yeah, five years," I say. And then, "What are you doing these days?" I remember years ago someone telling me that Benji Brown graduated at the top of his class at Duke Law School.

"I work for the DNC," he says.

"The DNC?" I say, and believe you me when I tell you, I can hardly get the words out.

"The Democratic National Committee?" he says.

"Oh, I know," I say quickly, not wanting him to think I don't know what the DNC is, or worse, that I'm not all for the DNC, or worse yet, that I'm (I'm whispering now) a *Republican*. "It's just," and I pause as it occurs to me just in the nick of time that to tell him all about my theory, how what I really need, even more than Patrick Dempsey, Jason Bateman, Ed Helms, Stephen Colbert, Adrien Grenier, Joaquin Phoenix, and David Duchovny, is a Democrat, might be a bit weird. I nod my head instead. I smile some more. He smiles, too.

"That's really interesting," I say, "that's terrific." And yes, I know, I probably could have said something better, something smarter perhaps, but really I think this was okay because he's smiling back at me, and saying, "I really love working there."

And then we just smile some more at each other for a minute. It's not at all a bored sort of okay-we're-all-caught-up-here-time-to-move-it-on-out sort of smiling, as there is something so sweetly goofy about it.

"What are you up to while you're out here?" I ask after a while.

"Oh, not much, just hanging out," he says, and pauses for a second, as if he's considering something.

"My dad just put his boat in the water and I was going to take it out for a sail." He turns his head a little bit as he says this, and I think, *Oh, good, he's going to invite me.* A second goes by and then I think that, also, maybe he isn't.

I'm just about to say, "Have a great time," or some approximation of that and then I think how once I say that, I'll go back to the house with Betsy, and spend a little more time with Annabelle and Captain. I'll say good-bye again to everyone and head back to the city, back to the Rothko and to the pugs at Pug Hill. Everything will be like it always was, which isn't a bad thing. But things, I think, could also stand to be different. I've learned these past few months about standing up straight, and enunciating and taking deep, calming breaths, and speaking clearly, and taking a room, one person at a time. But more than that, what I've learned is that, maybe, it really isn't even about all of that. In the end, I've learned, it's about being able to take a risk. I take a calming breath, because that helps, too.

"Would you like some company?" I ask.

"I would *love* some company," he says, all the emphasis on *love*. And then, as soon as he says it, I realize that I might not be hearing church bells after all. What I might be hearing—actually, what I am most certainly hearing, loud and clear and unmistakable—is Erasure. Track number eleven from the *Pop!* album: the song that starts with the guy screaming, *We'll be together again!*

"Sounds good," I tell him, and I think it's probably best that he has no idea I'm talking about a song lyric.

"Great," he says smiling, and looks down at his watch. "Want to say, two o'clock? I'll sail over and pick you up at the dock?"

"Two o'clock," I say, a little loudly, and it's all I can do to not ask him if he hears Erasure, too, because I'm pretty sure he must. Betsy starts barking again and not just one bark, like usual, but barking continuously until Ben looks down at her and says, right to her, "You can come, too," and she stops barking and looks up at him, quite taken. "Does she like sailing?" he asks me.

And of course, as you know, Betsy likes almost nothing so much as she likes the wind, and I tell him she does. Betsy's still looking up at him, silent and perfectly still. I don't think she can quite believe how completely he gets it.

"See you at two," we both say, at exactly the same time. I think, but don't say, *Jinx*. That's something, I think, the not saying it.

I pull very lightly on Betsy's leash, just to test the waters, so to speak, and surprisingly, she gets right up and runs ahead of me, back over the hill to the field. Betsy and I walk across the field together, and then turn around and head toward home. The whole time, the whole way back to the house, the Erasure song is still playing, really loudly, in the background.

* * *

Before I know it, Betsy and I are back at the beach, and we're a little early, because let's face it, we're a little excited about the boat ride. We walk the small stretch of beach together, down toward the edge of the dock and then, as we've got a while to wait, we both sit together in the sand. I reach over with the life preserver I've been carrying and help Betsy put one front leg in, and then the other. Heaven help you and your eardrums if you ever tried to put Betsy in a sweater, but because I think she so surely associates the life preserver with the wind, she gives me no problem at all as I click the straps together.

"Ready?" I ask her, and Betsy looks right up at me, and our eyes lock. I feel the way I've always felt in the presence of a dog: loved. As Betsy stands up and moves the entire back portion of her body to wag her tail, I can hear the gurgling in the back of her throat, and I know a conversation is going to start.

I look at the water and feel the salt on my skin and watch Betsy point her nose up to feel the breeze over her head. I think how I feel lighter than I've felt for as long as I can remember. There is, at this moment, a very big part of me that wants to lie on my back and kick my feet in the air with delight.

Betsy barks out a non-barking syllable and I can't help but think that she wants to point out here that this feeling isn't all because of Ben. And I have to say, I do agree with her. I think that however this day turns out, there isn't any way it could turn out badly. I look at Betsy and think that, yes, of course, there is the thought of sailing off into the sunset with the man of your dreams. There's that, but there are so many other things, too. There's walking along a small stretch of beach with your best friend, for starters.

I look up and see a sailboat approaching; the sails aren't up yet and it's just motoring over. I shield my eyes from the sun to get a better look and at that moment, Ben reaches up to wave at me. As he pulls up to the dock, Betsy barks again. I get up and we walk the length of the dock together, out to meet Ben's boat. Ben is gazelle-like up there: jumping from the sailboat to the dock, tying a rope to the dock, jumping back on.

When we get to the boat, I reach down to pick up Betsy, and

Ben reaches down to us. He takes Betsy from me and puts her in the captain's seat, and you'd think she'd be happy about that, you'd think she'd really like that seat, but she doesn't seem to like it at all. She's looking intently into a basket next to the steering console, and looking back at me a little frantically with what I'd really have to say is quite a lot of jealousy.

"It's okay, Betsy," I say, and she looks at me like she doesn't believe me. She takes another look into the basket and reaches her nose to the sky and starts a round of high-pitched shrills.

Ben takes my hand and pulls me up from the dock and into the boat. As he lets go of my hand, as Betsy goes from shrilling to screeching in the background, he says to me, smiling, "I want to introduce you to a friend."

And I have to be honest, my heart kind of sinks for just a moment, because for a horrible second I am absolutely convinced that some poised and beautiful girl who has perfectly matched her foundation to her skin tone is going to emerge from the cabin, smile at me toothily, and introduce herself as Ben's fiancée.

But instead, Ben turns to the basket that upon closer inspection is actually a dog bed. He lifts out a little black bundle wrapped in its own tiny yellow life preserver. I look closer and I swear I never would have believed it, not in a million years, if I weren't looking into its soft, angelic eyes. Inside the yellow life preserver, looking up at me sleepily, is a little black pug puppy.

"This is Max," he says, and somehow I stop smiling just long enough to say, "Hi, Max."

In the background Betsy's screeching has lost its sense of urgency and has become much more conversational in tone; also it's gotten to that point where it's so high-pitched that you can barely hear it. In fact, if you don't focus on trying to hear it or not hear it, the only sound you can hear is the sound of water splashing against the side of the boat.

"Ready?" Ben asks me.

"Ready," I say, and I can't help thinking that maybe this is all a dream. But a girl can dream. And a girl l ike me, I'm pretty good at that.

Following is a special excerpt from
Alison Pace's newest novel

a pug's tale

Available from Berkley Books!

For a moment, as I stood off to the side in the Temple of Dendur Hall, surrounded by pugs, I had the feeling that everything was right with the world. Usually I'm a firm believer that you should avoid such a feeling, because surely it's written somewhere that as soon as you feel something like that, everything in your life will go very wrong. But still, I felt it. I felt as if my only care that night, other than maybe my hope that Gil Turner didn't cotton to the fact that I wasn't on the guest list, was finding a photographer for a portrait of Max for my boyfriend, Ben.

Sometimes, just because it's easier, I call Max "my pug." Technically, he's not. Technically, Max is Ben's pug and I'm his caretaker ever since, eight months after we began dating, Ben took a job with Lawyers Without Borders and left, full of hope and purpose, for a five-month stint in Kinshasa.

Really. In case you're not familiar—I wasn't—Kinshasa is in the Democratic Republic of the Congo, in sub-Saharan Africa. It is not ideal. But I love Ben and admire what he's doing. I love Max, and I'm grateful that even if I do not at this moment live in the same country as my boyfriend, I have his pug. It counts for something. It counts for a lot. Perhaps I had more on my mind than the portrait, but the portrait was up there.

Then, quite slowly at first and then faster, the whole system began to melt down. I watched as a fawn pug, a long-legged, remarkably slender pug, the Lara Flynn Boyle of pugs, skidded on the marble floor and slid across the entirety of the eastern side of the room, barking as she went. In a different corner, a rather large, almost perfectly round pug in an orange leather harness first showed tooth, and then lunged with a great deal of snarling at a much smaller pug who'd been outfitted for the occasion in a tartan sweater. A black pug who for a second I thought to be Max, but luckily wasn't, vomited in a corner. Another one skidded across the south end of the room, making a soft howling noise as he progressed.

I scanned the room quickly for Max. He was still fixated on the amuse-bouche. Assorted pugs were peeing on several different surfaces. One left what could be viewed as a calling card on the polished marble floor. Maintenance men appeared with rolls of paper towels and spray bottles. Party guests fell silent, hushes ensued, and then people began to talk again.

In the background, Daphne Markham could be heard calling out "Ahoy!" over and over again as if a record were playing, one that no one realized had skipped.

"Ahoy!" she said to everyone who passed her. Her voice crescendoed throughout the room, over the din of conversation, over the clink of champagne glasses, punctuating the occasional pug-mishap-related hushes that broke out. "Ahoy!"

I leaned back against the wall. From this vantage point, I saw Gil Turner enter the hall. As he entered, he paused for a moment and straightened his tie. He took an iPhone out of his pocket, glanced at it with a half sneer, and then looked out across the room. As he did, his half sneer turned into a smile. He shifted his shoulders back and strode into the room like a famous actor onto a stage. He glided across the floor, almost like a pug who had lost his footing, and headed over to Daphne and her famed, held-aloft pug, Madeline. He looked happy, confident, pleased with himself. He didn't yet know that his party, along with the pugs within it, was teetering very close to the precipice of out of control.

"Ahoy!" Gil called out to Daphne, and I smiled, I think because something about Gil calling that out to her didn't quite work and it fell flat. He sounded foolish. Not nice, I know, but Gil didn't always bring out the best qualities in me.

I looked again toward Max, still way over at the far end of the buffet table. Suddenly he perked up and stood very alert, at attention. Then, it was as if everything else in the room had gone dark and a single bright spotlight had been shone upon Max. I looked across the room at him standing so still and watchful. He reminded me of these two German shorthaired pointers we sometimes see in Central Park. Like pointers who'd just seen a gunned-down grouse, Max was frozen, rigid, determined, moments away from bursting into action. Right then, he was the absolute embodiment of the calm before the storm. The calm part I could see; the storm part I knew was coming. Keeping an eye on Max was no small task in the sea of serpentining pugs, but it was made at least a little easier by the fact that Max is a black pug, and also, by his waistline.

I believe that just as the animals in the tsunami knew to get the hell away from sea level, I somehow knew something not good was a-coming. I also somehow knew that that moment was as good a moment as any for a fortifying sip of champagne. I took a sip of my champagne. I took a step toward Max, still statuesque beyond yonder buffet table. And then he wasn't, neither statue still nor beyond yonder buffet table.

Max took off like a bullet in my direction. For one last delusional moment I allowed myself to believe he was running right toward me, that this was nothing more than a dramatic outburst of affection. But it was not so. Instead of bounding into my arms in a pug reenactment of the final moments of *Lassie Come Home*, Max stopped several yards away from me. He stopped right at Daphne Markham's heels and began barking up at her and her pug, ferociously. He barked more ferociously than I believe I have ever seen any pug bark.

Someone I recognized from photographs in magazines turned to another and said, "That's not okay."

"No," someone else who happened to be wearing a tiara agreed. "It's really not."

Daphne's pug, Madeline, safe in Daphne's arms but perhaps outraged at the assault, angled her face ceilingward and began to howl. And then (then!) she jumped down from Daphne's arms and began running, at full speed, in the direction away from Max. Completely unfortunately, that direction also happened to be on a collision course with the reflecting pool. I hastily put my champagne on the tray of a passing waiter and hurried through the crowd.

"My goodness!" I heard someone say as I passed.

"Oh, dear God!" someone else exclaimed as Madeline lost her footing and slid several feet before landing directly in the reflecting pool. It is to date the only time I have ever